A DICKENSIAN CHRISTMAS MYSTERY

SCROOGE AND CRATCHIT

DETECTIVES

CURT LOCKLEAR

ISBN: 978-1-7357280-7-0 (hard cover)
     978-1-7357280-8-7 (soft cover)

Edited by: Monika Dziamka

Published by Warren Publishing
Charlotte, NC
www.warrenpublishing.net
Printed in the United States

Scrooge and Cratchit, Detectives: A Dickensian Christmas Mystery *is dedicated to my children (Catherine, Nathan, and Erin) who are the delight of my life; to all persons who love literature, the writings of Charles Dickens, and a good mystery; but most importantly, is dedicated to the greater glory of God.*

PRAISE FOR CURT LOCKLEAR BOOKS

Scrooge and Cratchit: Detectives

"Curt Locklear's mystery adventure novel, Scrooge and Cratchit: Detectives *reads like a good Dickens novel ... The plot evolves with vigor and excitement, and readers familiar with Dickens's original will be thrilled to welcome back some of Ebenezer's ghostly personages, including Marley (there are others too). Overall, a lively and fun read."*

—5-STAR REVIEW BY READERS' FAVORITE REVIEWER,
EMILY-JANE HILLS ORFORD

Splintered

"Splintered by Curt Locklear is one of those novels that demands your attention because of its well-crafted and well-developed plot line. Everything was connected so well, every character was so perfectly drawn and described that I felt at one with them. The story itself was very engrossing. You can feel the emotion right from the get go and you will find it till the very last word of the novel."

—5-STAR REVIEW, TABIA REVNEER,
READERS' FAVORITE REVIEWER

*"Like Mr. Locklear himself, the book is full of passion ...
for a good story, for history, and for the Civil War."*

—ROBERT HICKS, *NEW YORK TIMES* BESTSELLING
AUTHOR OF *THE WIDOW OF THE SOUTH* AND *THE ORPHAN MOTHER*

STAVE ONE

A DISTURBING BIT OF NEWS: A MURDER

Approximately 250 miles from London, in the vicinity of Cornwall, a man lay dead, his face smashed in by a shovel. The large man, who everyone in the vicinity said had done the deed, rode a lathered steed hard through the night.

He drove his horse, the fifth one in his long sojourn, to the outskirts of London, wherefrom he would hasten to the office of business associates of his—Ebenezer Scrooge and his money-lending partner, Bob Cratchit. He kept telling himself, *Scrooge is a changed man from two years ago. Surely, he will help.*

On the fourth day of his escape, two stout constables had laid their hands on him when he slept in a barn loft under a pile of hay. He eluded them because the frost that had gathered on his coat while he slept in the frigid night allowed him to slide loose from their grasp. He leapt to the ground and mounted a stolen plough-horse. He rode bareback, clinging to the horse's mane.

Ultimately arriving at the outskirts of London in late afternoon, the man released the horse and slipped into the city afoot.

About the same time, in the countryside outside Bristol, Lucy Tamperwind, a young woman with a fresh face and golden hair in ringlets, stepped into a coach. In one hand, she clutched a clumsy, heavy leather bag; and tight in the other fist, she crumpled a troubling letter from her uncle, Erasmus Tamperwind.

Her uncle's ink-smudged missive in scrawled letters beseeched her to come in haste to his sickbed, err he die before he could tell her some secret, dreadful news. The last words of the letter stated, *a vast fortune and my life are at stake.*

Her cheeks were blushed not from the chill air, but from fear for her uncle and the distressful warning.

In his London counting-house, Ebenezer Scrooge sat smug and content, unaware that the criminal was heading straight for him. He was reflecting on the fact that Marley was still dead to begin with. With a slight smile, he said to himself, "That much is still true as much as the certificate of burial is true." Scrooge had signed it, and his name was *good* upon it.

Yet there was a lot more *good* in Scrooge's name now, coming upon the second year after that eventful Christmas when Scrooge became re-acquainted with Marley. He was ruminating about the fact that Marley had been and still was as dead as a doornail, and that his ghost had not been lurking about for two years. He shuddered just thinking about his encounter of two years past.

"Bob Cratchit," he whispered to his new partner sitting across from him at what used to be the desk of Jacob Marley. He did not want to alert their new office boy, who was painting their walls with fresh paint.

Cratchit looked up from his perusal of a line of numbers on a page.

"Bob," Scrooge continued in a hushed tone, "I was just thinking that there can be much discussion about how dead a doornail is or was or ought ever to be. But I think that a coffin nail would probably suffice better as an analogy of how dead anything is. What say you?" He immediately regretted even bringing up the subject.

Cratchit looked up as though pondering the posit with much consideration. He then looked at Scrooge. "I believe you are right, Ebenezer. The coffin nail is a better analogy." He dipped his pen in an inkwell and continued his work.

While Scrooge reflected on Marley's death and his own changed life, and while Cratchit worked diligently and the office boy splashed paint on the office wall with furvor, the huge fugitive from the law barrelled through the London streets. He passed several buildings with posters of his likeness glaring at him.

He came face-to-face with a policeman who recognised the giant from a poster as the man wanted for the murder. The big man instantly grappled with the policeman, then picked him up and tossed him into a passing hay cart. He continued his race down alleys and byways, knocking over food carts in his mad rush. He would not be stopped in obtaining the offices of Scrooge and the new business partner, Bob Cratchit.

On this dismal day of advent, only one week before the nativity of the Lord, not all was right with the world, surely not in London, nor in Camden town, certainly not in Cornwall, nor even in Paris. In London, the manhunt was on.

The broad-chested bloke, intimidating by his very size, rushed through the snow-laden streets like a runaway train. The frosted vapour huffing from his mouth was like the smoke of a steam engine. He stopped momentarily and leaned against a brick wall, catching his breath. Looking about, he saw passersbys eyeing him. "Stay away from me!" he roared, then sped down an alley.

Lucy Tamperwind looked obliquely at the letter on her lap while the four-in-hand coach jounced along a rocky, serpentine road. Another older woman rode opposite her and was nodding in sleep. "I feel so conflicted," Lucy said to herself. "I hope I arrive before Uncle Erasmus dies."

The coach rolled to a stop at a crossroads. She heard the grumbling of the men who paid a smaller fee to ride, but only enough coin to sit atop the coach, hanging on to a rail or to tied-down luggage. She heard a loud burp from one of them. Pulling her blonde curls back with one hand, she peered out the coach window and, looking up, caught sight of a shabbily dressed man wiping his mouth with his sleeve. The man took a swig from a rum bottle, then turned suddenly and leered at Lucy. She jerked her head back inside. Something about the man made her stomach churn. *I don't trust him.* She wrung her hands.

❧

In the counting-house, Bob Cratchit perched on a stool behind Marley's old desk, Scrooge in a chair at his desk, both in the office that was connected at the rear to a great warehouse that housed all manner of goods brought in on the many ships that sidled up to the wharves attendant to London. There were ores of all sort, primarily iron, but copper and tin in abundance, furs for hats, exotic silks, and cask upon cask of wine or salted fish or merely brine or lemons or apples or spices or beaver pelts or whatever anyone could imagine to be stored in a cask.

Scrooge thought briefly about the fortunes of the shipping magnates and yearned for their wealth.

He set that thought aside, sighing. "I'm so glad Marley's dead," he mumbled, "and I shan't see him again."

Cratchit looked up at the comment, but Scrooge waved him off, and the partner continued copying a letter.

Scrooge, over the past two years, had become more observant of the machinations of the world and, also, had developed an astuteness in sizing up people as true human beings rather than as potential wealth-providers for himself. He perceived aspects amazing about the human form that, in his previous mindset, he had never noticed.

He looked out of the smoke-smudged office window near his desk and observed the palmprints and fingerprints of numerous hands that, at one time or another in the pursuit of checking if anyone was about in Scrooge's business chambers, had endeavoured to shade the light in order to see inside.

As he scrutinised these smudged prints, quite unaware of the coins spilt hither skither about his desk, which of itself was a new fashion of his behaviour, he took notice that each print, be it either hand or finger, had different markings, no two the same. And he marvelled at such a peculiarity.

His partner of a year and a half, Bob Cratchit, had gained a new measure of financial stature and ability to acquire adequate food. Therefore, he had grown quite formidable in his dimensions. He was lean in the waist, but his biceps fairly tore at his breech coat. His thighs were powerful, like those of the wretched prisoners who dragged the bowlines to tow the ships at the wharfs.

He was taller, or so it seemed, and he always made sure he was warm while he sat at his new desk with a bright flame in the coal stove in the corner. His cheeks were a cherry tone, his brow strong, his eye keen; indeed, his features had become quite attractive to many ladies who often would dally at the window of the office to take a peek, or perhaps a gander, at him.

Cratchit seldom failed to notice the becoming women who gawked at him, and though he loved his wife, he would often fantasise about involving himself with a fair maiden. In noticing, this day, one such young women batting her eyes at him through the window, he drew a deep sigh and tried to focus on the letter.

Scrooge left his perplexity of thought about thumbprints and fingerprints and smiled at his hardworking partner. Cratchit's good example had worn well on Scrooge. He had learned a lot about the true *business of mankind*.

While the accused criminal careened through the streets like an errant missile, a newcomer of a handful of months worked in the office of Scrooge and Cratchit.

It had come to Bob Cratchit's attention that the company sorely needed an office boy, and he had often mentioned as much to Scrooge, who, in battling his old miserly nature, had put off the inevitability until that day when a delightfully pleasant street urchin named Lockie appeared at the door of the Scrooge and Cratchit firm asking for a loan to buy his sister a pony. The young man's confidence and cheeriness won both their hearts, and though they issued him no loan, they put him to work.

"And how old are you now, young Lockie?" asked Scrooge the day he hired him.

"I wish that I knew, Master Scrooge, but I'm guessin' around seventeen. Old enough to marry and to fight in the army. I had some learning in Mr. John Pound's Ragged School, got my letters and my cyphers. Soon I hope to work in the morgues and be about preparin' the dead, and hammerin' and nailin' up coffins and the like."

Scrooge shrank like a withered flower, thinking back on his own dire exposure to the exactitude of death when he was visited by the Ghost of Christmas Future. He slumped, placing his hand on his heart. "No, no, I won't allow it. You shan't work there. I forbid it. To the morgue, I say *humbug*! Instead, you will work here in this office and grow up forthright and, and … at four shillings a week."

"Hear, hear!" Cratchit applauded. "We've needed an office boy for eons."

So, their enterprise flourished with the abundant energy of the indefatigable ragamuffin.

༒

On the morning of this dreary day, when the man who was intensely sought by the police was racing through the streets, Scrooge had finally relented to Cratchit and funded Lockie to purchase white paint for the walls. Lockie bought blue, much to Scrooge's chagrin, but since there was a "no return policy," Scrooge had little choice, and so Lockie was set to painting the dismal walls a cheerful sky-blue.

Scrooge returned to observing the smudged fingerprints on the windows, then took out documents signed by various individuals. Some used only their thumbprint in ink next to an "X." Peering at many loan agreements, Scrooge saw again and again that every print was different in its lines and squiggles, tiny scars, and mole marks.

The *old* Scrooge turned his thoughts to Lockie and determined that when the lad had completed the painting task, he would dismiss him. The heart of Scrooge had not completely turned.

He was pondering this matter and passively watching Lockie applying paint when the door to the office burst open to the point of clattering against the wall.

Scrooge, Cratchit, and Lockie stared in awe at a portly, muscled man of substantial height, dressed in a heavy, black cloak who bore a most distressed visage. Indeed, he looked horrified. Scrooge and Cratchit recognised him as their business acquaintance, Hezikiah Hiram Grumbles, a man of great charity and untarnished repute.

"Scrooge, you must save me!" Mr. Grumbles pleaded.

STAVE TWO
A TALE OF WOE, A GENEROUS DECISION

Scrooge arose from his chair and hastened to this colleague. "My dear Hiram Grumbles, whatever is the problem?"

"Ebenezer, I need a loan, just enough to pay for passage to France and obtain succour. I have relatives in Normandy." Grumbles noticeably shook. "I've been accused of murder in Cornwall. I cannot go to my bank, for surely the police will be waiting for me there. I was barely able to shake the sheriff's men who were hot on my trail, then a constabulary here in London just a few blocks away."

"Murder?" Scrooge asked, placing his hand on Grumbles's arm.

Lockie dropped his brush in the splattering paint on the floor. His mouth was agape.

"Who was murdered?" Cratchit asked.

Mr. Grumbles, flushed and out of breath, parked his large rear in the nearest chair before Lockie, with cloth in hand, could dust the seat. Grumbles waved his hat about his sweating face. "I have been running, ducking in and out of alleys. Several times, I saw posters with my likeness sketched on them. The sheriff must have sent a description ahead of me by train. I am completely undone." He fanned himself some more.

Scrooge took a chair opposite Grumbles. "Pray tell us, Hiram, what is at issue here?"

"Very well then, but may I first ensure that you will give me a loan of forty pounds, enough to give me passage to France?"

"Of course, yes, but you must tell us about how this dire fate came to be."

Cratchit pulled up another chair and sat, his elbows on his knees, leaning upon his fists in earnest attention. Lockie tried to emulate the posture while standing, thus smearing paint on his face.

"Seven nights ago," Hiram began, "I was working late at the Tamperwind tin mine, which abuts up to the shore in Cornwall. I was studying some ore samples, experimenting, when in bursts the owner's grounds caretaker, yelling. He is deaf and his speech is mumbly, but I ultimately understood that he thought that I had killed the mine manager, and that the police were forthcoming."

The three attendants gasped.

"He was so fervent and threatening to do me bodily harm, for he held a pickaxe in his hands, that I fled for my life. Without even time to gather a change of clothes, I found a horse already saddled, mounted it, and rode away. In passing the owner's house, but a small distance from the mine, I stopped. All the lights were on in the house, and a crowd of the tin mine workers, both women and men, were in the yard, talking in earnest. I heard one woman say, 'Old Miz Owsley, she's the deceased mine manager's wife. She saw the murderer. It was our own Mr. Grumbles that done it!'"

Lockie wiped off his blue-painted hands on a cloth, poured a glass of water from a pitcher for the distressed, *wanted* man and handed it to him.

"Thank you kindly." Grumbles downed the drink. "Have you something stronger?"

Cratchit rose to gather a flagon of rum from a desk drawer. He gave Mr. Grumbles a sizeable tumbler of the brew. He quaffed it off, drew the back of his hand across his mouth. "Thank you, Bob."

"Pray continue," Scrooge admonished Mr. Grumbles.

"There I was, sitting on the horse at the outskirts of the crowd, trying to understand what had happened. Each piece of conversation I heard verified that everyone thought I did the deed to my dear friend and fellow worker, Mr. Owsley, and simply because someone had said it, they all seemed convinced it was true. It has been hard enough in my life trying to overcome a name like 'Grumbles' and show the true Christian spirit that I have, and to have so many good folks so quickly turn on me with no proof. I am at a loss."

"Well, then what happened?" Lockie broke in.

The three men momentarily looked at Lockie.

"As I was delaying there, listening," Grumbles went on, "and hoping to gather any shred of information that might allow me the possibility of dismounting and putting an end to this misunderstanding, behold the caretaker came running after me again, shouting. Then another voice from a young boy that I took to be Mr. Tamperwind's ward, Michael, called out, 'There he is. There's Grumbles. He killed Mr. Owsley.'

"The crowd turned and rushed towards me. I had no choice but to ride away, fearing for my life." Mr. Grumbles fanned his sweaty face. "I'm so sorry to put this burden on you, dear Ebenezer, or you, friend Bob. I have ridden seven days and nights on four stolen horses, but I must away post-haste to France. Might I have that loan? On my honour, you will be repaid as soon as I am able."

Scrooge went to his desk, pulled out a cumbersome gangle of keys, found one, and opened a drawer. He counted out forty pounds into a small, cloth bag, tied it shut, and placed it in Mr. Grumbles's eager hands. "I do wish we knew more of the case," Scrooge said. "Surely if you turned yourself in, the police would soon set you free once the truth came forth."

"No, no. I cannot take that chance. I must catch the next tide. Wish me well. Say a prayer for me at church if you can." Mr. Grumbles leapt from his seat, wrapped his large cloak around his protuberance of a belly, and raced out the door into the snowy streets, almost knocking down a spice vendor.

The three attendants, Lockie, Scrooge, and Cratchit, gawked for a moment. Then Scrooge, realising he had not had Grumbles sign for the loan, reached for his keys, fumbled one of them into a drawer keyhole, and drew out a paper, pen, and an ink bottle. He sped to the door, but Grumbles had melted into the fog. Scrooge hung his head. He had always counted himself a "good man of business" even since that eventful Christmas of two years ago. Charitable, yes, but not foolhardy. "How could I have let him go without signing?" he called to the walls of the office.

"Why should you not be aware that Mr. Grumbles, our friend, would be a man of his word?" Cratchit remarked.

Scrooge gave him a sniping look.

"Ebenezer!"

"Yes, yes, Bob, charity. I remember."

"Do you remember on that Christmas Eve when he and Leggitt came here asking for a donation and you turned them away so cruelly?"

"Yes, yes."

There was a long silence. Lockie began whistling as he plunged his brush in the paint bucket and continued painting. Cratchit returned to his desk and began copying a document. Scrooge locked his desk drawers and plunked hard in his chair, and in a moment, was staring at the ink-smudged documents and then at the window fingerprints.

The bleak, grey buildings across the cobblestoned street looked to him like monoliths of an ancient race, faceless, charmless, perhaps hiding all sorts of secrets and evil-doers. Scrooge supposed that maybe any good person might, of an occasion, do an evil deed, perhaps when surrounded by evil; that individual might relent of his own scruples and toss them aside, even if momentarily, for whatever reason—for an ill-gotten item, to repay a grievance, or to assuage an insult.

Perhaps his friend, Mr. Grumbles, *had* committed the crime, *had* murdered the poor man in an act of rage, then concocted the whole story to cover his escape, using Scrooge as an unwilling accomplice. Had he just given a sizeable loan to a murderer? Yes, Grumbles was a good friend, but how well did he know him?

"So," Lockie interrupted Scrooge's thoughts, "does this Mr. Grumbles have a family that needs to be informed of his calamitous straits?" He returned to painting and took to whistling "God Rest Ye Merry, Gentlemen."

"He did," Cratchit called from his office. "A wife and six children, all of whom died last year in a fire."

Lockie set down his paintbrush, his face showing immediate remorse. "I lost a sister in a fire." He slowly picked up his brush and re-commenced. "Well, what about sisters or brothers?"

"His sister died of the dropsy some years back. He has no other relatives that I know of," Cratchit responded.

"Cousins?"

"For the sake of all that's good about our dear Queen Victoria," Scrooge called. "Why are you asking so many questions? The man is a friend. We helped him. He is on his way, and we likely will never see or hear of him again unless the authorities apprehend him. Forty pounds is as good as gone, and the man may be a wanton murderer." Scrooge's face was red.

"Come now, Ebenezer," Cratchit intoned placidly, "surely you don't think Hiram Grumbles is a murderer. He's not of that ilk. I'm astonished you would even consider such a thought."

"Do you know him, Bob? Do you really know him? Yes, we've had dinner with him on occasion, had business dealings, even given money to his charities. How do we know he wasn't dipping into those funds for his own use, and when he was caught red-handed, he took woeful action?"

"Ebenezer, I believe you are more concerned about your money than your friend's welfare."

Scrooge's face fell, acutely aware that Cratchit had surmised the truth of Scrooge's rantings.

"Bob," he said. "I apologise. It is so hard to put a filter, as it were, on my thoughts. Old habits die hard. Still, the man is a criminal at large, hunted by the police. What if they come here, asking of his whereabouts, and we have to—"

Scrooge halted his remarks when he gazed out his window and saw a dozen bobbies going door to door on the street. He sank into his chair. One bobby was headed straight up the steps of Scrooge's office.

STAVE THREE
A CLOSE CALL

A bobby, tall and moustached and fierce-faced, entered and clumped about in his heavy, sodden shoes up to Scrooge. He held up a poster. "Your pardon, sir. Seen this man?"

Scrooge was speechless. He dared not look at the face on the poster. Trembling, he sat clumsily in his chair and began fidgeting with papers, daring not even a peek at the policeman. Cratchit came up behind the man, stood on his tiptoes, and tried to eye the poster.

"I said," the bobby demanded, "have you seen this man?" He slammed the poster on Scrooge's desk. The middle-aged miser, turned charity-giver, could not raise his eyes from the keys he fumbled with in his hands. Two years ago, he had seen the Ghost of Christmas Future, reminding him of his own mortality. And this man reminded him too much of that vision. If he tried to hide the knowledge of Grumbles visiting the office and securing a loan, he would fail at it. If found out, he would go to prison for aiding a felon. His heart ached, and the room began to spin.

"Why, I know that fellow!" Lockie had come up and pointed a blue-paint finger at the poster. "He calls himself the 'Duke of Tarrytown.' Everyone knows him."

Scrooge gasped and looked at the poster. The rendered drawing was not of Hezekiah Hiram Grumbles, but of another man.

"That's the Duke, all right," Lockie continued. "He'd steal from his own mother, he would, and I'll bet you could find him over in one o' his hideouts on Winston Street. For sure, try that street."

The bobby straightened.

"What's he wanted for?" Cratchit asked.

"Robbing a bank. Fancies himself a Robin Hood. Steals from the rich, but he don't give none to the poor. This time he's going back to jail for good." He exited, slamming the door, then called the other bobbies around him, and they all took off running down the street.

Scrooge and Cratchit turned towards Lockie.

"You know this Duke fellow, Lockie?" Bob asked.

"Er, uh, not really. Only heard o' him. He hung around a few of us sometimes, taught us some things. You know."

Cratchit patted Lockie on the shoulder. "So, does the Duke hang around Winston Street? Is that where you're from?"

"No, to both questions, Master Cratchit. I just sent him that way because it's in the opposite direction of the docks, so as they'd be less likely to come upon that Grumbles fellow."

Scrooge and Cratchit were wide-eyed.

"Well done, Lockie," Scrooge said. "Now, back to work. I see several spots on the wall that you missed. Get busy, or I'll hold your wages. Let us give no more time to this murder issue. It is behind us."

"Besides," Cratchit mentioned, "it's near closing time. What say we shut down early? It's growing dark. See, there're the lamplighters out already."

Scrooge rubbed his eyes and nodded. Lockie began wiping the paint from his hands and face.

When the three stood outside the counting-house door, their comforters bound tight about their necks and hats pushed down on their heads, they enjoined some light banter about it being an obstreperous day, not odious, but excitingly out of the ordinary. Then Scrooge asked, "How now, Bob, about Tiny Tim? How does he fare? I've not seen him in a fortnight."

"Well, you might hardly recognise him," Cratchit responded. "His strength has increased, as has his stature. He seldom uses the crutch anymore, nor does he wear the iron brace. The surgery and medicines being admittedly successful."

Scrooge smiled broadly. "Excellent. That is such agreeable news. And the family?"

"Markedly healthy. I am a blessed man. So much so, Ebenezer, come this time next year, I may have enough saved to buy a new home."

Lockie, who during this time had transferred his gaze from one master to the other, remarked, "I should like to have a home someday." With that remark, he capered away like he had not a care in the world.

Lockie, from the first day of his employ two months previous, had been a boon. He was always prompt, and he stayed busy without being told to do so. He cleaned out the back rooms, swept out the chimney flues, brought in the coal, dusted the chairs just before the clients would sit, shovelled the horse muck that lay in the streets before the door, wrote the day's undertakings on a chalkboard with fairly legible hand, swept the floor, boiled the tea, and gave numerous clever compliments of the like of, "Master Scrooge, I most certainly hope my hair is as white as yours when I turn fifty, so that I may have the look of wisdom that you have."

After a month of such efforts, Scrooge, at Cratchit's behest, sent Lockie out with papers to an important client. He did the task so well, returning with the signed documents, that he was given the rank of courier. He was busy every day. Unbeknownst to the two towers of monetary industry, Lockie, on his travels, made excellent use of his pickpocketing skills. He supplemented his salary thus, so much, that he appeared one day with a brand-new hat of the tallest sort. He said, "It makes me look dignified, like a true proprietor of industry, like my two kind masters."

He gained smiles from his employers, and they trusted him with his work. However, the eventful day arrived with the constable at the door, his grip tight upon the collar of the courier whose tall hat was in his hands and who bore a contrite look on his countenance.

"Filched a lady's purse, he did," announced the constable.

Some quick thinking on Cratchit's part convinced the officer that Lockie was his ward. A *new programme*, Cratchit's invention, that the reformatories allowed certain individuals a chance to remake their lives under the watchful eye of a keen master.

"He is my affair, Constable," Cratchit said. "I will take him in hand and give him a harsh thrashing at the very least."

The constable, after several harrumphs, decided to allow Lockie into the custody of Mr. Cratchit and to the chastisement of both owners of the firm. Lockie vowed never to pickpocket again, but he owned that he had only done it for medicine for his dying cousin. In the end, he remained in their employ, and Cratchit never lifted a hand to him.

"Has it occurred to you before this moment, Scrooge," Cratchit asked, watching the ragged urchin disappear into the fog, "that Lockie may actually *not* have a true home?"

"Nary a thought." Scrooge rubbed his chin thoughtfully. "I'm not sure I want to know where he is living, be it under a bridge or in a brothel, inside a whore's closet. This day has been entirely too much. I plan to put it all behind me. If Grumbles is a murderer, then good riddance; if he's innocent, I wish him well and will pray for him at church."

Just then, Cratchit eyed four men struggling with hefting a wide coffin down the street. They needed two more to bear the weight. Cratchit took his partner by the sleeve, and each helped bear the coffin to the graveyard. At the grave, after doffing their hats, shaking hands with the bereaved, and joining in the simple prayers offered by a minister, the two well-doers departed.

The newer Scrooge felt a surge of joy for his magnanimity.

It was Bob Cratchit who had shown Ebenezer the benefits of benevolence—of the warm feeling in the heart. Bob would drop a coin in a beggar's cup, and Scrooge would do the same. Cratchit would take the arm of an old woman to escort her halfway across a thoroughfare, and Scrooge would take her the rest of the way.

Cratchit would offer to help bear a coffin of a poor mortal from the streets and Scrooge would lift a corner of said coffin.

Cratchit would pick flowers or purchase a bouquet at a flower cart and take them to his wife. Scrooge would follow suit and bring daylilies or some such to his nephew's wife, who was so appreciative, she often gave him a kiss on his cheek. To this, he was much obliged and blushed a tinge of red that many might say was more maroon.

He would then be invited in for a dinner of roast chicken with sage, potatoes, greens, and a plum pudding. Hence, Scrooge had gained a few pounds, much to his liking, and a new appreciation of good food.

Exiting the graveyard this late evening, with the light fast fading, the two friends shook hands and departed for their homes. Strolling happily along, Scrooge thought, *Thank goodness, I have no more problems for today.*

STAVE FOUR

MARLEY'S GHOST RETURNS

The winter night was falling fast, and Scrooge automatically clutched his chest where his change purse hung on a cord around his neck. He thought hard about his hard-earned money. Do not think Scrooge's previous bad habits did not often creep back into the wiles of the old miser. He was not so much a changed man, but a changing one, who often needed someone to remind him of his new focus. So, when no one seemed to be watching, he would slip back into that squeezing, clutching, wrenching, hand-to-the-grindstone malefactor he had been for so many dreary years, and his whole demeanour would show as much. The battle within him often raged, and the craving for accumulation of wealth never to be utilised for good was his greatest challenge.

His battle with the demons of his past still lingered, and those new demons who roamed the earth to spurn even the saints and make them howl in pain and fall again on their knees and beg for God's mercy would show up at Scrooge's ear often enough. Of course, the mercy for Scrooge would come later, but at what cost?

The battle in his heart was unending. Knowing as much about himself, he made a point every day, and maybe twice on Sundays, to go about doing one good deed, hard as it often was for him.

✌✍

The night slunk like a weasel around Scrooge, darker and closer. Suddenly remembering the encounter with Grumbles who, for all he knew, was a murderer, he sought the solace of his lonesome abode. He hurried along broken pavement and icy patches in environs that never saw the sunlight, shaded by the close-built edifices that seemed to squeeze closer every night. Along some narrow passageways, he shuffled sideways so as not to brush his shoulders against the bricks.

Even two years after his visit from the ghost of Jacob Marley, Scrooge had not moved out of his old chambers, the dark warehouse with rooms above, sprinkled down a long, constricted hallway. Nor had he let out the rooms to any other.

He neared the warehouse yard, dark even for Scrooge. He knew its every facet and was careful not to brush a single bush or grotesque statue that stood hither and yon about the grounds. Fog and frost hung about the house like a mourning drape. It seemed as if the lord of cold lodged there in mournful meditation. Scrooge, at last, breathed a little easier when his walking cane clattered against the steps of the old, sham palace.

He had gathered the one key and plunged it into the lock when, lo and behold, he glanced at the knocker, and there it was. Marley's face, with ghostly spectacles, turned up on its ghostly forehead. The hair, just as on that particular Christmas Eve night in Scrooge's recent past, was amazingly stirred as if by an errant breeze, and the eyes stared motionlessly through Scrooge, intent on something in an unfathomable distance, be it in space or time. The face's colour was pallid, but occasionally flushing to rose in the checks.

Despite what he had learned of ghosts and their habit of showing up unexpectedly, Scrooge was astonished. "Marley?" he said, his voice trembling. No sooner had he said the name than the spectre faded, revealing the knocker. Scrooge's mind raced. Was this the night he would pass into the afterworld? Had he made sufficient recompense for his past life? Had he been contrite enough? Charitable enough? Had he truly been about the "business of mankind"?

The manner in which his body quivered now was far more than when the policeman had entered the counting-house. Now, he was sure he would faint. Certain he was, also, that this was the night of his demise. He could think only of unlocking the door, for he did not want to die out in the cold on colder stone steps. He turned the key in the rusty lock. It did not give. He pushed hard, all the time his brain swooning. With one last jerk, the lock sprung, and Scrooge forced his way into the opaque hall and crumpled to the floor in a heap.

He did not faint, but his heart fairly endeavoured to leap from his chest. He finally stood, felt around until he found the flint box by the door, struck the marker against the flint, and lit a wick. He transferred the flame to a candle. He grabbed another candle from a nearby hall desk and lit it as well. He doused the wick, and, his eyes darting to all the dark corners of his abode, he stealthily climbed the wide stairs. His mind fled to all the fearsome corners of his cognizance. Was Marley here to mark his passing? Was he here to warn him again to change his errant ways?

Arriving at his chambers, he tenuously opened the door and shone the candlelight about. The room, its high ceilings clothed in gloom and fending off the light, was bare of any phantoms. There was only his stuffed chairs, a small table, a lamp, and a sideways-hung painting covered with so much dust that the premise of the painted scene was lost. He had never done a thing to adorn his dwelling in the near-two years. He had thought about it, but felt again and again that his wealth should be used to help those less fortunate than himself. Hence, he lived in a squalor of negligence.

He lit another wick from the candle's flame, and in short order, had built a blaze of fresh logs in the fireplace. He warmed his hands, then his backside, all the time glancing feverishly about the room. At last, he began to think this last apparition was merely a figment of his tired imagination, and that was all it was. He finally went to his cupboard, pulled out crackers and cheese and a tired slice of apple pie he had put off eating for no good reason. If he was to die tonight, he wanted to have one last bite of sweetness. He sat ponderously by the fire, both candles on his little table.

He had munched but a while on his repast when the little servant's bell that was never used began to tinkle. It then grew more vociferous that it sounded quite like the bell of a great church. When the bell hung silent at last, Scrooge turned towards the doorway, and there was the unmistakable clanking of chains and coin boxes and padlocks and cumbersome metal devices dragging slowly up the stairs. His attention was full upon the door as the sounds drew closer. He held his hand to his chest.

The raucous sound ceased.

He turned his head from the door, and there before him, stood the phantasm of Jacob Marley, looking no different than Scrooge had witnessed him almost two years previous. Jacob still maintained the cloth death-wrap about his jaw and appeared to be working said part of his face in order to speak.

At last, Scrooge said, "Good evening to you, friend."

"I am not your friend. Had I been your friend in life, I would have endeavoured to turn you from your evil, miserly, decrepit ways. And yet, here I am once more, forced by an unknown presence to visit you as part of my everlasting penance."

"I surmise it is to tell me of my approaching ... death." The last word screeched out of him like an unoiled door. He swallowed hard, then clasped his hands together, and turning his eyes upwards, began to pray in whispers.

"No!"

"No, what?" Scrooge trembled at the fury of Marley's pronouncement.

"No, I am not here to tell you of your impending death. I am not privy to such information." Marley's ghost, wearing the same waistcoat and stockings and just as transparent as that long-ago Christmas Eve, began wandering about the room, looking intensely at every stick of furniture and every wall. "Strange. Have I been here before?"

"Yes, you have. You lived in this building before. We were neighbours of a sort for a while. Though you never stepped foot in my chambers, I can say ..."

The ghost turned and wailed. Scrooge held his hands tight to his ears until the tortured spirit quit. "Ah, yes," Marley's ghost said, "I am not here to tell you of your demise. I only know of the here and now, and that is pretty sketchy. I can also tell you that you have made a grave error."

"Yes, I'm quite afraid that every error in this short time on earth for me is a 'grave' one."

"Don't! Don't joust at humour when your soul is at stake."

"They drive a stake in vampires' hearts to keep them dead, don't they?" Scrooge could not tell why he had let poor puns slip from his lips. He was entirely beside himself with dread.

Marley's ghost gave him such a look that it seemed to tie his vocal cords.

"You must take action!" the ghost demanded. "You cannot wait until tomorrow. You must act!"

"Yes, of course," Scrooge's timorous voice squeaked, "but about what?"

"About what? About what!" The chained spirit began clanging his chains and boxes and rose in the air.

Scrooge fell to his knees. "I beg you, Spirit, please tell me what action I must take, and if it saves my soul, I will do it."

Marley's ghost settled back to the floor, and he went about twirling one of the great boxes fettered to him on a chain as if it were a watch on a fob. He sauntered about the room like he was the chairman of the board of some corporation. He turned dramatically towards Scrooge, who, by this time, was cowering behind his chair. "Hear now, Ebenezer Scrooge, you have been given lately a special grace, one that you are to use, lest you lose a spectacular inheritance."

"I have?"

"Yes, your mental faculties have been enhanced. Certainly, you've noticed."

Scrooge searched his recollection and gave the ghost a dumbfounded look.

"Surely, Scrooge, you have noticed you are now observing things more than you ever did before."

"For example?"

"This very day, did you not notice the delicate form of holly leaves on a bush as you plied your way to work?"

"Yes, but ..."

"And did you not notice that the blue paint your hired help is painting on your walls is of a particular shade of blue, not just any blue, but it was a *shade* of blue?"

"Yes. As I recall, it was a pleasant blue like the sky on a sunny day."

"Precisely." Marley's ghost took to twirling the loathsome boxes again, creating a swirling sound like the whole room was being sucked down in a whirlpool. Scrooge cringed.

"And were you not," the apparition continued, "paying particular attention to the prints of people's hands and digits on your windowpane? And on the small weed flower in a crack in the pavement? And on the enormous shoe size of Mr. Hezekiah Hiram Grumbles when he invaded your office?"

"I suppose you are right?"

"Of course, I am. It is the one thing I am allowed to feel at this moment, for I have this burdensome task to tell you." Marley's ghost stopped short and leaned down to the crouching Scrooge, face to face. "Listen well, Scrooge. My time runs short." No sooner had he said that than an unseen forced yanked at his neck, and he gagged.

Finally, "Yes, yes, yes," he said while coughing. "Ebenezer Scrooge, Mr. Grumbles said he was accused of bashing in the head of his employer. Did he not?"

"He said as much."

"And did he not say he did not have any time to gather even a single change of clothes when he embarked in haste from the tin mine?"

"Yes, I believe he did."

"Now, with your new faculties, as you surveyed your friend from head to toe, identifying the dab of mustard on his vest, and the red clay and black soil on his shoes, the torn fingernail on his right index finger, the dark circles under his eyes of a man who had not slept for days. Do not tell me that you did not gather this information without so much as thinking on it."

Scrooge stood, his mind recalling every detail of Grumbles's appearance that the ghost had listed. "Yes, I did notice all those things, whereas before I would never have cared even about the colour of a man's eyes. In fact, I did not even know your eye colour when you were alive."

"*Hmmph!*" Marley's ghost appeared incensed. He folded his arms about his chest. "For your information, they were blue ... sky blue, as a matter of fact."

"Praise be."

"Indeed." Again, some fearsome force began dragging the spirit from the room. He attempted to grab the arm of a chair but in vain. "Listen, Scrooge. Did you notice any spattered blood on your late visitor's clothes? Any at all?"

"Why, no."

"My time is up. Think on it and take action now. A good man who has an important task in his future life cannot be detained from it. You must prove him ..." The ghost made a horrible gurgling sound, like he was being strangled. Some force was dragging him away.

"Yes, yes? There was no blood on his clothing. But what does that mean?"

The spirit was almost at the door.

"What am I to do, Marley? Speak comfort to me. What portent have you left me?"

Then the ghost was gone. Scrooge stared long at the room's smoke-stained, dingy walls. He sank again to the floor. "Whatever does he mean? The man he spoke of that needed to do something. Was that Grumbles? Old Hezekiah Hiram? What important thing must he do? And what did that comment about no blood splattered on his garments mean? I am dreadfully confused." He buried his face in his hands.

Why did I walk all those years with my eyes turned away from the very beings we are all sent here to serve? Why did I not look to that glorious Star, which led the Wise Men to a poor manger? Now I have a task to perform, and I know not what it is.

STAVE FIVE

DESPERATE PLANS MADE EVIDENT

Scrooge rose unsteadily, thinking he might go to bed. Perhaps a good night's sleep would clear his mind. He decided first to gaze out the window at the stars if they were not hidden by smoke and fog, for the London chimneys belched even more smoke into the air at night. When he threw back the heavy, velvet curtains, he saw a familiar man, but now *dead for many years*, whom he had known quite well when alive. The spectre of the long-gone corpse floated alongside a lamppost. He wore a pale waistcoat and translucent trousers, and a monstrous, iron safe hung taught on his ankle. His face, both grotesque and piteous, was flooded with tears, and he pointed to the street at a derelict woman with a small child upon a doorstep a few buildings down from Scrooge's abode. The misery in the woman's face told all clearly. The spirit sought to help the woman and her child, to divvy out some measure of goodness, but had lost any element of influence for all eternity.

The ghost vanished like a vapour while Scrooge stared at the poor woman and child. He tore his eyes from the sight and looked up to see a blanket of stars, bright and twinkling. No smoke, no fog. It was beautiful, and he beheld it as a gift.

He looked again at the tragic scene below and knew at once what he had to do. He gobbled a few more mouthfuls of his repast, flung his coat about him, and hastened out into the streets. When he came upon the woman and tiny girl, he placed three shillings in the woman's hand, then helped her to her feet. Holding her arm, for she walked unsteadily, he guided her down the street to a public eating house and inn, still open. She held the tiny girl, who was wrapped in a threadbare blanket, and the child whimpered pathetically.

He directed the woman to a seat in a booth and ordered from the owner a bowl of stew for the woman and large glasses of milk for both her and the child. He paid the man and told him to put the woman and child up for the next week. He dropped a bag of coins in the initially reluctant, then ecstatic, proprietor's hands. "I'll be back in some few days and will pay you any more due."

He smiled at the pitiful pair. The woman gave a grin from a somewhat toothless mouth while stew dribbled down her chin. The child was busy slurping the milk.

Scrooge was immediately out the door and hurtling along the pavement, his walking cane clacking generously.

At one point on Scrooge's sojourn, he was accosted by a drunkard who was squatting to peer at his own vomit in the gutter. Scrooge helped the man up, stood him against a wall. He always carried a small flask of laudanum in a coat pocket. He gave the derelict a dram of laudanum to calm his stomach.

Hurrying along the streets, he smelled the muck wagons that were being pulled along by sturdy horses, while curmudgeonly muckers shovelled the reeking mounds of horse excrements into the wagon. They then whispered in hoarse voices, "Ho!" The horse plodded a few feet farther to the next pile. Despite there being no wind, elements of the manure, mixed with hay and dust, drifted into the air each time the muckers shovelled it.

The tall street lanterns gave off an eerie glow, so much so, that Scrooge once perceived yet another haunt floating about, and he stopped short, seized with trepidation. Then, seeing the haunt only as foggy vapour and light, he proceeded in his left turns, then right, then left, then left again until he arrived at Bob Cratchit's still-humble dwelling in Camden Town. He shook his head, remembering the night he first peered in the window at a happy family of little means with a single child who was sick to death and crippled, yet the warmth of Christian joy had streamed through them all.

Looking once more in the window, he perceived a small candle lit on a stand, and lantern light spilt throughout the aspects of a small bedroom. He saw the male children crowded in makeshift beds, tangled in the blankets, sleeping soundly. He knew the parents' room was behind that one. Another room for the girls was above in a croft. Turning his gaze again to the candle in the corner of Cratchit's kitchen, he recognised his partner, who appeared to be working at a small desk, furtively scribbling some notes on a page.

Scrooge rapped lightly on the window.

Cratchit turned and, seeing his friend, rose and sped to the door. He stepped out, and though his face showed amazement, he shook Scrooge's hand with vigour.

"Scrooge," he whispered, "we are well-met. I have much to tell you. Come, let us move away from the door so as not to wake my family."

The two men stepped under the stars and into the streetlight, their visages now clearer to each other.

"I have much to share with you, much that we must do. You see—" Scrooge began.

"Good grief, I was about to say as much to you. Grumbles needs our help!"

"Yes, yes, that is why I'm here. I had thought of going alone to the tin mine, but I know nothing of that part of the isles, whereas you do, and—"

"Ebenezer, I was just sitting, marking out a route and plan that I would take alone, taking leave of work, if you were to allow it." He paused. "In fact, I know you would. Further—"

The two men continued to step on each other's conversation; such was their sense of immediacy and robustness of heart.

"We must somehow solve this crime for him," Scrooge said, his voice ringing in the night, "for I've been told he has something of immense importance to do in the future and I, or I guess, *we* must—"

"Wait a minute, kind sir. Did you just say you were told? In the middle of the night? How come that? For I can say as much."

"It's hard to explain, Bob."

Both men stood staring at each other, then for a moment at their boots, or up into the celestial sphere. Both cleared their throats. Then as if a starting bell had rung, both men began to tell the events of their evening.

Scrooge stopped mid-sentence. "Bob Cratchit, did I hear you say in the midst of what I was saying that you believe you were visited by a ghost?"

"Yes, I had but fallen asleep beside my wife, Alvina, when I awoke to see a bright, vaporous form, glowing and smiling abundantly. Surely, he was the very essence of cheer and communion with man. And he said as much. Not believing my eyes, I attempted to wake my Alvina, who, though I shouted at her and pushed on her shoulder, would not awaken."

He took a deep breath, long enough to see the look of amazement on Scrooge's face.

"Go ahead, Bob," Scrooge said, "for my story is not unlike yours. Please proceed."

"In due course, though I, at first, was filled with fear, and though I had often heard of ghosts walking abroad, I had never seen one. Then, he assured me that he was not an errant spirit, one doomed to walk the earth in incessant misery, but a blithe spirit, one sent hence from the heavenly abode. He told me that I was to find the means to clear the good name of Mr. Grumbles. And—"

"Did the ghost give you his name?"

"Yes. He said you would have known him in this life, indeed that you worked for him at one time of your life. Let me think. Ah, yes. He said his name was Fezziwig!"

"Ah ha! Good, old Fezziwig! If ever a man was bound for heaven, it was he." Scrooge felt a great sense of satisfaction knowing that the good work and positive demeanour of the man, who had always been a *man of business*, would indeed be installed in heaven.

"So, Fezziwig," Bob continued, "relayed some of your dealings together but mostly focused on what I was to do immediately. I'm to go to the mines and by some means, find the real killer. Say, Scrooge, did you say you had a similar story?"

"Yes, and I will relay it to you momentarily. But neither you nor I know much about mining. Under what auspices would we be able to abide there, surreptitiously I would say, in order to have time to solve this mystery?"

"Therein is where my plan involves your very nephew, Edmund, who is an engineer, is he not?"

"Yes, but his work is with building bridges and such, not with mining."

"It doesn't matter. He's an engineer, and the spirit of Fezziwig told me the mine has already advertised for an engineer to replace Grumbles. I say we convince Edmund to apply for the job via the post, attach a *black stamp* to it, and his resume will be the first name they see. He will say we are his apprentices at no extra cost. We can do that all on the morrow."

"That plan sounds good, but I'm wary that my nephew will agree. I feel there is some danger involved."

"Yes, quite! Fezziwig's ghost told me as much. The murderer is at large, and we will most assuredly be in mortal danger."

Both men allowed the concept of bodily harm or death foment in their minds. Just then, a troop of colliers aboard a trundle wagon passed on their way to work their shift in the coalmines. Among them, some boys no more than ten years old, sat huddled with them. Cratchit shook his head. "There goes one of the great tragedies of our time. Those poor children."

Scrooge felt astonishment. He had seen the orphan children huddled in alleys or under bridges, and he knew deeper in his heart that the practice of forcing small boys to work in the mines was rampant despite the recent law forbidding it. "I hadn't considered their plight."

In the bare, foggy light, Scrooge observed one wafer-thin waif seated with his poorly shod feet dangling off the end of the wagon. The boy's face showed such misery and despair; Scrooge was reminded of the horrid creatures the Ghost of Christmas Present had hidden under his vast cloak—one ignoble child was *poverty* and the other *ignorance*. Impulsively, Scrooge stretched out his hand as if he would snatch the boy from his dismal life and save him. But then the wagon was lost in the fog.

Turning back to Cratchit, he said, "Let us repair to your desk, complete our plan. I will fill you in on my own events of the night, and you must tell me of what good old Fezziwig imparted to you."

"And on the morrow, we must catch your nephew before he leaves for work and beg his participation."

The friends hastened inside.

STAVE SIX

CAPABLE WITH A GUN

When Scrooge's nephew, Frederick Edmund Nuckols, plodded sleepily to the door of his home, he had no idea who would be knocking at such an early hour. He looked at the grandfather clock. Four-thirty! He took a wick from a sideboard, lit it from his own lamp, and lit several others about the living room. Then he opened the door. "Uncle!" he exclaimed. "What brings you out at such an early hour?"

"Nothing, save the most urgent doings," Scrooge remarked, barging past Edmund into the room with Cratchit close on his heels. Turning while Edmund was closing the door, he minced no words. "We have been up all night, but our task requires immediate action, and you are the key to its success. A very important man's life is at stake, and much more for what he is deigned to do in the future."

Edmund plopped into a stuffed chair, rubbed his sleepy eyes, and attempted to listen.

"Who's there, Freddy?" a sweet female voice called from the upstairs.

"It's my dear uncle, Bernice. No cause for alarm."

Bernice, cloaked in a robe, came to the top of the stairs and called down. "Good morrow, dear Ebenezer, and the same to you, Bob Cratchit."

"And to you, as well, good lady," Cratchit said.

"Good morning, Bernice," Scrooge said. "I wish we had time to chat, but I'm in need of your husband for at least a few days in an urgent and, perhaps, life-threatening course."

"What? Well, let me put some tea on, and we'll listen." Bernice, her blonde curls dangling below her nightcap, bounced down the stairs and into the kitchen. Soon the three men heard the clattering of cups and saucers and the tea kettle clack upon the stove.

"There she goes, the only person in the world whom I allow to call me 'Fred.' Such a common name. In my line of work, I go by 'Edmund' and much prefer it. It is dynamic and forceful. But she is the angel of my goings and comings, the most beautiful woman I know."

"Well," said Scrooge, "'Frederick' *is* your first Christian name."

"I still have no taste for it, except when she says it." Edmund looked admiringly at Bernice in the kitchen. After a long moment, he yawned and turned to Scrooge and Bob. "What is all this about?" he asked. "Here I am on the first day of my vacation, hoping to sleep in."

"All the better that you are not required at your employ, for we need your expertise and your cover for our endeavour," Scrooge continued. "Like I've said, a man's life and much more depends on ours and your help."

"Who is this important man?"

"No other than Hezekiah Hiram Grumbles," Cratchit intoned. "He came to our office but yesterday, much affright. He's been accused of a murder that he did not commit. It is imperative that we go to the mine where he served as the engineer and save his good name and, perhaps, catch the real killer."

"Mr. Grumbles?" Edmund was in disbelief. "*Our* Mr. Grumbles?" He sat back in the seat. "That's impossible. The man wouldn't kill a fly. But I fail to see how I can help."

Scrooge leaned closer. "Edmund, you are an engineer. The company has already advertised for a replacement for Grumbles."

Bernice shuffled in with a tray of a teapot, cups, and saucers. She set down the tray and began pouring. "I've been listening. For goodness sakes, we need to do what we can for the sterling Mr. Grumbles."

The men nodded and took their cups, but none sipped the tea.

"But, Uncle Ebenezer, I'm not a mining engineer. I build bridges."

"It doesn't matter, nephew. We need only have you pretend for a few days while Bob and I gather evidence. We will be acting as your apprentices."

"Before I say yes, who is the man who was murdered? And, by what means?"

"We obtained a copy of the *Times*," Cratchit said, "and the murder is detailed in a small article, primarily giving the details known by the police—that Hiram is the accused and not yet apprehended, some cursory remarks of what supposed eyewitnesses said. The man's name is ..." He ruffled through the newspaper and upon finding the article, said, "His name is, or was, a Mr. Mortimer Owsley, manager of the mine. The sheriff had been immediately called and took control of the case."

"What do you think we are going to uncover that the constabulary has not already found?" Edmund asked.

"That is what we do not know," replied Scrooge. "Neither of us knows anything about gathering clues, nor of inspecting a site of a murder, nor of asking questions of witnesses. We are pure novices. Quite frankly, I am at a loss as to how to proceed, but *proceed* we must."

Cratchit nodded. "It's as if it is our sum token in life to do this. At some point, you deserve a fuller explanation, but now, time is of the essence. Will you help us?"

"Dear nephew," admonished Scrooge, "please help us."

Edmund closed his eyes as if in prayer. "Let me gather some clothes and sundry items for the journey." He stood, guzzled his tea, and handed the cup and saucer to Bernice.

"Dear Fred," Bernice said, "please promise me you'll be careful."

"I am the epitome of caution, my dear." He hustled up the stairs to fill a bag of clothes.

When he came down, Cratchit had just finished proscribing a vita announcing the excellent work history of *Edmund Nuckols, Esq., Mining Engineer Extraordinaire*. He handed the still ink-wet resume to Edmund who read it, chuckling at various points. Handing the page back to

Cratchit, he said, "Bob, I had no idea what an eloquent liar you are." He laughed heartedly.

Scrooge, for his part, had written a letter of introduction for Edmund. The nephew signed the letter in a broad hand. When the ink had dried, both pages went in an envelope, a penny black postage stamp was attached, and the three stood, ready to depart.

Bernice came forward, tears dotting her eyelashes, accompanied by two strapping lads, sleepy-eyed and yawning. Edmund hugged the boys, then gave his wife a loving embrace and kiss.

"You must be careful, Freddie," Beatrice said. "I must hear from you. Please write and tell me all is well."

"I will, my love, and look here." He opened his bag. She, along with Scrooge and Cratchit, peered inside the bag. Atop the clothes lay two pistols and a sack of shot and a horn of powder. "I tell you now. I will be the soul of caution. If I had been there, Edward Oxford would never have even gotten close to Queen Victoria when he tried to assassinate her." His voice fairly rang.

Bernice smiled but a little and patted Edmund's shoulder. "I shall miss you, my sweet."

"Farewell, my love."

Scrooge and Cratchit bid Bernice goodbye, and the three men strode out the door into the still, dark streets. Cratchit went to his own home to gather a few belongings for the journey and say farewell to his own family, thence to the rail station to purchase three tickets and wait for the others. Scrooge and Edmund walked to Scrooge's abode where he packed a simple bag, then they strode quickly to Scrooge's office.

STAVE SEVEN

THE PERILOUS JOURNEY BEGINS

When Lockie raced through the street to the Scrooge and Cratchit countinghouse, he feared he was late. He grabbed the knob, slammed against the door at full tilt, and was thrown back when it did not open. He fell off the steps and onto the wet cobblestones. Rising and holding his sore backside, he endeavoured to wrench the door open. He realised the place was locked up tight. No light shone in either window. No smoke poured from the chimneys. He posted himself on the step and waited, bewildered by such a turn of events.

Just as streams of sunlight from the morning sun began to flicker on the buildings, Scrooge and Edmund arrived at the office and beheld Lockie sitting on the step, a distressed glower on his face. "Where ha' you been?" he yelled indignantly. "Was I to wait here all day? Was I to hail a policeman to see if you had died, a murdered bloody corpse lying in an ally?"

"How now, brave, young Lockie," replied Scrooge. "You have not been put out. Is it raining?" He looked up at the sky. "Well, no, it is not. Is it snowing? Are you frigid from the cold?"

Lockie hung his head. "Beggin' your pardon, Master Scrooge."

"Not to worry. Now step aside, for I must open the office, and you shan't see which key I use. Step back, I say." Scrooge was becoming aware that he would have to leave his office with all its money and legal papers for an indefinite period, and he was loath to do so. Fumbling in his pocket, he fielded a broad key and stuck it in the lock, looking side to side to make sure no eyes saw him. He swung open the door and, catching sight of a passing ward, called him hither.

"See here, Constable," Scrooge demanded. "I must leave this edifice for an extended time, and I insist. Do you hear me? I insist you watch it with the wary eyes of an eagle. No one who comes to this door should enter it, save me." Scrooge's face had grown red, almost like in a rage. "Swear it, I say!"

Lockie stood at Scrooge's shoulder, nodding and giving a tight-lipped scowl at the policeman.

The constable appeared quite unruffled by Scrooge's tirade. He stepped back, brushed some dust from his lapels. "I'll do what I can, sir, but I ain't promisin' nothin'."

Before Scrooge could respond, he walked away, twirling his nightstick.

Scrooge turned and trudged inside, followed by Edmund and Lockie.

All was silent in the office. The walls were half sky-blue, half dismal-grey. Coal dust sat in the stoves, and a few papers were strewn on Scrooge's desk. He looked past his desk at a door at the rear of his mark. He had unbolted the long-sealed-shut doorway in recent weeks, whereupon he could open it of an occasion, and the rich effluvium of the spices from the wharfs, when they arrived, spilt into the office. He had begun to feel the rich things of the earth had been deprived of him those many past years; granted, they were deprived of him by his own doing, but he now so much more appreciated the simple pleasures of life.

Suddenly sad again, he remembered he had dwelt day after day in this sullen office, even after the wonderful, fearful, mysterious Christmas of two years past. He had never missed a day, save two holidays, inside the walls.

While he became less and less aware of the presence of his nephew and office boy, he found himself deeply yearning for a book to read, a fiction, something to take his mind off the task ahead of him. Yes, he could read *Robinson Crusoe* again and yield to its adventure, safe within the confines of his book, away from the real danger that seemed fast approaching. He understood this office had been his island, a place of solitude, away from danger. Now he must embark to a new future, less certain. Less tedious. Potentially more deadly.

Suddenly, after thinking of Crusoe's exploits, he felt enthralled with the aspect of an adventure, even facing danger. He was a new Crusoe. And who was his Friday? Edmund? Cratchit? Why! If his solving of this case made the news, he might gain recognition by the Lord Mayor himself. He felt quite proud.

Turning, he said to Lockie, "Your new job is to keep an eye on this place. I will leave a note on my desk that if any crime is committed here that whichever constable arrives here to inspect, he will know to contact you and that you must be here every day between noon and one o'clock. Do you understand that, Lockie?"

"Yes, Master Scrooge."

"Good." Scrooge went to a locked cabinet, opened it, and removed two bags of coins and set them in his deep coat pockets. He locked the cabinets, placed the key in a side coat pocket and scribbled the note he had described, leaving it on his desk. He wrote in a broad hand a placard he then placed in the window: "Closed. Come back tomorrow." Lockie remained near to him, peering over his shoulder.

With that, the three exited the building. Scrooge locked it up tight, turned quickly, almost knocking Lockie from the steps. With no apology to the young man, he and Edmund advanced to Scrooge's home to gather what he needed for their journey to the Tamperwind mine in County Cornwall. Lockie was left standing in the lurch on the steps.

When the two men were out of sight, Lockie said, "Begging your pardon, Master Scrooge, but I don't think I'll be followin' those orders." Then he took two keys he had pickpocketed from Scrooge and laid in a scarf. With one key, he let himself inside the office. With the second one, he went to the cabinet Scrooge had just used. He opened it. Inside were sacks and sacks of coins. He could be a rich man if he took even one of them. But he considered. *If I'm suddenly rich, I will soon be suddenly dead. I'll pass on taking the riches.* He untied one of the sacks and removed two crowns and two shillings. "That ought to get me to the Tamperwind mine." He shut the cabinet door, locked it, left the office, and secured the door, then thrust the keys deep in the pocket of his ragged trousers. He smirked a little and walked off in a jaunty fashion, his tall hat cocked to one side. After a few strides, he tossed the tall hat to a crippled man who had no hat. He put on his old cap. "Best not be conspicuous."

Across town, Edmund and Scrooge hastened to the Victoria train station. Just outside the gate, they spotted Cratchit, looking a bit worried, for it was almost time for departure. Coming closer, Scrooge recognised the apple of his eye—Tiny Tim—though he was hardly *tiny* anymore, and he stood straight as an arrow.

"Hello, Mr. Scrooge, my second father!" Tim called. "How are you this fine day?"

"It is indeed a fine day, the bright sun is shining, the air crisp, and I see a boy growing into a man!" Scrooge dropped his bags and shook the lad's hand vigorously. "You look to be faring quite well."

"Yes, sir, dear friend and second father. The alkali salts and the lengthy stay on the sunny cliffs of Dover in the sanatorium have done me good. Thanks so much to you." Tim leaned but a little on a much taller crutch. His smile was infectious. "I couldn't let Father carry the bags all the way to the station by himself." Tim held a heavily laden satchel in the hand opposite the crutch. "And good morrow to you, Mr. Nuckols. How fare thee and your family?"

"Quite well, as a matter of fact—"

"We've no time, Edmund," said Cratchit. "I'm sorry, but the train is preparing to depart. Hark, even now the conductor is calling for all to board."

Clearly, they all heard the conductor's admonition. The train's bell clanged. Audible steam gasps filled the air, followed by the engine whistle's shriek.

"Hurry now!" Cratchit said. "Tim, give again for me my fondest regards to your mother. Stay well, son. I'm counting on you and Peter to keep the household running like clockwork. And keep an eye on Belinda. She's become quite comely, and too many beaus at the door will swell her head. Keep a close eye on her. Bar the door if need be."

"I will, Father." He handed the suitcase to Bob, who took up a second, long cloth bag that looked inordinately heavy for clothing. "God bless you, Father, and you as well, goodly Master Scrooge, and Edmund. God bless you, everyone!" he called after the three retreating figures.

Each man waved back. They raced towards their passenger car.

No sooner had they boarded the train than it lurched forward. The three found seats. Edmund sat across from Scrooge and Cratchit.

Scrooge looked a long time at Cratchit's long bag. "Whatever do you bear in that long piece of cloth, Bob?"

"I wish I had a true gun case, but that is the best I can do for my musket."

"Musket?"

"Yes, some time back, I purchased it and have been going out of a Sunday now and then to the forest and taking some target practice. I think I've become rather proficient in its use."

"Have you shot anything?"

"Other than a target, no. Deer, rabbit, and muskrat have had little to fear from me. Still, I feel if a need arises in our endeavour where I should need a gun, I'd rather have one, than not."

Scrooge nodded. He became acutely aware that both Edmund and Cratchit seemed adept at handling a weapon, yet he knew nothing of self-defence, not even the basics of fisticuffs. His last scuffle with any adversary had been in the schoolyard when he was only ten. While Cratchit peered at a map, Scrooge attempted to move his arms rapidly, dodging his head left and right, as if he were in a real duel of fists. When Cratchit looked at him with a puzzled look, Scrooge stretched his arms high and yawned. "I'll wager I'm a bit tired, having not slept."

"Yes," Cratchit said. He turned back to the map.

Edmund was browsing a heavy book.

"What are you reading?" Scrooge asked.

"Well, if I'm to appear to be a mining engineer, I'd better know a little about it. This is a book I happened to have that is a *handbook for mining*. Quite interesting. Care to look?"

"Oh, no, not now." The lack of sleep was beginning to overtake Scrooge, and the rocking of the train was lulling him to welcomed slumber. His eyes drooped.

"It looks here," Cratchit announced, jabbing a finger at the map, "that it's 245 miles to St. Austell where we will disembark. We pass through the towns of Bugle, Luxalynn, Ponts Mill, St. Blazy, and we will pass over that great viaduct."

"Yes," Edmund called above the racket of the clacking wheels. "I helped design that viaduct as part of a team of engineers. One hundred feet above the chasm, six hundred and fifty feet across it. Quite a feat of engineering."

Scrooge tried to listen to Edmund and Cratchit's conversation, but he soon nodded to sleep.

Unbeknownst to them, eight rows back, Lockie sat gazing out the window in amazement.

STAVE EIGHT
THE IMAGINARY UNCLE

Lockie bent low behind the seat back and kept his cap pulled down. As best he could, he glimpsed out the window at the bucolic countryside of short stone walls, rolling brown grass hills with spots of white snow, sedgy creeks, haystacks, and flocks of sheep in every other pasture.

Lockie was purely mesmerised. He had never been out of London, in fact, never more than a few blocks' radii of Scrooge's office. He felt a thrill, enamoured by the entirety of it. His world had grown significantly. Farther from the city, snow glistened in patches, and in some areas, the white fluff stretched for miles, so different from the grey-sludge snow of the streets of London. Whenever the train made a stop for water or to pick up and drop off passengers, Lockie sprang from his seat and raced about the town to see everything he could in the moments before the train again departed. He was gorging himself on the outside world. He was satiated.

When the train arrived at St. Austell, the three men disembarked, and Lockie slid out a back door of the car.

The men trooped from the train station, then across the cobblestone central courtyard to an inn where from, on the next day, they would take a coach to the Tamperwind mine. Snow had drifted up against the walls of the inn and the stable. The coach horses pranced and nickered in a corral while a hostler, bundled head to foot in a heavy coat, scarf, and wool cap, waved his arms to make sure the horses got their exercise. Though Scrooge and his comrades hustled inside the inn, Lockie raced to the corral fence, jumped on the top rail, and gazed, entranced by the rugged, yet comfortable sight. In his mind, he was in heaven.

After the hostler had herded the stout ponies inside the stable, Lockie noted the icy snap in the wind and began to concern himself about his own bedding situation. In London, he had always had a willing family to take him in for a farthing, or a woman of the evening who had no man for the night and needed someone to snuggle with for warmth only, or a gaggle of urchins like himself who huddled in some unencumbered shanty. Out here, on his own, he would have to depend on what resources he could attain.

The sun was receding rapidly in this day that was approaching the winter solstice. Lockie posted himself outside the stable door. When the hostler, a broad-shouldered hulk of a man with great strands of black hair spreading from under his wool hat, strode out the door, he turned and padlocked the door. Lockie's face fell. He would have to find another way in. The big man muttered as he strode away, "Well, Mavin, you done your little ponies good. You're a decent man, Mavin, you are. Now, where's my pint that I deserve?"

Lockie did not wish to delay, for his fingers were growing numb. He had no gloves, and his clothes were generally threadbare.

He scrambled around the side of the barn and was attempting to climb to the open hayloft window when the hostler appeared at the corner. "What ho! What are you doin' there, vandal?! You won't be stealin' any o' my fine animals, nor the eggs of the missus' chickens. I'll throttle you, I will!" He raced towards Lockie and leapt to grab at the young lad's dangling foot, for the other foot barely found a toehold on a crossbar board, while his hands struggled to maintain a grip on a slippery pipe. The hostler leapt again and again to grab the dangling foot. Lockie kicked and kicked and hung on.

"If you be that highwayman that's traversin' about and stealin' from the good folks on these coaches," the hostler called, "I'll drag ye right now before the magistrate!"

"Highwayman?" Lockie whispered. "He thinks me a common robber."

"And they'll hang ye for sure."

Finally, the man grew weary of his toil and bent over, gasping for air. Lockie used the moment to climb inside the open hayloft window. He turned and peered down at the man who was still trying to gain his breath. Lockie came up with a plan. When the man looked up, shaking a fist at him, Lockie smiled his brilliant, toothy grin. "Why, Uncle Mavin, is that you?"

The man looked a bit bewildered and a bit suspicious.

"Don't you recognise me? It's me, your nephew, Lockie."

The man pinched an eye at the lad. "I don't know no Lockie. And I ain't got no fambly to have a nephew from. So, who be ye?"

"Why, of course, I'm not your real nephew. We all know that."

The man scratched his head. "I can't say that I know you at all."

"Very well." Lockie continued to smile. "What's the town next over that you've visited over the years, the one where you go for a pint at the pub?"

"You mean, Ponts Mill?"

"Yes, of course. And what's the name of the pub?"

"Ponts Mill public house."

"And the name of the barmaid there that you've often spoken to?"

"Can't say that I ever said two words between us."

"Well, of course not, not while you were sober." Lockie let the words sink in.

"What'd ya mean? I keep my liquor well 'nough."

"Yes, you do, except on those occasions when you and she would share a bottle."

"I don't recall as much. Are you tryin' to prevaricate agin' me?"

"No, Uncle Mavin. How else would I know your name?"

"I ain't your uncle."

"No, but you've met me several times after you'd had a few and you were a whistling and singing and laughing with me dear mother, the barmaid. I remember distinctly you saying to her, 'If there's ever anything you or your boy needs, I'm the man. Consider me your brother.' Now don't tell me you don't remember saying that?"

"Well, I guess I did, but I don't recollect it."

"So here I am, fetching after the *anything* that you promised. You see, I'm on a journey. All I need from you, Uncle Mavin, is a good coat and a place to sleep here tonight. I'll even muck out the stalls to show you my goodwill."

Lockie could tell Mavin was mulling over the proposition. At length, he said, "Well, I am a man who keeps his promises. You come down here. You show me an evening's work of cleaning those stables, breakin' the ice in the horses' water buckets, and I'll find you a coat. You can sleep in the loft. That's all I have to gi' ye."

"Perfect!" Lockie scooted out the hayloft, traversed the sidewall, and plopped to the ground. Mavin helped him up and dusted him off. He took him to the barn door, opened the lock, and showed him the muck basket and pitchfork.

"Get ye busy now," the hostler said. He put his hands on his hips and watched Lockie.

Though unfamiliar with the task and only having seen the muckrakers cleaning the streets in London, Lockie went about removing the piles of horse ashes and lowering them into a large woven basket. After he finished, Mavin dug in an old burlap bag and fished out a ragged and torn but heavy coat. Lockie tried it on. Too large, but he was happy to get it.

Mavin tousled the boy's hair. "You sleep in the loft tonight. I'll not wake ye. It's up to ye to wake yourself. I hope you're not leavin' your poor mother without means of support."

"No, good sir, she's fine." Lockie beamed his winning smile, and he climbed the ladder up into the loft. "I'll be fine here. Thanks again, Uncle Mavin."

Mavin plodded out the door. Lockie heard him turn the key in the lock. Gazing out the open window, myriad stars sparkled like the diamonds in an Arabian night's treasure. He settled back into a heap of straw and watched the dark sky. No fog, no smoke. Once, a shooting star sped across the sky. Lockie was content. What could possibly be all this danger his masters spoke of anyway?

STAVE NINE

UP THE MOUNTAIN, AND A BRIGAND

Lockie awoke the next morning at the sound of the coachman trumpeting his horn, announcing the arrival of the coach at the inn. The sun was full up, the air crisp, and a few snowflakes drifted lazily down. Lockie sat up, threw on his coat, and immediately felt pangs of hunger. He climbed down the ladder onto the barn floor. He went immediately where the chickens sat on their nests. He reached under one, drew out the egg, cracked it gently on his noggin, then supped down the contents. He did the same to three more hens, stealing their eggs.

The sound of female voices just outside the barn startled him. "That would be the housemaids coming to gather the eggs and milk the cow," he said to himself. He climbed the ladder and hid in the hay. Two maidens came in and began their tasks. One of them said, "I certainly hope they catch the robber that's been stealin' lately. I heard he struck a coach last night near St. Blazy. I'm afraid to go anywhere alone."

"Me too," said the second.

Lockie was not about to stay and listen. If Scrooge and his partners were leaving on this coach, he needed to be handy about it. He stealthily climbed out the loft window and grappled down to the ground. The snow was falling harder now. He thrust his cap low on his brow, and with the heavy coat about him, he looked to be the size of a robust man.

Cratchit, Edmund, and Scrooge emerged from the inn along with several other men and one pleasant-looking damsel with curly blonde hair peeking from under her bonnet. Most of the men wore top hats, though one wore a shabby cap. While the hostler undid the harnesses of the four charges, then hitched the new ones in place, Lockie followed suit of three other gentlemen—two amiable-looking men, one a tinker, one a merchant with a heavy case, and the third a hulking man who smelled of liquor and sour cheese. They all climbed atop the vast coach, seating themselves amongst the sundry luggage. Lockie kept his cap low and faced towards the back. Scrooge and his companions were waiting to board the inner seats of the coach, for Cratchit had spared no expense on their accommodations, including the coach.

"Fine thing, Bob Cratchit," Scrooge bemoaned, "spending a full crown for our journey. I'd have been just as comfortable riding atop. And furthermore, the tips required for service! Sixpence for the chambermaid. Tupence for the bootjacks. I tell you, by the end of this journey, we shall all be paupers." He grimaced and thrust his hands into his long pockets.

Suddenly, a strange look overcame his face. He began searching all his pockets.

The driver called, "Get ye in, if you're travelin'. Now where's me guard?"

No sooner had he made the statement than the broad-chested guard burst out the door of the stable, pulling up and buttoning his trousers. A young maiden followed quickly after, "Don't forget your gun, Ferlin!" Her voice fairly twinkled while she handed him a bulky blunderbuss. She was blushing, and her dress and apron were untidy.

The guard's face turned rosy as well. He took the gun, smiling unabashedly at her. "See you next trip, Arlise."

"Bye, bye," she tittered while he mounted the seat beside the driver. She vigorously waved a hankie and blew him a kiss. He grabbed at the air like he was catching it, putting his hand to his heart.

Scrooge was still fumbling in his multiple pockets as he got into the coach. Cratchit allowed the young woman into the coach, then he and Edmund entered and seated themselves. The young woman, trim at the waist and erstwhile of face, and having a small bottom and the slightest bosom, sat next to Edmund who maintained the largest backside of the four. Scrooge sat opposite him while Cratchit sat opposite the woman.

Scrooge, scowling, announced, "And at the end of our journey, we are required by whoever decides such things to tip both the driver and guard a shilling. Why does everything cost so much? And, and ..." He floundered for words, flummoxed by the feelings that had plumbed his heart for so long. He felt anger at the expense and remorse at his own lack of charity. *I probably should have given an even bigger tip to the chambermaid.* Lacking the wherewithal to console himself, he looked down at his boots. *I must have put the keys in my bag.* He took off his tall hat and attempted to make himself comfortable. When he glanced up, Edmund was looking out the window. The young woman across from Cratchit was smiling and almost giggling. When he turned towards Cratchit, he saw his partner smiling back at her.

"What's the humour?" he asked, his voice showing he was peeved.

Cratchit turned to him. "Oh, 'twas nothing. Just every time the coach hit a bump, my hat fell off, and we found it funny."

"Oh, yes, sir," the young woman remarked. "I'm altogether sorry. I couldn't help myself from laughing. It was quite a lark to watch your hat jostle off so many times."

"Bob Cratchit, at your service, miss." Cratchit tipped his hat then set it in his lap.

They smiled again at each other, the young woman ducking her head demurely. Cratchit cleared his throat and looked out the window, fiddling with his wedding ring.

Fine thing, Scrooge thought, *the man is married and with children. We've not time for this malarkey. Humbug!*

Scrooge's demeanour grew darker because now he knew they would soon arrive at the mine. Things were not right. They had not had time to plan any strategy. He sensed impending doom. His throat tightened, and his heart raced. For a moment, he wished for the counsel of Jacob

Marley, but the ghost's words seemed to have mixed messages. Maybe the ghost was doing the devil's bidding to find evidence to exonerate Grumbles, when in fact he *was* the killer. His thoughts plunged deeper and deeper into fear and despair. He had not slept well, and despite his wariness of the threesome's future, he fell into a fitful sleep. His dreams careened madly from one shadowy corner to the next with dark, cloaked murderers carrying bludgeons in their fists fast upon him.

He awoke with a start. They had arrived at the last way station, and the hostler there was hitching a fresh set of horses, plus a large cock horse in the lead.

"This big, cock horse," the driver said, "is needed to pull the coach up this steep incline." Scrooge leaned out to see the forbidding hill and was amazed. Its height and angle of ascent were stupefying. On either side were steep drop-offs into craggy pits. Scrooge had trouble imagining that they would be able to reach its top.

He looked at his fellow passengers, all nodding in sleep. He rapped on the coach sidewall. "See here, driver, are we supposed to mount that hill?"

"That we are," the driver called back. He popped his whip, and the horses struck out. Then he said, "Usually we make it. The ice may make it a tad slippery."

Usually! What does he mean by that? Scrooge looked out at the ice-covered road. He further flinched at the wheels sliding not gracefully about on the road. The coach jerked again and again. The driver popped his whip regularly. The riders atop the coach began bewailing and called for the driver to slow down.

"Can't slow down or we'll never make it up the hill!" He snapped his great whip and called loudly at his charges.

Edmund, Cratchit, and the woman all awoke, being they were jostled like puppets in a Punch and Judy show. "What the devil!" remarked Edmund.

Cratchit rubbed his temple, for he had hit his head hard on the sidewall. The woman clung to a wall strap for dear life. Soon they were ascending the pinnacle. Scrooge looked out and saw the side of the road falling away into a precipice a bare two feet from the wheels. He saw two of the men from the top of the coach leap to the icy mud of the road, and one of them slid precariously close to the chasm. They got up and tried in piteous fashion to run after the coach.

The coach felt to Scrooge, for all the world, to be ascending straight up, his weight plastering him to the back wall. The woman was whimpering, Cratchit had great dread upon his brow. Edmund closed his eyes and gritted his teeth. The jerking of the coach, the stamping of the horses' hooves, the calls of the driver and guard. The hostler, riding astride the cock horse, yelling at the top of his lungs.

Then as if all their efforts were doomed, the coach began to slide backwards, weaving from side to side.

"We shall all perish!" Edmund called.

The woman screamed in terror.

Scrooge heard a small, sweet woman's voice. "Tell the driver to stop. Use the brake."

Scrooge called as loud as he could, "Pull the brake, you idiot. Stop us!"

The driver pulled the brake, and the coach shuddered to a stop only a few feet from slipping into the chasm.

The voice, a whisper light and airy, said, "Now tell all the men to get out and help the horses pull the coach."

Scrooge was alarmed. He looked about him. The voice was not ghostlike, but familiar. Where had he heard it?

He struggled from his seat and out the door. Standing in the narrow road, he said, "Driver, for all our lives, let all us men help pull or push the coach to the pinnacle."

The driver frowned, then said, "All right, me hearties! Let's push this coach."

The men who had evacuated the coach earlier came up, and soon, Edmund, Cratchit, the guard, and the men from atop were pushing wheels or pulling on the horses' harnesses. Lockie was careful to keep himself opposite the side Scrooge and Edmund were on, and well behind Cratchit who pushed a front wheel.

With much effort and sweat, muddy hands, and mud to the tops of their boots, the coach reached the hilltop. The group looked down on the opposite side of the steep road to a gentle slope into a crag-filled valley with a few outcroppings of wild grasses and barely a tree in sight. All the men, save Lockie, who hid behind the coach, stood in a group, breathing hard, but generally smiling. The guard took out a large kerchief and began wiping his muddy hands.

At that moment, the man who smelled of liquor and sour cheese wrested the blunderbuss from the guard, backed a few steps away, cocked the weapon, and aimed it at the group. "Now!" he announced. "I have your attention, and I'll be having your valuables. Let's start with the wallets, gentlemen." Stuck in his belt was a flintlock pistol.

"You craven highwayman!" the driver called.

"Wait till I get my hands on you," growled the guard.

"Oh, but you won't," the robber sneered. "I'll be long gone, and I 'ope I don't have to kill any o' you." He was a big man with hulking shoulders.

Each of the men, except Scrooge, took wallets from their person and tossed them at the feet of the large man. Scrooge, too reticent to even think of departing with his money, stood with his hands up and his head down.

"And what about you?" The robber poked his gun in Scrooge's ribs. "Come on, fellow, don't be the one to die. You'll find more money. I'll bet you're good with money."

Scrooge appeared to boil, his face reddening, his eyes like sparks. "You'll not have a farthing, not a ha' penny, you scoundrel, you varmint!" Scrooge kept backing away while the large man was attempting to gather wallets from the ground with one hand, but he kept spilling them.

"Old man, don't press me!" he growled. "I'd love to use this gun."

When reaching for a wallet, the highwayman had the gun aimed down. The distraction of Scrooge's tirade was all Lockie needed. He had slipped like a stealthy fox at the chicken coop behind the broad man with the gun. He leapt on the man's back, put a finger on the trigger of the gun. The big gun discharged straight into the mud with such force, it knocked both Lockie and the thief to the ground, the gun spinning to the feet of the guard. When Lockie bounced to his feet, he held the man's pistol, aimed at the man who was pulling himself to his feet. His dark, woolly coat was covered with mud.

Lockie handed the flintlock to the guard. "Here you are, sir. I don't know how to use it."

"Well, I do, lad." He cocked the hammer back. "And I'd be glad to use it."

The robber tossed the one wallet he still held at the feet of the guard. When the guard looked down, the robber raced pell-mell back down the treacherous hill, weaving in his escape. The guard could take no shot.

Lockie turned and saw the dumbfounded look on Scrooge's, Cratchit's, and Edmund's faces.

"Well." He shrugged. "I couldn't let you go off without your best office boy in the entire money-lending world, now could I?"

Cratchit strode forwards and hugged the boy. "You are a brave one, Lockie!"

He quickly released the boy, who received backslaps from all the men. The woman called grateful words from inside the coach. When Lockie looked up at Scrooge, his master bore a dour scowl. "We will talk later, young man." Scrooge looked a long time at the boy as if he were a stranger. The skinny street kid, who said he was seventeen, was not tall, but he was muscled. His threadbare clothes needed mending, especially the knees of his trousers that were torn wide open, a bloodied scrape on one knee. The brown locks spilt like a waterfall from under the measly cap. The freckled but ruddy face showed youthful exuberance, but a depth of wisdom as well. "When we get to the tin mine shop, we must get you some reasonable clothes."

Lockie smiled.

"But we will most definitely talk later." Scrooge climbed in the coach. "Well, get atop the coach. You didn't pay to ride inside."

Lockie climbed up. The others took their seats and the coach wound along the ragged Macadam road. In the distance, Scrooge, leaning out the window, his face seared by an icy wind, witnessed the mine, and to the immediate left of it lay the shanty homes of the workers' village and a shop or two and a forlorn church facing the road. Farther to the left, but a quarter-of-a-mile atop a small verdant hill with the only trees in the area, stood the mansion of Mr. Tamperwind.

Ducking his head back inside the coach and lowering the curtain, his mind was refreshed, somehow glad that Lockie had come along. Further, he recognised the voice that had spoken to his mind when the stage was sliding backwards was not one he had never heard, but one he had almost forgotten—his fiancé, Isabelle. Pity. She was such a beauty both in appearance and in spirit. And he had let her go.

The words she had said had never been lost to him and burned now in his heart. She had bemoaned of his growing coldness towards her as his heart had warmed to *monetary gain*, "In a changed nature, an altered spirit."

He had indeed changed in those past years as if some horrid creature had gathered him in with stinging tentacles, a great octopus that held his spirit tight until it blackened into the man he became for twenty plus years. Where had the years gone? No day during that time stood out, no moment was any different from another. Put the key in the lock of his counting-house door, complain for any reason, fear for the slightest loss of any of his accumulated wealth, reminding himself to pinch every penny and to keep his nose steady on the grindstone. *Did light ever enter into that place in those days?*

He remembered a distant event when he had been Isabelle's suitor, himself a young man of twenty, but sure that he wished to marry her. That incident was somewhat similar to the recent harrowing traverse up the icy hill, and in that moment in his and Isabelle's past, when the four-in-hand could not negotiate a muddy tract, she had whispered the same words to him then. He and the other men got out and pushed the coach along to drier soil. He smiled a ginger little smirk, remembering that when the deed was accomplished, she gave him her gentle kiss upon his cheek and the glow of her smile.

He ran his hand through his prematurely white hair. The frost-icy rime that adorned his head had become more like a friendly snow in which children might play at snowball fights and build snowmen and go sledding down its snowy hills. His gait was springier than it had been those many years as a miser; his smile was purer and, let us say, winsome. A tired hypocrite had become a sort of good-natured sprite.

Scrooge had changed. Or had he?

STAVE TEN

JOURNEY COMPLETED; A NEW MURDER FOUND

The coach slowed and came to a stop at the weigh station near the mine. A more dismal place would be hard to find. All the ground was tamped-down, grey, sticky mud. Not a sliver of green anywhere. The opening to the mine was dark and imposing with vast timber columns supporting it. Glimmers of lantern light flickered from within the opening chamber, which was a sort of tall cavern where the pump houses were stationed. The gaping cavern of the mine sat in a high, craggy hill that looked like a jumble of boulders that had been tossed in the air and then landed haphazardly on top of each other. Each rusty red and black, jagged outcropping more imposing and rugged than the one below it. Along a narrow avenue between the village and the mine itself, Scrooge could just make out in the distance the tumultuous sea with grey and whitecapped waves.

The tinker and the other merchant dismounted quickly and set about knocking on the doors of the shanties, each home with only a single window, slats for panelling, piteous roofs of thatch, and spare boards, cobbled together. When the doors opened, though, each travelling vendor was shuttled in like he was family. Lockie stayed atop the coach. The driver and guard dismounted. The guard set to cleaning the mud from his gun; the driver helped the hostler with the harnesses and feeding and watering the team of horses.

"I say," Cratchit said to the driver, stepping down from the coach. "Can you not take us as far as the Tamperwind mansion? We have business there."

"No, I'm afraid you'll have to make the trek yourself. Company policy. We stop here at the weigh station, rest the horses, and attempt to make it back to the inn down the road before nightfall."

"But—"

"There're no buts to it, sir. Please excuse me."

With that, Cratchit called to Lockie, "Toss down the bags; we've got to hike to the mansion. I hope they are cordial enough to put us up for the night." When Scrooge came around beside him, Cratchit whispered, "And I certainly hope they hire Edmund on the spot."

Scrooge nodded, but remembering himself, he took shillings from his pocket and paid the gratuity to the driver and guard. Surreptitiously, he shoved a few coppers into Lockie's palm. "We'll get you some gloves too."

The young woman, who had been waiting in the coach until the bags were lowered, exited and stood before Cratchit. She was petite and kind-faced. Though a simple beauty, her smiles were abundant, as were the golden curls cascading about her shoulders. "Kind sir," she asked of Cratchit, "might I ask you to help me carry the trunk up the hill as well? I'm sure my uncle, Erasmus, will pay you well."

"Your uncle?"

"Yes, my Uncle Erasmus Tamperwind beckoned me here by letter but two weeks ago. My name is Lucy Tamperwind. According to his letter, he has important information to share with me, the content of which I do not know. My father died years ago. My mother, weighed down by consumption, passed away a mere two months past. I've spent these last months putting her estate in order. I'm only seventeen, and to have the burden of my mother's death, the estate in disrepair, and then this urgent letter from my uncle, I'm quite undone. Now I'm to visit my uncle whom I have not seen since I was a very small girl. I'm looking forward to it, truly I am. But I am beside myself."

"Well, that is a heavy load you have shouldered, but good to know that after that harrowing robbery attempt, we at least made it here alive." Cratchit reached up and took the large trunk from Lockie and lowered it to the ground with a thud. "My name is Bob Cratchit."

"I'm pleased to meet you, Mr. Cratchit." Lucy extended her hand, and he shook it.

"I am here with Mr. Edmund Nuckols, a mining engineer." He pointed at Scrooge's nephew. Then he pointed at Scrooge. "Mr. Ebenezer Scrooge, there, and I are apprentices. We are here in response to an advertisement for the chief engineer position. It seems the previous one had to leave unexpectedly."

"Oh," she said and looked up at Lockie on top of the coach.

"Yes, that is our assistant apprentice. He's a blessing I would say, especially after today. Not an expected blessing, but still here. Yes, here." Cratchit stammered at what to say next.

Lockie tipped his hat at Lucy. "I'm pleased to meet such a gorgeous creature. God's earth is a better place for your being here."

"Lockie has a gift of gab, Miss Tamperwind." Cratchit gave a smirking smile.

Lockie leapt to the ground beside Cratchit. Lucy looked at her heavy trunk.

"Yes, quite." Cratchit blushed, then lifted one end of the trunk. He held his musket in the cloth case in his other hand.

Lockie threw Cratchit's suitcase atop the trunk and hefted the other end of the chest. The five travellers trudged up the long, muddy slope past the shanties, a handful of the miners and their families toiling about their pitiful yards. They gained steep, paved stairs of about fifty yards in length. Arriving after many tedious steps at the top of the stairs, a polite, low, white picket fence girded the estate. Tangled vines grew about it, and some of the grounds seemed to be in shabby order. Bare trees with a sliver of ice on their branches stood like dark, goblin guards. The gate was locked, so the five of them took turns hollering until, finally, a hefty man with bulging muscles and a timid expression trotted around the house and appeared at the gate.

"We're here," stated Scrooge, "in response to the advertisement for the mining engineer. This young woman is Mr. Tamperwind's niece."

The humble-faced man cocked his head and waved both hands beside his ears. He mumbled something on the order of his being deaf, but he smiled, unlocked the gate, and in subservient fashion, bowing often, led the group up the house steps and opened the door and allowed them inside.

The mansion was aglow with light. Candles and lamps burned everywhere. Hung on every wall were great boughs of greenery, primarily holly with its red berries. The parlour and dining room fireplaces fairly roared with the logs crackling and popping, and the oaken aroma filling the vast parlour was appealing. Some fancy streamers of red intertwined with green pine boughs ran up the bannister and along the sidewall. The appearance was entirely festive as if Christmas day had already arrived.

They stood in the doorway upon an ornately woven rug when a thin woman of about thirty with an aquiline nose, dark eyes, whitish skin, and pitch-black hair tied in a bun strode quickly into the room, carrying a new-made ribbon bow. She stopped full, dropping the bow. "Who are you? Who let you in?"

The deaf-mute hastened to her and handed her a note he had scribbled on foolscap. She read it and bade him to withdraw. He stood to the side of the room, head down, ringing his cap in his hands.

"The gardener's note really tells me nothing. Who are you?"

Scrooge took the task of introducing them all, last of all the niece, Lucy.

"Ah, dear Lucy," the pretty but severe woman said, "I'm so glad to finally meet you. I'm your cousin, Abigail. Samuel, my brother and your cousin, is around here somewhere. We've only arrived yesterday and are slowly becoming appraised of the disturbing situation here. Lucy, we've never been able to meet until now, for I believe the two sisters-in-law, our mothers, had a falling out just before either of us were born." She gave her cousin a warm embrace. "Now, a new friend, my cousin, that I will surely treasure is here at last."

She then introduced herself to each of the men and exuberantly shook their hands, jabbering like a child about each one's name and personal story. Lockie sat on the trunk, weary from the journey. When she came to him, she asked, "And who is this fine gentleman? He looks a bit worse for wear." She bent forwards right into his face, smiling intently.

No sooner were the words out of her mouth than her brother, a stark, pale-skinned man of her equivalent height, emerged from the back of the house and walked to the group, one hand in his coat side pocket, his fingers in, his thumb out. He wore no smile, but held a pipe tight in his teeth in a sort of grimace. His suit was impeccably maintained, an ascot about his neck. When he came up beside her, Scrooge could see the definite family resemblance in their faces. "Dear sister," the man said, placing his arm around her waist and pulling her away from Lockie, "aren't you going to introduce me?"

"Why, yes," she said, her facial expression changing from light-hearted to a subdued, demure look. "Samuel Jiggins, I'd like you to meet Mr. Ebenezer Scrooge, Mr. Bob Cratchit, and Mr. Edmund Nuckols. Oh, and their page, Lockie. They are here to apply for a job in Uncle's mine. And this young woman is our dear cousin, Lucy Tamperwind."

While Samuel made the rounds, greeting and speaking with each individual, Scrooge felt compelled to notice the nuances of the persons they had met. Samuel maintained his dark hair trimmed close and wore a suit of a fine weave, indicating either wealth or putting on a show, for his shoes were badly scraped, a hole forming at the toe of one. He seemed to be visibly stiff, not because of formality, but perhaps from a back injury. Scrooge had seen other individuals with pinched backs behave so.

Samuel's sister, Abigail, seemed much less vivacious than at first. What was the cause? When she reached up to straighten her hair, he noticed several white scars on her left wrist. Attempts at suicide? Her fingernails were bitten to the quick, indicating a nervous temperament. A tea stain was on her dress about knee-high.

The gardener appeared as humble as anyone could be. His hands were grimy and rough, but if he was the gardener, why were his boots of high quality? His swollen nose showed the reddened corpuscles of a drinker; his hands shook like a drunkard's.

Scrooge took in the beautifully appointed home. To the right of the entrance was the dining room, then the kitchen and firewood room. To the left was an extensive parlour with a high ceiling. The furniture had elegant floral designs. A huge grandfather clock and hall tree stood as sentries to the doorway. No family portraits hung about, something he felt was odd for a family of wealth not to have any at all. And why was the house so lit up, even to the upstairs?

He was pondering this when Samuel asked his sister to explain the overabundance of lighting.

"You see," she began, "we have been in terror ever since we arrived and learned of the death of the mining manager, a gruesome tale that the housekeeper and Uncle Tamperwind's young ward has told us. Some of the miners have said they have seen the black-cloaked killer, a Mr. Grumbles, skulking about, even as late as last night."

Scrooge, Cratchit, and Edmund flashed astonished looks. Scrooge wondered, *Something is indeed amiss. Grumbles is supposed to be on his way to Paris, or so I thought.*

Abigail drew a deep breath. "What is more, last night, there was yet another murder, a miner, a Mr. Smyth. Before the body was found, some miners saw a big man in a black cloak running away. They are quite frightened, as are we all if a murderer is prowling about."

"Speak for yourself, Abigail," Samuel intoned.

"Wait!" said Scrooge. "You say, a second murder has taken place?"

Edmund, Cratchit, and Lockie looked at each other, amazed. Scrooge's face showed more dread than amazement. Samuel and Abigail nodded solemnly.

"Please continue, Miss Jiggins," Edmund said.

"Please, call me 'Abigail.'"

"At your pleasure, ma'am. Please go on."

"Very well. Mrs. Owsley and I—she is the manager's wife and housekeeper here—are frightened. I had the gardener lock the gate and keep a watch. In addition, I want to keep the house as lit as possible to hopefully keep the murderer away. Not having anything else to do, I decided to brighten up the place with holly and streamers, for it so needs cheering up. And … that's all."

She ducked her head and withdrew a few steps behind her brother.

"Well said, sister." Samuel cringed suddenly, arched his back, and groaned. After a moment, he said, "I've had a back injury, a fall from a horse, you see. I would show you up to Mr. Tamperwind's room, but I have difficulty climbing stairs. He is quite ill and bedridden if you didn't know."

"Certainly," said Edmund, "but might we meet the housekeeper and the ward?"

"Agatha Owsley, the housekeeper who lost her husband, and Michael Tamperwind, the ward. I'm not sure where they are, perhaps in the garden in the back. You will meet them soon. Abigail, would you mind escorting the gentlemen up to Uncle's room? If he's looking for a replacement mining engineer, I'm sure he'll be excited to meet Mr. Nuckols. And even more so to see his niece. I must tell you, sirs, that Uncle Erasmus has been ill for some time and remains in his bed. He may be tired and, shall we say, crotchety. Gentlemen, Lucy, if you'll follow my sister. His bedroom is at the top of the stairs."

Lockie stood to go as well.

"Stay with the luggage," Scrooge directed.

Lockie plopped again on top of the trunk.

Scrooge came last in the group. Samuel stopped him at the bottom, pulling him aside. "I hope that your friend, Mr. Nuckols, can assuage Uncle's guilt and get the mine working again. He feels responsible in some ways for the death of his foreman at the hands of the former mining engineer. I wish I knew more to tell you all, but everyone here is pretty closemouthed about it. I believe our dear uncle suspected something was amiss, which is why he sent the urgent letters to Lucy and us. He'd not seen us, nor us him, in eons, so why would his letter sound so ... so filled with fear?"

"Has he not told you the reason for the letters to you and your cousin, Lucy?"

"His sister and brother, our mother and Lucy's father, are both dead. He had no children of his own; hence he's occasionally taken in children as wards. The one he has now is about ten years old. Extremely smart lad. To answer your question, Uncle Erasmus has been rather brusque with us, appearing preoccupied and wary. We've tried to bring up the letter twice, and he's diverted the subject elsewhere."

"Thank you, Samuel, for that information." Scrooge began to climb the stairs.

"Oh, and, Mr. Scrooge," Samuel called. Scrooge halted and turned. "Do not be surprised at my sister's behaviour. She was quite buoyant with you when you arrived, but her mood changes on a whim and she becomes quite aggressive. Please don't be taken aback by it. She's been that way since her youth, and I do my best to care for her."

"Thank you." Scrooge proceeded up the stairs. Glancing out a window, he saw a boy of about ten who was talking to a cat on a tree limb. He remembered a fondness for cats at one time of his childhood.

STAVE ELEVEN

THE MASTER OF THE HOUSE

Reaching the top of the stairs, Scrooge joined the group outside Mr. Tamperwind's bedroom. Abigail was lightly knocking on the door and calling his name. There was, at first, no response. Suddenly, the door sprang open, and a woman with grey, tangled hair falling about her wrinkled face stood in the doorway. She wore a sullied cap and a dirty apron over a twice-turned dress. With a few teeth missing, she bore a sort of snarl. "Why would you be bothering Mr. Tamperwind? He needs his rest, Miss Abigail, *miss high and mighty* niece from Lancaster. Have you not troubled him enough in these awful times? He is torn in pieces with grief over miner Smyth's death. Not to mention my husband's demise." The woman was working herself into a tither. She stomped her foot. "Now, who are these people with you? I demand to know."

Scrooge wondered if the man needed his rest, why was she making such a racket?

"First of all, Agatha," Abigail calmly said, "this woman here is Uncle's other niece, Lucy." She lightly pushed Lucy forwards.

Agatha Owsley eyed Lucy suspiciously. "When was the last time you saw your uncle, young woman?" She fairly spit the words out. "Do you know him at all, or how would he know you're telling the truth and not some thief?"

Lucy, taken aback, said, "Well, I am certainly his niece. I have little else to tell you. I have not seen him since I was a very small child. I remember him as kind, but beyond that, I can show him a small painting of his brother, my father, that I carry with me."

"How am I to know that's true? You look like someone who'd take advantage of an old man."

"Here, let me show the portrait to Uncle Erasmus. Surely—"

"Let them come in, Mrs. Owsley," a weak voice called from inside the room in the darkest corner where the bed stood. "I'll be the one to decide."

With every aspect of her demeanour showing intense reluctance, the old housekeeper let them enter. Lucy ran to the uncle's bedside and threw her arms about the old man who was propped up by pillows on an imposing walnut, fourposter bed. "Oh, Uncle, I'm so glad to see you. I wish my mother had let me visit you earlier. She only just passed two months ago."

"I'm aware of that, dear," said the old man in a scratchy voice. He reached out a pale, blue-veined hand and stroked her hair. "You are a pretty thing. You look like your mother."

"Really?" Lucy straightened and smoothed her dress. "I always thought I looked more like my father."

"That cuss? Never! He drove my dear sister from me. He's the one that drove the wedge between us. But not to worry. I'm sure you loved your father. Pity they're both dead. They are both dead, are they not?"

"Sadly, yes." Lucy hung her head and wiped a tear from her eye. She handed the ailing man a hand-sized portrait of her father.

He looked at it a moment, then began coughing and could not seem to stop. Abigail grabbed a glass and pitcher and poured him some water. He took the water gratefully and guzzled it.

"That's my job, Abigail," the cranky housekeeper said, her hands on her hips. "Don't be thinking you'll take my job from me."

"No one's here to take your job, Agatha," Abigail retorted. "Now be quiet. You are but a servant, and we are family." She gave the woman a severe look.

"Yes, yes. Family," The old man whispered, nodding his head. "And who be these gentlemen? Are they claiming to be family as well?"

"No, sir," said Edmund, stepping forwards, his hat in his hand. "I'm applying for the mining engineer job. I sent my resume just one day back."

"I've not received it."

"Perhaps the mail has been delayed."

"Perhaps."

Edmund looked back towards Scrooge with a distressed look. He returned his gaze to his potential employer. "Sir, I assure you I have the experience and talent to make this mine a wealth-filled project. What I've read about it is that it has not reached its potential."

"Is that so?"

"Yes, and to boot, I have these two apprentices with me, Mr. Scrooge and Mr. Cratchit. I'm a professor in London, and I see this as an opportunity to get my hand back in the trade and train some highly capable individuals. Mr. Scrooge has run a successful business for many years. Mr. Cratchit is highly capable with financial books, having worked at London banks. You see, Mr. Tamperwind, you get three for the price of one."

The old man eyed Cratchit, then Scrooge. He pointed a shaking hand at Scrooge. "That one looks quite old to be an apprentice."

"Quite ..." Edmund was at a loss for words.

Scrooge stepped forwards. "It is a pleasure to meet you, Mr. Tamperwind. I assure you that I am here to learn the mining trade. I work in commodities, futures, and the like. The more I learn about how mining works, the more capably I can invest and help others to invest. I assure you, from what Mr. Nuckols tells me, this mine is on the verge of a great spike in growth. I'm here to learn and be a good worker for you as well." Scrooge was amazed at himself for how quickly he prevaricated his credentials.

"I see," the man barely whispered with a weak voice. "Right now, I'm rather tired. We'll speak more tomorrow. Mrs. Owsley, would you see to accommodations for our guests?"

Scrooge took in the bedroom upon their departure. An immense, finely-crafted desk sat across from the bed. An expensive carpet on the floor. A chest of drawers and an armoire posted on separate walls. One tall, windowed door beside the bed led out to a small balcony. Beyond the lampstand beside the bed, the room was barren.

Agatha Owsley showed each man a room upstairs. Lucy shared a room with Abigail. They had not yet met the mine owner's ward, Michael. Agatha had her own room off the kitchen downstairs. Samuel, with his bad back, slept on a couch in the parlour. Lockie was sent to make do with a trundle bed and spare blankets in the wood room off the side of the kitchen.

After Mrs. Owsley prepared a simple repast, the night dropped its curtain, and the dark surrounded the house. Before retiring to his room, Scrooge noted the weariness from their journey displayed by all in his company.

In his room, Scrooge searched his bags for the missing keys, but never found them. *Did I drop them by the door of my business or in boarding the train?* He was totally despondent. He hoped whoever came upon the keys would not know what doors they opened. He resolved to dispatch a message to the London police on the next outbound coach.

Sitting on his bed with only his boots off, he felt a compulsion to plan with Cratchit and Edmund what their next move should be to solve the murders. Too anxious to sleep, and wanting to know more about the second murder, he decided to slip out and go to his cohort's rooms and hold a conference. When he opened his bedroom door, Edmund and Cratchit stood before him, Cratchit's hand was raised as if to knock. "We have to plan," he whispered.

The three, like sailors planning a mutiny, seated themselves with heads together and spoke in hushed voices.

"What are we to do?" Edmund asked. "He hasn't hired me, not even an interview."

"I believe we should use this evening to look around," Cratchit added.

"Look where?" Edmund asked.

The men sat quietly for a long time.

"I've been noticing things," Scrooge began. "First, all the cousins received letters calling them here urgently but for an unknown reason. When Samuel and his sister tried asking the old man about it, he dodged the question, perhaps fearing reprisal from an unknown assailant. Maybe someone in the mining town is suspect to him. He may have been threatened by some unknown person. And Mrs. Owsley seems a bit too ornery, instead of in mourning for the loss of her husband."

"But the young boy, the ward, was a witness to the event," Cratchit said. "According to Grumbles, others claimed to be as well."

"Precisely, I think someone dressed up like him and did the deed," Scrooge said.

"What if, tomorrow," Edmund interjected, "we go to the mine, under the auspices of familiarising ourselves to it, and ask the miners what they know?"

"I was thinking as much," Scrooge said, "and we can go into the nearby town of Hopworth and speak to the sheriff there. Maybe we can learn some details about the death of this miner. What's his name? Oh yes, Smyth."

"I say we get a look at the body if it's not been buried yet," Cratchit added. "And see if we can find anything there that would help us solve this mystery."

"Capital idea, Bob," Scrooge said. "So tonight, we get a good night's sleep. For goodness sakes, I've not had one lately. Then let's go on our search at first light."

With all in agreement, the men retired. Scrooge lay in his bed but did not fall asleep immediately, for the idea of Marley's ghost or another such phantom appearing sprang to his mind and would not leave. Finally, too weary to keep his eyes open, he drifted off.

STAVE TWELVE

THE HUNT FOR CLUES AND MORE
MURDEROUS ATTACKS

Scrooge awoke with a start. It would be vain of him to not feel the difference of the cold upon his face, for the fireplace was white with ash, not a spark of coal to warm the room, and the warmth the rest of his body felt beneath the blankets and coverlet was sufficient to make him want to stay where he was. Turning his head but a little to peer out the room's window, he saw that the sun had risen in a dismal sky, dreary with low-slung clouds like deep, grey curtains.

Seeing the ice accumulated on the bare tree limbs outside the window and the frost upon the windowpanes, he fathomed a safe guess that the temperature was a long way below freezing. Still, he mustered the courage to crawl from his bed, slip on his house shoes, and pace around the room, slapping his arms about him, attempting to warm his bony body. Feeling his blood finally moving—albeit at a sluggish pace, for he was not as fit as Bob Cratchit—he tossed off his nightcap and gown and dressed hastily, throwing not one but two scarves about his throat.

He went to the basin, poured a trickle of icy water into the bowl, and sprinkled his face, shivering. Next, keeping himself as clothed as possible, he relieved himself in the chamber pot from under the bed. Afterwards, he buttoned up his breeches and threw on a sweater and a heavy coat. When he exited, he ran full tilt into Mrs. Owsley. She looked up at him, but she might as well have been looking down at him, for she bore such a ferocious demeanour of condescension towards him. He was quite taken aback.

"Your breakfast is ready downstairs," she said coldly, and Scrooge thought her very words could make a hot meal turn chilly. "And you better join your friends already there." She waddled away.

Scrooged trotted down the stairs and at that moment, he met Samuel standing as before with his one hand in his jacket pocket and looking about like he was surveying his handiwork of running the world. He removed a snuff-box from the pocket and placed a pinch of snuff in each nostril. His eyes began to water and his nose twitched, but seeing Scrooge descend the stairs, he extended the box of coarse tobacco to Scrooge. He then sneezed violently and smiled, delighted at the result.

Scrooge begged off the offer with a wave of his hand. "Thank you, Samuel, but I do not indulge. I found it too expensive a habit." He strode past Samuel, who sneezed again. Scrooge went to look out the front door's windowpane. "Tell me, Samuel, how far to the shantytown and to the mine? What would you guess?'

"I'd say a good hundred yards to the shantytown and the shops," Samuel said, walking up beside Scrooge. "Another fifty to the mine entrance."

"Yes." Scrooge was pondering a method to obtain evidence. "Do you know where the body of Mr. Owsley was found?"

"I believe the sheriff in Hopworth could tell more. Like I say, everyone here has been rather closedmouthed."

The two men heard hooting and hollering from outside. They looked out the windows to behold a young boy of about ten years riding a shaggy Shetland, endeavouring to get the sluggish beast to gallop. The animal barely trotted, but the boy kept kicking his heels into the pony's sides. In a flash, another pony appeared, ridden by none other than the impractical Lockie, cheering and batting his tiny steed with a willow branch, using it like a jockey's whip.

"Ah, to be young again." Scrooge reminisced of a time in his youth when he had partaken in just such an activity. Turning to Samuel, he said, "After breakfast, I think I'll take a stroll down to the mine. Just look about. And how far would you say it is to Hopworth?"

"I'd hazard a guess at less than a mile, just to the northwest, though the path, I cannot call it a 'road,' is a bit tricky. I started down it the first day we arrived, just to stretch my legs, and found it almost comical, and it was getting late. I don't know how the town survives economically. One poor way in or out. Perhaps we should make the trek there together in the light of day. I'm curious about it too. The walk would probably do my back good."

"Yes. Well, let's see what is for breakfast."

"I've already eaten, but you go ahead. I believe your friends are dining there."

Scrooge walked through a dining area, then through a narrow hall lined with pantries and cupboards laden with dishes. Great stacks of ruddy, brown onions were on the counter, their aroma steeped with scattered cloves of garlic. A pyramid of apples sat in a varnished maple bowl, and mossy, chocolate brown filberts crowded a sort of canister to overflowing. Nutmeg and ginger inundated the crowded kitchen. In the pie pantry, a lemon pie, half gone, sat amidst a dozen or so lemons. The smells fairly swatted Scrooge's nose, but he had to halt and relish several deep whiffs, for his own abode never smelled so pleasant. He wondered what the abundance of seasonings were for.

When he arrived at a meagre table where his friends were seated, sipping their tea over generally empty plates where eggs and sausage had lain, he quickly noticed the chalk markings of intricate problems of geometry and algebra on the dark grey walls and on the table.

Cratchit noticed Scrooge's wonderment. "That's the young ward's doing, according to Mrs. Owsley. He seems to be quite the mathematician."

"Oh."

"Charming young man," Edmund said. "When we came downstairs, he was forking pie into his mouth as fast as possible and studying a chess game puzzle in that book on the sideboard. He stopped his study and began a truly adult conversation with us. He was ebullient and pleasant, a little gentleman. He appears to be quite intelligent and well-schooled.

He told us the game of chess began in India, at least the game we know now, and it was called ..."

"Chaturanga!" Cratchit called.

"Yes, a remarkable boy. Quite a pleasant boy."

"He began explaining one of these geometric problems," Cratchit pointed to one set of chalk marks halfway up a wall, "saying that it was one of Newton's questionable theorems."

"I understood the concepts but could really only nod my head," Edmund said, sipping his tea.

"I wonder," remarked Scrooge, "that he knows how lucky he is to be here, getting an education, having plenty to eat and a fine upbringing rather than being a mine rat like so many young boys are."

"Come now, Uncle Scrooge," said Edmund, "surely you of all people know that the mines could not operate properly were it not for the cheap wages a young boy draws, and that they are the ones small enough to climb up those narrow tunnels to bring the material down. And what is more, they are providing income for their families."

"Are they?" Scrooge retorted. "Would not the family have more money if they paid the grown men instead of giving the job to a child? I say, make the tunnels larger for the men to go through. Raise the wages to a liveable amount. I know how little I used to pay Bob and how his poor family barely survived, and had I not changed my thinking and my ways, his son, Tim, would not be alive today."

"But, Uncle, you know my heart."

"Edmund, your two boys. Would you have them doing the job that so many of these poor waifs perform, many of them working in the mines rather than living in a workhouse?"

Edmund hung his head. "I can't believe that after so many years of trying to get you to see the reason for spreading goodwill and fighting the good fight that I am taking a comeuppance from you. Well said, Uncle. I value your point."

"And well you should, nephew. What is there to eat?"

"There's some cold, soft-boiled eggs in the pot, some cold toast and marmalade. Some pathetic gruel," Cratchit replied.

"I'll do without all of it," Scrooge said. "Bob, I want you to go with me to Tamperwind town, then to Hopworth. Let's see if the sheriff can tell us anything about either murder. Edmund, you go to the mine. Meet some of the miners. See what they know. We'll meet at the mine's entrance come two o'clock. Oh, and Edmund, tell Lockie to stay here and to keep his ears open."

In short order, the men alerted Abigail and Mrs. Owsley of their desire to get to know the area. Before they departed, Scrooge asked Lucy to put in a good word to her uncle regarding Edmund's obtaining the mining engineer position.

The three plodded down the stairs then onto the grey-sludge snow towards the mine's shantytown. Exiting the gate to the fence, the men heard the crashing of waves, for the ocean was nearby, the tin mine being dug into the craggy rocks that stood beside said ocean. They veered to their left some eighty yards, then climbed some jagged, black- and red-streaked rocks, sprayed wet by occasional large waves. Below them was a frightful range of rocks, splashed by the thundering waves that towered over their obstacles in great plumes of milky foam. The waves rolled and roared and raged their way through caverns in the crass, seaweed-strewn rocks like they were trying earnestly to tear the earth apart.

In the distance, a quarter-of-a-league or so from the shore, stood a lonely lighthouse, white and grey, almost the colour of the sea itself. It stood on a craggy outcropping, its light shining in the dismal fog of late morning. Scrooge felt hypnotised by the surging, rhythmic sound of the waves. He thought of the lighthouse keeper, alone every day. Always alone.

He realised how he had made his own life like that of a lighthouse keeper, seeking solitude, not in order to read books, nor reflect on scripture, nor to tirelessly toil to make the briny deep safer for seafarers so that the sailors of a great many vessels could come home safely to port and to their families.

He had made himself a tragic lighthouse keeper who toiled not for the sake of mankind, but solely for himself. He had been a prisoner of his money. He said a silent prayer for any other being who might have walked down life's road like he had, that they would turn from their safe, soft, solitary ways and instead sacrifice for their fellow man. "Amen," he said aloud.

His wakefulness sped across the heaving sea, and in his mind, he spied the ship that the Ghost of Christmas Present of two years before had borne him. When they had landed, unseen, on the deck of the vessel, he heard fully the helmsman, the lookout, and the officers of the watch each humming a Christmas carol. What was it the officer of the watch said to the drowsy deckhand? Ah, yes. Scrooge remembered. "Dream on, my friend, of Christmas dreams, of sugarplums and festive parties, and of a sweet kiss from a pretty maiden." Scrooge smiled.

"There's a small wharf down there." Cratchit pointed. "Surely, that's not where the ore ships anchor. 'Tis awfully small."

Scrooge barely looked where Cratchit indicated. He was thinking of what it must be like to sail out in the moaning wind in supple darkness over the great abyss of the ocean. What secrets the great ocean held—of glorious battles, of fine fishing locations, and of death. So lost in his thoughts, he barely heard his two companions' conversation.

"I agree," said Edmund. "The wharf must be for fishing boats and small schooners. The large, deep-draft ore ships could not tie up there."

Edmund and Cratchit, quite wary of the wet spray landing on them, headed back to the path. Scrooge remained, peering out into the vast, deep coverlet of secrets.

"Coming, Uncle?" Edmund called.

Scrooge broke from his reverie. Solemnly, he climbed down from the crag and followed his nephew and partner.

While Edmund went straight to the mine, Scrooge and Cratchit stopped at a meagre café in Tamperwind town where Scrooge ordered a tea and a crumpet. In less than five minutes, they were on their way to Hopworth. They passed Edmund talking with a crowd of miners.

After passing the opening between two boulders of the path to Hopworth twice, they finally located the narrow byway and trod down a gentle slope between crags and boulders of coral granite and tar-black bismuth. Turning a corner around one boulder, they came upon Samuel seated and wheezing. He looked up and seemed beside himself.

"Are you hurt?" inquired Scrooge.

"Your back?" asked Cratchit.

"Neither," he responded. "I've had a most frightening encounter."

Scrooge and Cratchit waited for him to tell his tale.

"All right, all right," he said, attempting to calm himself. "I took off before you, Scrooge, knowing that since I have to walk carefully because of my back, I didn't want to slow you down. I figured you would catch up with me. Not five minutes before you arrived, I turned this very corner and came face to face with a large man in a black cloak wearing a mask over his face. He wanted no money, although he was large enough that he could have throttled me entirely. I was at his mercy, for he grabbed me about my throat."

Scrooge noted the red marks, smeared with black coal dust, clearly made by hands, on Samuel's throat.

"His voice was like none I'd ever heard. Like a bear or a vicious hound. He said he would have his revenge and that my sister and I should leave immediately if we knew what was good for us."

"Which way did he go?" Cratchit said, wishing he had brought his rifle.

"He went up those boulders there and disappeared. He moved agilely for such a large man."

Cratchit scrambled a short distance up the escarpment, but seeing the rocks gave no evidence of the man's retreat, he returned.

Scrooge looked down. "Was the man standing just here?"

"Yes," said Samuel.

"Look at the size of the shoe." He pointed to the deep indention in the muddy snow.

Samuel took a flask from his jacket pocket and poured the liquid down his throat. "There, better." He attempted a smile, but his back was obviously paining him.

"I think you should go back," Scrooge said. "Cratchit will accompany you."

"What about you, Ebenezer?" Cratchit asked.

"I'll be fine. The accoster has gone. I doubt he would try to threaten another. Besides," Scrooge opened his coat a modicum, revealing a long pistol, "before we left, I had Edmund load one of his guns for me. Even if I have never fired one in my life, just its presence should drive away any ne'er-do-well. I want to find out about the two murders. So far, we have nothing."

Cratchit looked surprised. "Good for you, Ebenezer. But do be careful." With that, Cratchit supported Samuel by the elbow, and they trod slowly back to the mansion.

Scrooge proceeded up one slope, then down one, and began wondering where the town of Hopworth lay hidden.

STAVE THIRTEEN

THE ATTACK ON SCROOGE

s if by magic, grey shake roofs and chimneys appeared nestled in a small valley after Scrooge rounded a large, granite outcropping. Hopworth was no glittering city, nor hideaway hamlet. It was a collection of shanty buildings, smaller in size than the mine shanty town that had no name other than "Tamperwind." One building bore a sign that hung lazily on a yardarm—*Vittles* was all it said. Scrooge, sensing no other place to begin, went inside. A robust, apron-clad proprietor stood behind a counter in the shady place, but the shop had its share of baskets of fruit, sacks of flour and the like, sundry items for sewing such as bolts of cloth and needles, plus spades and hoes and other implements of gardening and formidable tools for mining.

"Hi, ho!" the proprietor called. "What say you this fine day?" The man beamed like he had not seen a customer all day, and Scrooge guessed that he had not. "We just received a fine shipment of pears yesterday, fresh and ready for pies and cobblers and very sweet."

Scrooge glanced at the large basket of pears the man pointed to and saw a remarkable pile of the green and yellow fruit that looked as fresh as what would be ordered for Queen Victoria. Scrooge chose one, asking, "How much?"

"A ha'penny for one."

Scrooge dug in his pocket, produced the coin, and then set the fruit in his pocket. "Tell me, sir, where might I find the sheriff of Hopworth?"

"Why, you're lookin' at 'im." The man's smile broadened. "Are you in need of a sheriff? Has there been a crime? For I assure you, we've had no shortage of crimes here lately, murders and the like."

"And the like?"

"Well, only murders, but two of them. Dastardly deeds, they were." The man shook his head. "I am Sheriff Malcolm Pickens. That's who I be."

Scrooge shook the meaty hand of the sheriff. "I'm Ebenezer Scrooge, new to these parts, as, uh, part of an investigation through the college and St. James Hospital. We became aware of a recent mine death here, and we are attempting to gather information for medical reasons." Scrooge was surprised at his own ingenuity.

"Indeed, indeed." Pickens clapped his hands together. "How can I be of service to the medical arts? We are often in need of a surgeon here, with the mine and all. A broken leg here, a collapsed lung there, and all manner of disease. Last year, we had a typhus epidemic, unlike any I'd seen."

"'Tis a pity. You say there is not a surgeon of any sort nearby."

"Nary a one. Now, let me be of service." Sheriff Pickens was all ready to assist.

"I'd like to see the body of the recently murdered miner if I could, and perhaps ..."

"You can see both murdered bodies if you'd like."

"What? Owsley hasn't been put in the ground?"

"No, I have them both back here in what I call the 'anti-room' where I store the meat." He beckoned Scrooge to follow him.

They walked down a long, dimly lit stairway into a sort of vault with dank, rock walls propped up by timbers. "This tunnel was an original attempt at the Tamperwind mine. The 'primary shaft,' you might call it." The sheriff lit a lantern for himself and lit a second one and gave it to Scrooge.

Upon reaching the bottom of the stairs, they descended at a very steep rate through the narrow-walled tunnel. They stopped at a landing where the sheriff pointed to a long, human-sized slew extending down into the gloom of the mine. Scrooge could only see the top of the smooth wooden trough.

"That's the fast way down into the mine," Sheriff Pickens announced. "It's like slidin' into hell."

Scrooge stretched his lantern over the dark opening near the trough—a slide. It appeared in the glow of the lantern to go on forever and ever into darkness.

"But over here," said the sheriff, "is where I keep dead bodies when we get them."

Scrooge followed Pickens into a room with wooden plank walls, perhaps at one time used as an office for the mine manager. A simple desk and chair were pushed into the corner—torches, unlit, perched in sconces on the walls. Scrooge turned. Before him, on slabs like tables of what appeared to be a combination of rock and ice, lay the two dead men. Nothing covered them. The first one appeared, for all the world, merely to be sleeping, though a huge maroon splotch covered half his shirt under his jacket and just above his breeches. Scrooge surmised that was the miner, Smyth. Judging from his unwrinkled face, Scrooge guessed the man to be no more than thirty.

Beyond that body lay the second that Scrooge could only guess was Owsley's. The face, battered and dark black from the blood, was entirely unrecognisable. The body was contorted from rigour mortis, one arm bent up at the elbow, the hand like a claw. No worms or beasties crawled about either body, and Scrooge noted why. As cold as the weather above ground was, the cutting cold of this place was difficult to ignore.

When the sound of a scraping chain sounded behind him, Scrooge fully expected, when he spun around, to see the ghosts of the dead men. What he saw instead was the sheriff removing the chain from a locked chest of cheeses. He breathed a profound sigh of relief and turned to the corpses.

Scrooge was unaccustomed to looking closely at dead bodies. Whenever seeing one lying in a gutter of the London streets, or on a funeral bier, or piled up with other corpses in a wagon during London's epidemics, he had always turned his head. That was in the old days. In the last two years, his compassion had bloomed, and he had attended several funerals of people he knew and of some he did not. Always, he bowed his head and prayed for the deceased and their families. This, however, was different.

Gathering his courage, despite his shaking hands, he said, "Might I examine the bodies?"

"Of course, anything for science. But I caution you not to disturb them much. I've called for a coroner from Lazy Eye to examine them and to help me make arrangements. I must follow the course of the law."

"Why, pray tell me, was Owsley not buried? It's been over a week."

"I'm not sure, for we could easily have dug him up. In this hard ground, no one gets buried deep. But I was told to wait. You see, I'm primarily sheriff by the goodwill of Mr. Tamperwind. When he purchased the mine from Mr. Hopworth, my uncle, the agreement allowed that some of his best workers be allowed to stay in the little town here until they passed, you see. I was asked to look after the place, so here I am. Sheriff, shopkeeper, street cleaner, and sometimes medicinal procurer. That be I."

"Have you heard any more from the other authorities?"

"Not a word. And Mrs. Owsley has been jumpin' mad about it. She storms in here daily and demands he be buried, and I tell her I can't. Quite a conundrum."

Scrooge merely nodded, then proceeded to the first body. He picked up the arm, heavy and puerile. He examined the weight of it, for he really did not know what he was looking for. Then he noticed the blood had splattered about the rest of the man's clothes. He further noticed long strands of grey hair still clutched in the man's tightened fingers. Suddenly he knew. The man had been in a close fight and had been shot in the stomach probably while still grappling with his assailant. "Have you checked this man for clues?"

"Clues? He was shot. Anyone can tell that. Oh, and I've been doing my duty asking around. Grumbles is the one that done it."

"Has anyone given you any further information regarding the murder?"

Sheriff Pickens looked perplexed. "I really just have this job because my uncle wanted me to take care of his good workers. That's mostly what I do."

"I see." Scrooge turned back to the miner's corpse. He began to rummage around, though tentatively, through the man's pockets. In one pants pocket, he found a hefty pouch of coins. He thought at first to show this to the sheriff who was checking out a leg of mutton hung on a hook. Instead, he stuffed the pouch in his own pocket.

Next, he went to the battered body. The skull and face had been caved in. The body was clothed in filthy, ill-fitted miner's clothes. Scrooge surveyed the head, but had difficulty looking at it and decided instead to examine the rest of the body. The pockets of the clothes were empty. The stomach was distended. The smell of death was faint but definitely present. He was about to leave when he noticed the hands and fingers. He looked at them, then looked at the hands of the miner, then back to Owsley's corpse hands and fingers.

He had a theory forming in his mind. "That is enough for now, Sheriff Pickens. I'll be going now."

"What? No questions for me? The one that brought you here?" The once garrulous, overtly friendly man had suddenly turned hostile. His face was red, and he looked as though he would throttle Scrooge. He was big enough and strong enough.

Scrooge backed up, still holding the lantern, his hands outthrust. "No, of course, I have questions for you."

The man was not listening. He stormed about the small compartment. "No one ever listens to me. No one ever asks my opinion!" he repeated over and over.

Scrooge was quite afraid the man would stumble over him or one of the corpses in his raging.

Sheriff Pickens yelled, "Get out!" He pointed to the door.

Scrooge rushed away up the steep path, the dark walls seeming closer and the tunnel narrower than in the descent. Gaining footing on the stairs, he became aware of heavy footsteps behind him—a man was racing after him. He turned to look. But he saw not the congenial sheriff, but a huge man clothed in a black cape, his face masked by a black ribbon across his eyes. There were openings in the ribbon so the man could see. In the dim light, the eyes shone fierce and maniacal. Scrooge raced up the stairs, hearing the heavy footsteps behind him. He was almost at the top when he felt hands grab his coat. He fell back but caught a hand onto a rail and righted himself. Then he heard a heavy crash as his pursuer, instead of grabbing him, slipped on the steps and tumbled down into endless shadow. Scrooge sprinted up the remaining stairs, out of the shop, and kept going until he had gone a good distance up the path.

He stopped, leaning against one of the great boulders. He pulled the pistol from his belt, cocked it, and looked back. No one was pursuing him. Resting only a moment, he continued at a rapid pace, constantly checking behind him, until he reached the Tamperwind mine entrance. The noise of the steam engines in the mine, clattering and chugging, was almost ear-busting. Scrooge held his hands to his ears. Just at that moment, he saw Edmund and Cratchit approaching him. "I've just been in peril of my life," Scrooge announced.

"Whatever happened, Ebenezer?" Cratchit asked when the three men came together.

Scrooge led the men some distance from the mine opening in order that he be heard, then began relaying the astounding event in the old Hopworth mine tunnel, of first meeting the sheriff, trooping deep into the tunnel, and examining the body, then the horrific transformation of the sheriff. "I was hurrying to get out when the devil-man came at me with such force and vigour, all huge and black—at least he seemed immense in the shadows of the tunnel."

"Was it the sheriff?" Edmund asked.

"I cannot see a man in public service turning so, and the man who came at me seemed much larger." Scrooge still panted, and his heart raced just in the retelling. He sat on a large rock. "I guess that it could have been him. Or from what I can perceive, the sheriff may be dead."

Edmund and Cratchit began discussing the event with fervour, and Scrooge attempted to listen, but in his mind, he was again facing the dark Ghost of Christmas Future. He had seen his potential ignominious death foretold by the hideous phantom, and by comparison, this last event in the mine was like he had been trapped in a crypt.

"Ebenezer! Ebenezer, are you listening?" Cratchit shook his business partner's shoulder.

"I beg your pardon, Bob," Scrooge said. "That was an ordeal unlike any in my life."

"Well, listen enough to hear what we have to say," Cratchit continued.

"I'm all ears."

Edmund began. "When I was asking around about the death of the miner, Smyth, most of the miners, their wives, everyone was reticent to even mention a word, some fearing what they call 'the evil eye' if they did speak of the murder. They were aware of Mr. Tamperwind's lingering illness, though of what malady they knew not. They had not laid eyes on him in years. Only Grumbles and Owsley ever met with him and always in the house. At any rate, I was standing in a group of them who all were shaking their heads about my questions regarding the murder, and they were backing away when one wizened fellow said, 'I'm too old to care if it gets me killed. I'll tell you what I know.'"

Scrooge leaned forwards, his chin resting on his fists.

"As soon as the old man started telling the tale, everyone else began chiming in like all the church bells in London were in your bedroom. It appears that for some days even before the death of Owsley that Smyth was about dropping obvious hints that he was going to be, to quote them, 'rolling in silver.' Now, most of them ignored him, but when he announced he was heading out and that he knew how he was going to get richer still, they were alerted that something was amiss. He seemed wary of everyone, keeping to himself in a corner of the mine with the wall behind him, barely working, and nervous as a flea."

"I happened to come up to the crowd after I had delivered Samuel to the house," Cratchit enjoined. "One good wife was wringing her hands in her apron, and suddenly she yelled out that when all had left the mine last night, Smyth was the last to leave. No one was near him when he came out of the mine opening, save her, some yards away. She saw a huge man in a black cape, his face masked, rush on Smyth with such force, he knocked Smyth to the ground. Smyth leapt to his feet and pulled a pistol, but in the '*fit*,' as she called it, in the *fit*, the gun went off and Smyth fell to the ground. He was still alive in the woman's home, lying on a kitchen table when Tamperwind's niece and nephew, Abigail and Samuel, arrived by coach that had been long-delayed in the valley."

"When some of the miners went to the house to tell Mr. Tamperwind, the housekeeper, Mrs. Owsley, wouldn't let them in," said Edmund. "Only when Samuel came out were they able to tell of the event. Samuel sent someone to obtain the sheriff and to seek a surgeon down in the valley."

"We found out," Cratchit interjected, "that there is no physician in Hopworth or for miles around. Sheriff Pickens came, but Smyth had already died. He asked a few questions, then he took the body in a barrow to Hopworth."

"And I have seen the body," Scrooge said. "And in his erstwhile battle for his life, he fought with someone older, someone with grey hair. I found strands of grey hair in his fists." Scrooge thought to himself that Grumbles had grey hair. He let the thought lie. "In addition, I found this." He pulled the bag of coins from his pocket and dumped the contents into Cratchit's cupped hands.

The three men's eyes widened, counting the silver coins quickly: six crowns, plus two coin-shaped silver slugs with no coin markings. A fortune for some.

"This is why the man was killed, but how did he come by the money? This may be all that was left. The killer may have taken any other money he had," Scrooge said.

"I say we go up to Tamperwind's. It's nigh on noon. We'll have dinner there and press our desire to work for the gentleman."

STAVE FOURTEEN

MEETING MR. TAMPERWIND AND
SOME TRAGIC FAMILY HISTORY

Scrooge, Cratchit, and Edmund walked up to the mansion. When they reached the gate, the deaf gardener was waiting, smiled, and made some incomprehensible remarks in a squeaky voice about having a good day. The three nodded.

Reaching the porch, Lockie swung from behind a pillar and the young ward, Michael, swung around from the opposite. "Boo!" the little fellow called.

"Scared ya, huh?" yelled Lockie.

The men, so intense in their thoughts, were alarmed, each jumping back a pace, Scrooge grabbing his chest. "Lockie," he reprimanded, "whatever has gotten into you?"

"I've just been having fun riding horses, chasing the geese, playing mumblypeg, writing math with chalk on the walls. It's been a wonderful day!" Lockie beamed. "Let me introduce my friend, Michael, mathematician and jockey extraordinaire."

"That's a big word for you, Lockie. *Extraordinaire.*"

"Michael taught it to me. It means 'fine as alabaster.' Smooth as silk."

"Pleased to meet you, Michael," each man said, and shook the young tyke's hand.

He smiled almost fawningly. "I trust you've met my foster father, the great Mr. Tamperwind. He is so good to me."

"Yes, we have, and we were just going to meet him again, perhaps after dinner," Cratchit said.

"Oh, no. Let's go see him now. Come on." He raced inside, beckoning them to follow him.

The entire group went upstairs at a hasty pace, handing their coats and hats to Samuel who stood at the bottom of the stairs. He was much amazed.

"Now wait! Now wait!" Mrs. Owsley called from the dining room, but her admonitions were in vain.

The men and boy stood at the bedroom door only a moment. Michael knocked, called, then opened the door. The old man lay, looking weak as ever, in the sumptuous bed, pillows about him.

"Father," Michael said. "These men came with me to see you."

"Fine, fine," Tamperwind said, then coughed violently. He put a weak hand on the boy's head and tousled the hair, offering a tepid smile. Turning his attention to the men, "Ah, yes, the men applying for the mining engineer position. A post came just this morning. I read the resume."

"Hello, Mr. Tamperwind," Edmund said. "It's good to see you, but though I wish the employment, I am saddened to see you so ill. Do the mining crew know of your illness?"

"Thank you for your concern, but my illness is unattributable. It's best to leave me alone. Yes, the crew knows I'm ill, but they must also know that everything is to continue. Therefore, I'm in no condition to have a host of rabble marching in here applying for the job, so I'm giving you and your apprentices the position." He coughed until Michael gave him a drink of water. "I'm giving you the job on the condition I see results. You hear me?" he seemed the most excited since they had met.

"Yes, of course," Edmund said bowing. Scrooge and Cratchit bowed as well. "We'll start straight away tomorrow."

"You'll not wait until tomorrow. Begin today. I have no manager for the mine. They could be stealing me blind. I've too many worries. Now, act the manager and the engineer. Be gone. Let me be with my ward."

Michael turned, giving them the nod they needed to leave. "Father," he said, "may my new friend Lockie stay, just for a while?"

"No, no, son." He slumped back into his pillows. "Tell Mrs. Owsley to prepare them something to eat, then you show them around the mine. That's a good boy."

Michael, his face downfallen, trudged out of the room after the men. Lockie came last and closed the door. They trooped down to the dining table where a slumgullion in a heavy pot sat steaming on a side table. Rich, meaty aroma swelled around the room. Mrs. Owsley stood scowling beside it with her ladle upraised. "You'll not make me wait again. Come feed yourselves, or you can all starve."

The men and boys lined up and took a bowl. She served each one, and they took seats at an overlong, dark varnished table with heavy legs. A chandelier hung above them. Scrooge noted that the sideboards and decorative cabinets had not been dusted in a while. On the table, two huge loaves of sourdough bread sat on wooden boards with carving knives. Each man and boy helped themselves. Scrooge found himself hungrier than he had been in a long while, and the repast was good. Though hungry, he found himself swatting at Lockie, who demonstrated atrocious table manners, reaching across others for the bread, wiping his mouth with his sleeve, and slurping the stew loudly.

Samuel came in, served himself from the pot, for Mrs. Owsley had left to the kitchen. No sooner had he sat down than his sister rushed in. "Good to see you, Abigail," Samuel said.

"Well, it's not good to see you, you fiend. Why did you not wake me? I'm famished." Her face was as red as a beet and her voice as strident as a banshee. "I'll not deal with it. You hear me! Get these men out of here. I want to eat alone."

"They'll be finished in a moment, dear sister," Samuel said calmly.

"I told you they must leave now." She hastily took the ladle and splashed the liquid into a bowl, her hands shaking. A large amount splattered on the floor and her dress. "Oh, dear, my clothes, my clothes." She flung the bowl down, smashing it to pieces. She was a storm leaving the room.

Samuel shrugged. "Now you see, gentlemen, what I spoke of before. Amiable as a kitten one minute, a devouring lion the next. She's been that way since youth. Runs in the family I'm afraid. Her father, though not mine, had similar issues. My father died in a carriage accident, and Mother remarried. The new man was often as fine and as congenial a soul that ever walked the earth, but for various reasons, he would burst into violent rages. It got him killed one evening in a pub down at the London docks. Mother went looking for his killer, and the same man killed her. A pirate he was. They hung him on a gibbet. It did Abigail and me little good. We had to survive as best we could. Fortunately, we had an uncle, Lucy's father, who was wealthy, provided for us for a while. He was Mr. Tamperwind's brother. The two had a falling out years before and never spoke to each other. That benevolent uncle passed, then Uncle Erasmus insured we had a family to take us in until we were adults. So, there you have it."

"That's quite a story," Lockie announced, his mouth full of bread. Scrooge swatted the back of the boy's head, but he continued. "I never had an uncle to take me in, and if it weren't for Master Scrooge and Master Cratchit, I imagine I'd be in the dead house for sure. They've been my saving grace." He smiled.

Scrooge and Cratchit smiled also. Scrooge, instead of swatting him, patted him on the back. "Lockie," he said, "we go to the mine after we eat. On the way, we'll stop and get you some new clothes."

"Hear, hear!" Cratchit said.

Lucy, all smiles and curly hair, arrived in the room. "Am I too late to eat?"

"Not at all," Cratchit said. "Here, let me get you a bowl. It's really quite delicious." He arose quickly and served her a bowl.

Lockie, meanwhile, pulled out her chair. "Watch your step of the spilt soup and broken crockery. There was a bit of a mishap earlier."

"Yes, I know. Abigail told me. She is quite beside herself, saying she hates herself, so if you don't mind, I'll take this bowl of soup to her."

"Yes, of course," Cratchit said.

Lockie's face showed remorse and a bit of confusion. He watched her the entire way until she was out of sight.

Cratchit and Lockie sat again and finished their meals. Mrs. Owsley entered and began taking up the dirty dishes, then cleaned up the spill and broken dish.

"Gentlemen," Edmund announced, "it is time we go to the mine." He lowered his voice. "I am troubled by all the recent turns of events. I could barely eat, thinking that some man tried to accost my dear uncle and Samuel."

"I have an idea," Cratchit interjected, also in a whisper. "Why don't you go with young Michael to the mine and have him show you around? I'll go to Hopworth. Check out this sheriff and the goings-on in that store."

"Good idea," said Scrooge.

"What about me?" Lockie asked.

"You come with me to get you some clothes," Scrooge replied. "We'll buy you appropriate new attire. When we're done, you go back to the house and keep a sharp eye."

"But I want to go to the mine."

"No, you don't. The wrong sort sees you, he'll try to force you into labour, hauling the baskets in those narrow tunnels. No. You stay at the house."

No sooner had Scrooge finished the dialogue than Michael appeared at the door, munching an apple, and he held a small slate and chalk in his other hand. "Are you gentlemen ready to go? My father wants me to show you the mine. I go there often, looking for treasure like the thief, Ali Baba."

Lockie, though seven years older than Michael, having seldom played as a child, had enjoyed some playtime riding the Shetlands and playing at wooden swords with his new young acquaintance. He had missed so much of a joyful youth that any sort of play and perambulations into fantasy seemed overwhelmingly intriguing. He hung his head. New clothes meant nothing compared to searching for treasure in a mine.

STAVE FIFTEEN
NEW CLOTHES FOR LOCKIE, THE MINE, AND REMEMBERED SORROW

When Scrooge and Lockie arrived at the commodities store of the mining town, they found little to choose from that was at all better than the clothes he wore, save they were not torn and ragged. Scrooge made him try on trousers, shirts, boots, even socks, and lastly a coat and woollen hat. The fit was loose, but warm and clean. Lockie carefully slipped the keys for Scrooge's office from the old pair of trousers to the new.

Before Scrooge could pay for the new clothes, one of the women running the establishment gathered up Lockie's old clothes and bundled them into a sack. "We need rags all the time, for cleaning and staunching wounds. You won't miss 'em."

Scrooge saw there was no arguing with her and was reminded of the charwomen who had taken his bed linens to sell at the pawnshop in his terminal experience with the Ghost of Christmas Future. It was too remorse-laden a thought.

Shoving his loaded pistol deep under his coat, he sent Lockie trudging up the hill to the mansion. "Keep a sharp eye!"

Lockie did not turn back, nor wave. Scrooge observed Cratchit fairly jogging down the road towards Hopworth. He held his long gun in his hands.

Scrooge joined Edmund and Michael outside one of the two pubs in town. Each pub crouched on either side of a whimsical version of a church. The church was brick and rock and mortar along its lower tier; and the warped boards of the upper walls were patched together with tin plates, connecting the boards. Each plate was hammered in with nails. The walls of the squat, muddled establishment, after eight-feet-tall walls, arose further another fifteen feet in an astonishingly steep pitched roof of greying boards with various swaths of pink or blue paint and occasional green. Above the heavy, carved oak doors, a large circular motif of the "Three Hares" ran circling each other.

Michael pulled on a heavy brass knocker, and the door swung open. The place was all shadows, save for a single glowing red globe near the distant altar. Michael chuckled. "Funny place, this! I've no use for it." He turned away from the door and motioned for Scrooge and Edmund to follow him out. "But I have a great charge to show you gentlemen—the second tin mine ever visited by Joseph of Arimathea."

"What?" exclaimed both Edmund and Scrooge together, keeping pace with the boy.

"Yes, it's not well-known elsewhere, but the story is that Joseph of Arimathea travelled to the isles years ago and visited here and the Ding Dong mine down the road. He was noted as a tin merchant. I'm sure you knew that."

Scrooge and Edmund were astonished.

"What is more, on one such journey, he is said to have brought along young Jesus. He was an old family friend. So they say."

"Interesting," said Edmund.

"I doubt it's true," Michael said. "If Jesus did come here, he would not have left such a sorry excuse for a church and let it bide here all this time like a disfigured frog. Ah, now, here we are at the mine." He was hollering.

Five great steam engines, each in its own granite walled house, lined up, beginning just inside the entrance, and chugged and clattered like a hundred train engines. Each engine house stood some thirty yards from the next. In the coal houses adjacent, swarthy men, blackened with coal dust, shovelled chunks of coal into the furnaces. Great blasts of heat fomented the entire mine opening. Lanterns hung precariously on high hooks and swung like wind-torn ribbons with the vibrations that shook the entirety of the area that stretched in a slow slope into the shadowy cavern. A cloud of coal dust and mine dust hung in the air.

Michael took a kerchief, dipped it in a water barrel, and flung the cloth across his nose and mouth. Edmund and Scrooge did the same.

"Let us take a look here," Edmund called.

The three stepped inside one of the steam engine houses. "I'll wager each of these engines is near fifty tons," Edmund remarked. "That bob wall is massive, just as it should be to hold the beam and pistons." He pointed. "You see, Uncle, er, Mr. Scrooge." He was aware of his misstep in naming his uncle, but Michael appeared enamoured by the reciprocating motion of the pump rods. "You see," Edmund continued. "The bob wall, or the beam wall, must be strong else the entire building collapse, much stronger than the other three. I've built several when we dredged around some lakes to install the pillars for bridges."

Scrooge again took notice that the workers, though not staring directly at them, were listening, their heads cocked towards Edmund and himself.

"Hello, gentlemen," Scrooge announced. "We are the new mining engineers. Mr. Nuckols here is touring the facility. He will be happy to meet with you later and answer your questions."

Scrooge thought his remarks cordial, but the response of head shakings and shoulder shrugs led him to believe they had heard as much before but had no interest.

At that moment, a steam whistle blew. While the engines continued to chug and whine, the coal workers tossed aside their shovels and went to their metal lunch pails. Each one sat on the heap of coal and took out a pasty and gobbled it, then chugged beer from brown bottles. Scrooge marvelled at their muscled arms and backs. Their eyes were like tiny, white saucers on a black cloth. Never once did they look at Edmund or Scrooge, content to munch away in silence. Occasionally, one would mumble some comment to which the others would chuckle. One fellow looked weaker than the others. Though no more than thirty-five, his hair was greying, his face drawn, his eyes as red as the dawn. His hands trembled, holding the pasty.

Behind them, they heard the tramp of feet. Turning, they saw a long line of women and children returning from their meal inside the mine. They carried their meagre lunch pails. In their aprons' pockets sat a set of varied chisels and hammers. Not one of them smiled. Scrooge noticed the blotched red skin of three of the women who appeared anaemic, and they coughed unceasingly.

By now, Michael was racing and hopping about the wide opening area, leaping from boulder to boulder that rested in the entrance. "Come on, you sluggards!" he called, smiling broadly. "If you don't keep moving, the Knockers will do you mischief." He raced ahead of them. Scrooge and Edmund trotted in pursuit.

"Knockers?" Scrooge asked.

"They're sort of mischievous spirits that live in the mines," Edmund said. "They can cause you to have an accident if you're not wary. All an old wives' hoary tale to keep children away from the mine."

Scrooge had seen ghosts, so he was not convinced that the Knockers were purely imaginary creatures. They passed two carts, pulled by the stout cave ponies. Boys no bigger than Michael were dumping coal into the carts. The horses' eyes drooped; their manes and tails were bedraggled.

Edmund and Scrooge walked past the carts, and in a moment, they stood beside Michael, peering over the edge of a deep drop. Pump rods extended down into the cavity, and a large pipe ran beside them.

"The pump rods run the pumps at the bottom," Edmund said. "Pump out the water into that pipe that goes to that holding tank just outside the surface." Edmund was feeling quite at home. Though he knew little about actual tin, he did know about drilling.

Suddenly, Michael began twirling his arms as if trying to regain his balance above the edge. Scrooge and Edmund rushed forwards to grab him. He began laughing. "Fooled you. Ha!"

Neither Scrooge nor Edmund took his ploy lightly.

"That will be enough of that, young man," Edmund stated firmly. "Your job is to show us around. Not frighten us to death."

"Sorry, gents," Michael said. He pointed down. "This here is tunnel number one. There are five, you know."

Scrooge and Edmund carefully leaned out to see into the dark recesses of the drop. A single, sturdy ladder leaned against the rock wall of the opening. They could see glimmers of light in the cave below. Coming up from the cave, climbing by using but one hand to grasp each rung, a miner pulled himself up the steep rungs. On his back, a sort of peddler's pack was laden with hammers, picks and chisels, a tin pail, and cloths. On the wide brim of his cap, a tallow candle stuck in a clod of clay burned a flickering flame.

He reached the top rung and looked astonished at the well-dressed gentlemen and young Michael. "A hand, please," he said.

Edmund reached out and grabbed one hand and pulled the man the final steps up the ladder. The man sank to his knees, holding a bandaged hand up against his chest. "Wasn't sure I'd make it. Bunged my hand royal, I did." He held it up for them to see. The bloody cloth covered a bloodier distorted hand. He revealed a finger bone protruding from the first digit. "I'll be needing a surgeon to shove the bone back in, I will." Panting, he struggled to his feet. He meandered off towards the mine entrance.

Scrooge felt an inordinate need to succour the man but mentally grasped he could not, for he knew nothing of the medical arts. Reluctantly, he climbed down the ladder after Michael and Edmund. The men were cautious, but Michael essentially slid down the lengthy ladder. In the mine proper, the clanking of the pump rods racketed off the walls, and sometimes as one, long, ear-piercing syllable. Scrooge saw what he knew he would see. Numerous men were pickaxing at the walls, other men were picking up the broken rocks and placing them in large rolling carts. Other men shoved a massive timber up against the ceiling of a new tunnel. When the timber would not move into place, both Scrooge and Edmund assisted the team to shove the reluctant support into position.

"I wish Bob had been here," Scrooge said. "He's so strong now. As an ox."

Scrooge also saw what he did not wish to see. Several young men about the age of Lockie and younger had vast straw baskets hung from their shoulders and strapped to their waists. The boys worked in teams, taking rocks from the cart and piling them to overflowing into the baskets. The boys, walking in a long line, carried their loads to a series of ladders that led to a precarious landing, at which point they climbed another ladder, and Scrooge watched them climb the interior escarpments ladder by ladder until, struggling, they reached the top and headed outside with their burdens.

Edmund took notes on a small pad of paper and asked the miners questions. Some answered well; others seemed almost incoherent. At one point, the faux engineers reached a shadowy tunnel that led ever upwards. It reached a point where no man could go farther. At that point, several thin boys in the raggediest of clothes filtered out of the hole on their hands and knees, each carrying a basket with a modicum of rocks.

Scrooge insisted to Edmund he had seen enough. He had come to solve a mystery and save a man's life. His heart had changed from its tin ore hardness of the past and had softened in the glow of kindness shared with friends and family in the two years since the night of the ghosts. Now he wanted to get away from what was killing his fellow man—the mines were tombs awaiting the already dead to succumb. He wanted so much to flee.

Gaining barely enough composure, he hastened to what seemed like a mile-high ladder. He was panicked, for the climb now seemed much more perilous than the journey down. Panting, he clambered up the ladder, his feet slipping here, his grasping hand missing a rung there.

"Slow down, for heaven's sake, Mister Scrooge!" Edmund called from below him.

Still, Scrooge climbed on in distress as if a Knocker or other phantom was chasing him just like the black-clad man had done earlier in the morning. He reached the top and fell to his knees, his heart racing. He looked to his side, and arriving from another ladder, the emaciated boys with pale faces splotched with dust and grime stumbled past him, carrying their sacks of ore rocks. They stopped at a huge, two-wheeled barrow and dumped the contents of their baskets into it. Two large, muscled women took hold of the handles and shoved the barrow up the incline, straining at every step. The boys turned as one, like little machines, to scale down the ladders once again.

Edmund arrived, also weary from the climb. "I don't see how they do this work. I am tuckered. Quite tuckered."

Michael came up to them, bubbling with enthusiasm. "I feel ever so happy. The men and women are working hard despite having no manager to drive them. I am so pleased."

When he said that, several workers stopped and glowered at him. He paid them no heed. Instead he wished them a joyous day and skipped passed the grinding engines towards the entrance. Edmund and Scrooge followed.

Upon reaching the open air, the sunlight glared, and all three shaded their eyes. Along the front of the mine, long, heavy tables had been set up. At one end, girls of about eight to ten stood before a slew through which water channelled. They grabbed the chunks of ore from the barrows that were lined up, washed them under the running water, then placed the chunks into three piles on each of the three long tables. The poor girls' dresses and aprons were soaked from the sloshing water, as were their shoes. Their hands were filthy.

Older women took the ore samples from the stacks. Using pick hammers, they chopped at each chunk until it had been diminished to a pile of pebbles. They shoved the pebbles down the table to several other women, the stronger looking ones, who, with immense hammers, pounded the pebbles into a sort of ragged, black, oatmeal-like dust.

"I read about this," Edmund whispered to Scrooge. "The young girls doing the washing of the rock have to determine what type of ore is most extant in the rock. Tin. Copper. Granite. They begin *the spalling process*. The next group of women are *cobbers*. They, as you see, break up the rocks. The last women are called *buckers*."

"I see," said Scrooge, his hand on his chin. He was thinking of his sweet love, Isabelle. What if his abandoning her because of his miserliness had led to her being forced to perform such a job? A tear formed in his eye and trickled down his cheek. He stood there in the glaring sunlight while the women worked. He heard the rattling symphony of a hundred hammers and wished he was somewhere else.

"Next," Edmund said, "I read in that book that they do a process called *jigging* in the mechanical screens down the way to sift out the finer ore. Excuse me. I must go survey the final product and try to look like I know what I'm doing."

He did just that. Scrooge watched his intrepid nephew play the part brilliantly. He shovelled some of the ore with a small spoon tool. Fingered it. Held it up in the sunlight. Made some comments to the men working the jigging machine. Scrooge's emotions were running rampant. Sorrow for the loss of his one true love, fear from the day's earlier trials, and pride for his nephew. He felt suddenly very tired.

The sun had come out, melting the patches of snow, but the wind had picked up dramatically, blowing dust all about and whipping the women's dresses. "Come, Edmund. Let us depart."

The two men climbed the long hill in silence. Reaching the gate with the gardener there to open it, Scrooge said, "I should not have let Bob go alone. He may have walked into considerable danger. What were we thinking?"

"I believe you're thinking too much, Uncle. It is highly unlikely that a man would thrice attempt to attack. Twice was enough, I feel quite certain. He accosted Samuel in the early morn, you, a while later. Surely, the man has gone into hiding."

"I hope you are right. Still, we have no clues as to what has happened."

"Not to worry, dear Uncle."

STAVE SIXTEEN

CRATCHIT THROWN IN A HOLE TO DIE

ob Cratchit had spent much of the afternoon asking around the town of Hopworth if anyone knew anything about the two murders. Despite his carrying a musket, the handful of aged townsfolk were cordial and tried to be helpful. No one knew anything. Nor did they know where the sheriff had gone. Having no other recourse, Cratchit went into the open store and sat down on some sacks of oats. He placed the musket against the wall near him. Leaning back, though he did not mean to, he fell quickly asleep.

He awoke to a voice calling weakly, "Help, please help." The sound came from the back of the store. He rose quickly and rushed to the back of the store. Thereupon he found the entrance down into the old mine. He seized a nearby lantern and found a thin punk glowing in the metal box. He blew on it and touched it to the lantern wick; the flame sprang up, giving ample light. He stuck the punk with its tiny glow in his top jacket pocket. Again, he heard the voice.

In his haste, he left his gun behind. He rushed down the stairs and then into the narrow tunnel. The voice echoed louder. At length, he reached the landing. To his right was a darkened office room. To his left was the long, wooden slide. He peered down into the opaque, dismal night of the lower cavern.

The voice sounded again, but the echo threw the voice all over the place. He looked up to see a high cavern ceiling. He held up his lantern and witnessed a massive colony of bats, a wall of black spreading across the entirety of it. He heard, too, their squeaks, almost like a troubled call for help. Had he been deceived?

Then the lantern was knocked from his hand, clattering to the tunnel floor, the light doused. Two great hands took hold of his collar and throttled him. He pushed against a massive, shadowy figure, powerful beyond his imaginings. With barely any light, he saw gleaming, sharp teeth, gritted. He smelled foul breath like death itself. Suddenly, he was released from the grip and felt himself tumbling backwards. He fell body and soul into the smooth wooden trough and began sliding into total darkness and at a speed he had not ever experienced. He was sure that when the long slide ended, his head would be crushed against a wall. Faster it went, and for a time that seemed like forever, into the bowels of the earth.

Then the ride ended, and he catapulted off the slide and landed on what seemed to be a pile of mattresses. He could see nothing, but after feeling around, he surmised he had indeed landed on straw-ticking bedding. His body was safe, but his future was questionable. He twisted around and found the edge of a mattress. Beyond, it seemed to be solid ground. He hesitantly stood up, careful not to move in any direction. He was in abject darkness. He stretched out his hands and felt nothing. Bending down, he carefully surveyed the few yards around where he had set his feet. Solid ground, pebble-strewn. He took a tentative step. Sliding his feet ever so carefully, he attempted to ascertain the end of the slide he had ridden. Nothing.

His ears began to ring. He felt sure he was moving in the right direction, shuffling step after shuffling step.

"*Oof!*" No mistaking it. He had stepped against a man. The flesh felt squishy.

"Please don't hurt me," the squeaky voice said.

"I won't. I won't," Cratchit admonished the man. "I won't hurt you."

"Have you anything to eat?"

"No." Cratchit bent down and felt a man's arm.

"Don't hurt me!" the man screamed.

"I'm not going to hurt you. I just wanted to get a sense of who you are. At least we're not alone. That's good."

"I don't know. I was not alone yesterday. The other man is gone. I think he died." The man's voice was trembling.

"How long have you been down here?"

"How should I know? I'm going to depart this world, and that's that. The other man must've died."

"Do you know who the other man was?"

"How could I know? There's no light. I think it was the sheriff."

Cratchit reflected on the man's pronouncement, then squatted down. "Here. Reach out and touch my arm."

In a moment, a hand felt Cratchit's elbow.

"Very well," the voice called. "You're here. I'm here. It does us no good. We have no light."

"What did the other man who was here do?"

"He walked off like he knew what he was doing, then I heard a long cry and a … a crash, then nothing."

"Do you know why you're here?"

"The dark monster threw me in here. Then he laughed." Suddenly, the man was sobbing.

"Look," Cratchit tried to calm himself. "My name is Bob. What's yours?"

"Harold Wiltfang. I'm the proprietor of the store above us. Though I'm no better for it. I will die down here, a nameless pile of bones. In a million years, I'll be part of the rocks, the tin ore, whatever is here."

"Believe me, Harold, we can get out of here. But I thought the sheriff was the store owner. Yet you say you are."

"Yes, he stole it from me, by force, he did." The man sobbed again.

"We will find a way out."

"Not without light, we can't."

"There must be some torch or something down here. It was a mine, you know."

"Yes, I know. There were torches, but this is a big room, carved out eons ago by the ocean that is just beyond the wall. I can hear the ocean waves."

Cratchit had no idea what wall the man was talking about. "Do you know why there are mattresses down here?"

"Well, of course I do. Before I built the store above it, all the town children would come here and slide down the trough. They put these mattresses there so no one would get hurt."

"How did they get out?"

"They walked out. You see, they had lanterns, and there used to be a way out of here just a short distance, then walk up an incline to the top again and ride down once more."

"So, it was a game?"

"Yes, but without light, we can't find our way out. There are deep chasms out that way."

Cratchit sensed that the man was pointing in some direction.

"If only we had some light." Harold began sobbing again.

Cratchit had a thought. He checked his pocket. He pulled out the punk. Though small, it still glowed a tiny orange light. "We can light the mattress ticking. With that fire, we can find a torch or lantern or something."

"Hurrah," the other man said sarcastically. "Say, where are you going?"

Cratchit had risen, turned, and slid his feet along, hoping to find the mattress he had landed on. He shuffled along for some time. "Oh, no," he said at last. "I can't find it."

"Can't find what?"

"The mattress. Whatever ticking and fabric it has. I can light it with this wick in my hand."

"Oh, well, why don't you use the mattress I'm sitting on?"

"You're sitting on one? Splendid! Keep talking. I'll work my way to you." He turned and headed into the nothingness. "You must keep talking. I'll walk towards your voice."

"But what should I say?"

"How about a nursery rhyme?"

"Very well. I don't think your plan will work."

"Sure, it will. Now keep talking. I'll come to you."

"Little Jack Horner ... sat in a corner, eating a Christmas pie ..." Harold began blubbering. "I'm so hungry. I'd give anything for a pie."

"That's all right. Just keep crying. I'll head towards you."

Harold bawled so loud that the echo reverberated throughout the vast cavern.

Cratchit stopped. "Can you just talk normally, please?"

Harold ceased sobbing. "He stuck in his thumb and pulled out a plum, and said, 'What a good boy am I.'" He began whimpering.

Cratchit arrived beside him. He knelt, pulling a small penknife from his pants pocket. Feeling carefully, he avoided Harold's body and located the mattress. He ripped the fabric with the knife and drew out a wad of straw. He held it before his face. Harold was whimpering now. Cratchit blew on the punk; the spark glowed up. He touched it to the straw.

"It's damp." He blew again on the punk and touched it to the straw. It would not light. He bent down and reached farther inside the mattress, this time withdrawing drier elements. He blew on the tiny, remaining stub of punk and touched it to the straw. The flame flew up so quickly, Cratchit almost dropped the wad. "Quick! Get more ticking."

Harry was standing beside him in a mere moment with great handfuls of the straw. Soon they had a fire on the ground. The flames reflected off glass-like cave walls, polished by eons of ocean waves that receded eons later. Cratchit and Wiltfang saw each other's faces. Harold was as chubby as a turnip, with a childlike, pudgy face.

Cratchit knew they needed to search quickly for a torch or lantern before the flames went out.

"I'll keep the fire burning," Harold offered, wiping his tear-stained face. "You find a torch."

Harold was good to his word. He soon had the fire blazing, the two men's shadows dancing like tribal warriors in a war dance across the cavern walls. Cratchit raced to every wall, searching behind every rock, in the corners.

Then, "Praise God! I found a lantern." He held up the lantern. "And it's got plenty of oil."

Harold, a plump man in his mid-forties, balding and sporting a wide double chin, was leaping up and down. In a moment, the lantern was lit, and a good thing, too, for the straw fire was filling the cavern with smoke.

"This way, I believe." Harold strode into one of several cave tunnels that extended out from the cavern. Cratchit fell in behind. They travelled up the pebble-strewn incline a matter of about fifty yards.

"Yes, yes." Harold held the lantern high. When they turned the corner of the narrowing tunnel, he suddenly stopped. "This cannot be."

Before them, rocks were piled to the ceiling, blocking further progress.

"Are you sure this is the way out?" Cratchit asked.

"It used to be," Harold said.

"Perhaps you've forgotten."

"No, no. This was the way. The other tunnels end up in dead ends." He sat down on the cold ground, burying his head in his hands.

Cratchit took the lantern and began searching. He scrambled up the piles of rocks and held the light at any appearance of a hole. Whether by a landslide or purposeful piling of the heavy rocks, they were assuredly blocked in.

STAVE SEVENTEEN

THINGS COME UNDONE

Scrooge sat on the edge of a sofa in the mansion's parlour. He chewed on a hangnail. He seldom had in his life felt what he was feeling now—that a dear friend might be dead. Before Jacob Marley died, he had considered him only a business partner, more like a bare acquaintance. Sure, he called him "friend," but the intimacy stopped there. Marley had become more of a friend to him as a ghost than he had ever been in life.

Yet, with the rolling up and rolling down changing of his heart, he had grown inimically fond of Bob Cratchit. His partner, a confidant, a guide to all things of goodwill. He had been to the funerals of other persons he had known. He even attended the funeral in Scotland of a distant uncle, but he had never felt the pangs of distorted sorrow that ran through him now, indeed through his very soul.

It was late, the hour well past the arrival of darkness. The grandfather clock ticked like wagon wheels over rough pavement, a clack, then another clack, then the inordinately loud chime of the half-hour. Scrooge stood and marched about the room in front of the others of the household who were also holding vigil. "Where the devil is he?"

"Might we begin a search party?" Samuel offered.

"I think it's time, Mr. Scrooge," Edmund said.

"I will help," said Abigail.

"Yes, and I as well," said Lucy.

Lockie was already standing at the door, his hand on the knob.

"Well, you'll not have me going out on such a night, the wind howling like wolves," Mrs. Agatha Owsley proffered. "Someone has to stay here and guard the house, take care of Mr. Tamperwind. And I'll not have Michael going out in this night."

Michael had taken up a position beside Lockie, but seeing the fierceness in Mrs. Owsley's face, he retreated from the door.

The gardener stood, cap in his hand, his head bowed.

"I say, Mrs. Owsley," Samuel said, "if you would be so kind as to direct the gardener—what's his name—to go about gathering lanterns for us, I'll take him with me. Scrooge. You, Lockie, and Edmund, go together as well."

"His name," Mrs. Owsley growled, "is Clarence Dimwittle, and he's as *dim* as they come." She smirked at her crass pun. "But I'll send him with you." She went to the big man with the broad shoulders and meek face and made several wild and animated motions, and he seemed to ascertain her meaning. He went out while the others gathered coats.

"No, you shan't go on," Samuel said to Lucy and Abigail. "Someone should stay here and be guard. We don't know what to expect. We'll go down to the mine town and enlist some of the men there to help us. We need you and Lucy here. And use these for protection if you must." From under his jacket, he had drawn out two pistols, handing one to each. "You pull the hammer back. Place one of these little caps on the nipple here, and it's ready to fire. Be careful, don't let it go off unintentionally."

Lucy held the gun and firing caps gingerly while Abigail lifted it naturally and took aim along its barrel, pointing it at the grandfather clock.

Clarence arrived, lugging several lanterns, enough for many men.

He, along with Scrooge, Edmund, Lockie, and Samuel, pulled their coat collars up, threw on scarves and hats, and plunged out into the gale. The wind was like ice. "No rain," Scrooge said. "I'm grateful for that."

"Be careful, Lockie!" Michael called from the porch, his tone melancholy.

"Do be careful, Lockie," Lucy called, her tone admiring.

Scrooge wondered what might have transpired between Lockie and the young maiden who was perhaps half a year his senior. But he had no time to wonder about such things now.

In quick time, the five made it to town and enlisted support from six stout-hearted men. Five teams went forth. The wind, at first mimicking wolves howling, now sounded like several banshees at odds with each other, shrieking from one hill to another. Scrooge had never heard such a wailing wind in his life, and all the men had trouble keeping their lanterns lit. At length, the teams walked off into the darkness, and soon, their lanterns could not be seen from the mansion.

Scrooge, Edmund, and Lockie headed straight for Hopworth. Edmund had a third pistol in hand. Scrooge rested his hand on the hilt of his pistol. Lockie carried a lantern and a large stone he had picked up from the roadside. The path to the lost town was even more difficult to negotiate in the dark, and no fewer than five times did the threesome take a wrong turn. Finally, the tawdry town once again seemed to spring up from the valley incline. The light of a few hearths burned enough to glow from windows. Scant light fell out onto the dirt street to make their footsteps easier.

Scrooge recognised the sheriff's store and headed straight towards it. Edmund and Lockie followed. The door was slinging around and clattering against the jam and the outside wall. The wind had entered and thrown much of the goods into disarray.

"Say! What's this?" Lockie called against the wind. He held up Cratchit's rifle.

"That's Bob's. I know it for sure." Scrooge took the gun in hand.

"That means Bob was here," Edmund said.

Scrooge drew a trembling breath, for he knew what had pursued him in the tunnel behind the store might be there still. Fear was in his throat and in his bones. His voice shook. "Let us proceed."

The three crept through the back of the store, then down the steep steps to the steady incline of the narrow tunnel. The lantern light glanced off the walls, throwing wild, hideous shadows that marched up and down the walls and reminded Scrooge of that Christmas Eve night when he had seen the tormented spirits bound in chains, each of them so wishing they could have helped those less fortunate, but were powerless to do so. He had determined then and there he would do more for the Cratchit family, not just helping Tim recover, but ensuring an education for all the children and setting aside a tidy sum for the couple's old age.

All these thoughts raced through his head, but paramount was his desire to save his friend. They reached the landing where the mine manager's office was and where Sheriff Pickens stored his meat and the dead bodies. Scrooge peered over the edge of the down-spiralling trough-slide while Edmund and Lockie searched the office but found nothing, save some footprints. One of the sets of prints was quite large.

Lockie, in schoolboy fashion, followed the footsteps, placing his own small feet inside the foot patterns. He followed the steps up to a wall where they stopped.

Scrooge and Edmund were huddled, talking about their next move.

"Look here," Lockie hollered. "There's a sort of door. It's covered with plaster and made to look like the tunnel wall. See. Here are the seams and the hinges."

Scrooge and Edmund approached the door, made to look like a wall, and felt the seams.

"No wonder I didn't see it when I was down here before." Scrooge marvelled at how precise the fittings were. "Lockie, you're a wonder."

With not undue struggle, the three pulled the heavy door back, behind which ran a lengthy curving tunnel. Unlit torches sat in sconces at intervals along the wall.

Suddenly, a light flickered at a far turn in the tunnel.

"What ho!" Edmund cried. "Who's in the passage?"

In a twinkling, two figures appeared—the taller, thin one holding a lantern, the chubby one tagging along behind.

"I say. You've come at just the right time," called a voice. Immediately, Scrooge recognised his friend, Cratchit.

Cratchit continued speaking while he and his companion made their way to the three at the doorway. "We were far down in the cavern.

Our first passage was blocked, so we've been plying our way through various tunnels. We'd been this way once but thought it a dead end. Only by providence did you arrive as we were searching yet again. And furthermore—"

Cratchit had arrived at the wall-door and Scrooge embraced him with all the force he had within him, tears of joy pouring down his cheeks. "Dear Cratchit, I thought you might be dead. But here you are, alive. Alive! My dear boon chum. I'm so grateful you are still walking this earth. I shall add some additional prayers this evening in gratitude for your safety."

Harold Wiltfang stood rocking on his heels just out of the glow of the lanterns. Cratchit shook hands heartily with Edmund and Lockie.

"It was Lockie who discovered this hidden door," Scrooge explained. "There are other search parties out in the wind looking for you as well, including Samuel and the deaf gardener, Dimwittle."

"Then we must tell them I am safe," said Cratchit. "Oh, and let me introduce to you Harold Wiltfang. He had already been down in the cave some days. How many days, he does not know."

"And I'm quite hungry. Let me go into my storage locker. I believe I have some dried jerky in there." Not wanting to shake hands, the man rushed into the dark office turned into a meat locker. The others followed suit. In the lantern's glow, Harold endeavoured to find some dried meat, which he obtained from a wooden box, pulling out strips of jerky, and began gnawing on them. He seemed content to sit and chew voraciously on the meat.

"Wiltfang says," Cratchit said, drawing his companions aside, "that another man had been tossed down the trough-slide into the cavern. Apparently, the slide at one time was used by early miners as a quicker way to enter the deeper portions of the mine without the tedious descent down a ladder. When this mine closed, Harold says it was used by local children as a play park of sorts. They slid down it, landed on mattresses, then walked out through what was once an easy exit. Yet we found that exit blocked."

"What happened to the other man?"

"Wiltfang said the man was tossed down only this morning but attempted to find his way in the total darkness and fell in some chasm to his death. We never saw a body but did find some rather deep chasms where our lantern light would not penetrate. Any idea who the man was?"

"I'll tell you who I think he was," Harold said, having stopped chewing long enough to speak. "He was the town sheriff. Pickens. I heard him arguing with the other man. Probably the big man in all black clothes. Covers even his face, he does."

"When was this?" Scrooge asked.

"Just this morning. Being down in the hole, I could not hear quite well, though my cries for help apparently were never heard. I did hear the voice of an older gentleman up above this morning."

"That was probably me," Scrooge added.

"Be that as it may, I'm glad the sheriff is dead. He's the one who told me he was buying the store. Buying it forcefully I should say. When I tried to bargain with him, he was joined by this immense man. The big man in black threw me down the trough to die. Fortunate I was to locate the underground stream that ran there, or I'd have died of thirst."

"When did this occur?" Edmund asked.

"There was some big commotion happening up at the Tamperwind mine. I don't know what it was, but it was serious. Occurred in the night. The next morning, I was opening my shop, and the sheriff appeared, all nervous like. Said he wanted to buy the store. When I refused, that's when I was dumped down the slide into the hole."

The four Londonites looked at each other with amazement.

"When I came here just this morning," Scrooge said, "the sheriff acted as though he'd owned the store for years. He brought me here to show me the dead bodies, and ..." Scrooge turned to look at the slabs where the bodies had lain. "They're not here!"

"What?" all the others proclaimed in near unison.

"The dead bodies were here this morning. I examined them. Now they're gone!" Scrooge paced between the slabs, pointing. "I just saw them here and here."

"Two dead bodies in my meat locker?" Harold looked dubiously at the jerky in his hands. He tossed them down. "What did they die of?"

"They were murdered?"

"Not typhus, not the pox?"

"No, no," Scrooge continued. "Why would he show me the bodies only to have them stolen away?"

Lockie followed behind Scrooge while he strode back and forth by the slabs. "Lockie, do get out of my way."

"Certainly, Mr. Scrooge." Lockie stepped aside.

Suddenly, Scrooge bolted from the room and began examining the footprints in the ample dust of the landing. He walked back and forth, his head bent. He pulled out his spectacles from his pocket, got down on his knees. "Look here," he announced.

Lockie came up beside him. "Are you thinking what I'm thinking, Mr. Scrooge?"

Scrooge looked momentarily at the intrepid lad. "Perhaps. Gentlemen, gander at these footprints, the large ones."

The men circled around.

"Here," Scrooge pointed at a series of smaller prints. "These prints are ours, not petite but certainly smaller than these big ones strewn about. Up here, you see where the prints begin to be just the toes. I believe that is where the big man was chasing me earlier. And there." He pointed where the dust showed a wide indentation. "Must be where he fell from the stairs when he tripped in his pursuit of me."

The men went as a group back to the area of passage between the old office and the hidden door.

Before Scrooge could speak, Lockie interjected, "Here is where the footprints appear deeper in the soil. This indicates he was carrying a heavy load."

Scrooge patted Lockie on the shoulder. "Yes, Lockie, of course."

Lockie held his head high. "I conjecture he carried both bodies from the meat locker to the hidden door and exited out this tunnel."

"But we found no other exit when we were searching the cave," Cratchit said.

"Perhaps there is another hidden door," Edmund offered.

"Yes, and if Harold knows of the stream that runs through the cavern, it must come out somewhere."

"If we go now, we might find it!" Lockie was ready to pursue the idea.

"Not tonight, young man," Scrooge said. "We need to get back and alert the others that we found Mr. Cratchit and Mr. Wiltfang. Else they may be searching all night."

The men headed up the incline and onto the stairs. The chubby shopkeeper did his best to keep up.

Gaining the shop floor, Scrooge commented, "At first, the sheriff was most cordial to me. Perhaps he was trying to keep everything jovial in order to lure me to my death. If the big man had killed me, it would have been easy to hide my body."

"Yes," Cratchit said. "But if the big man and the sheriff were in cahoots, what part did they play in the murder of the mine manager, Owsley, and the miner, Smyth? And why did the big man toss Sheriff Pickens into the cavern? The longer we're here, the more unanswered questions we have."

"I have some ideas on the miner who was killed," Edmund remarked. "When I was asking around the town this morning, a few of them offered that he was bragging about coming into a great store of money. Perhaps he was too mouthy, and the big man put an end to him. I think he knew something about the manager's death. I would wager the sheriff was in on it too."

"With the sheriff supposedly dead, and miner Smyth dead, that leaves the large man dressed in black," Scrooge said.

"And he wears a mask," Cratchit said.

"What did they know and what did they stand to gain?" Lockie asked.

"That's a good question," Scrooge replied. "Let us call for the others."

STAVE EIGHTEEN
CRASS BEHAVIOUR OF MINERS
AND ANOTHER MURDER

The wind had abated markedly, and the town of Hopworth appeared quiet. A solitary figure leaned against a lamppost. Coming closer, the five men could see it was a woman, wearing a short skirt and a flimsy shawl. In the brash lamplight, her face seemed bruised red, but when they came closer, they saw that her cheeks were rouged and her lips red.

"Lookin' for sumpin to do?" the woman remarked and turned to face the men, her bosom's deep cleavage showing above a scanty blouse.

"A punk. A common whore," Edmund remarked. "I guess that the occupation is not limited to the cities, but even here in the outskirts of civilisation."

The men, purely by habit, tipped their hats but made their way around her by a wide margin.

Lockie looked back at her with pity. He knew so many like her, whose only possible occupation was to eke out a living in London. No other means to support herself, adrift in a sea of drunken, lustful men, and perhaps women, and she wishing for something to hang on to, some safe port o' call. He knew one such woman who always gave him a bed to sleep in with no expectations other than to keep her warm on frigid nights. Their body heat saved both their lives. Her name was *Rose*.

Scrooge and his companions began calling loudly, "Hi, ho! We found him! He's safe."

"Come forth! No more need to hunt!" Edmund yelled.

In but a few minutes, three teams of townsmen appeared, striding from different directions. All clapped their hands on Cratchit's shoulders. They, too, were surprised to see Mr. Wiltfang and hugged him.

"We thought you went off to the big city," said one to Wiltfang. "That's what the sheriff told us."

Wiltfang attempted to explain his plight of what turned out to be only one day, his disorientation like that of a caged animal, but the men were too joyous and too ready to escape the gale and return to their homes. Five of the six men were in their later years and had suffered through all the excitement they could have wanted for a month. At length, the miners had all gone home. Scrooge and the others waited for the last two in the search to arrive, Samuel and the gardener, Dimwittle.

They called and called. Lockie and Edmund went up several nearby short hills, hollering against the wind, yet neither Samuel nor Dimwittle appeared.

When they were back together in a group by the Hopworth general store, Cratchit said, "You know, the gardener can't hear, and Samuel has a bad back."

"Yes," Edmund said.

All were silent, worry upon their countenances.

After an hour of waiting and shouting, the group decided to head back to the mansion. Lockie surreptitiously remained behind, still watching, under the town's single streetlamp. He stood shivering, for though the wind finally settled, the temperature was falling as fast as an object might plummet from a height. An old cart rumbled by. Lockie wondered what the driver sought to do at this late hour.

A dark form appeared not too far away, startling him. He followed the shadowy figure, slowly striding along the walkway by the homes. The form turned towards him, and he could see a woman appearing in the dismal light.

"You lookin' for someone, sugar?" The voice was distinct, and he soon recognised her as she drew closer—the woman of the evening. She still wore her straggly shawl and looked, save her bosom, as thin as a post. She came up to him and laid a limp wrist on his shoulder. "You need someone to keep you warm, sweet one?" She smiled a grey tooth smile, trying her best to look appealing.

"No, ma'am. I'm fine. I'll be hustling on home now." He was almost afraid of her.

"No need to hurry. I'm here to help your night be warmer."

She continued to call after him while he ran up the hill. Soon he was even with the mine entrance. A few lights glowed at the entrance. A man with a musket patrolled outside. Another two men sat just inside the opening, also with muskets. Lockie decided to stop and visit with the men. Each man appeared as grim as pallbearers, dark circles under their eyes.

"What ho, gentlemen?"

They gave him not so much as a nod.

"I say, gentlemen, is the mine always guarded in this fashion?"

They looked at him but gave no response.

"It's a simple question. I'm new here."

"If you're lookin' for work, we don't have a foreman to hire ya," the meanest-looking one said.

"No, I ain't looking for work. I just want to know why the guard."

"There're too many murders goin' on." The mean one snarled like a wolf.

"Who's being murdered?" Lockie knew the answer but wanted to see what the men would say.

He received no response. After a long moment, he started to walk away. The mean man, so large he was like a piece of the mountain broke off, moved into Lockie's path. "Why you stickin' your nose in where it don't belong?"

"You're right. I just heard that a man named Grumbles was thought to have done the killin'."

"That's right," the mean one growled. "It was him that killed the foreman, Mr. Owsley, and him that killed ol' Creaker Smyth. I don't know what his issue is, but we're here to keep him from causin' more killin'. He's a villain, he is."

"Did you see Grumbles do the deeds?" Lockie asked in his most pleasant voice.

"Don't know why that matters to you, but none of us did, except his friend, the sheriff, saw it. Go ask the sheriff. He was a witness."

"So, you don't know about the sheriff?"

"What'd ya mean we don't know about the sheriff?"

"Oh, nothing. Not at all. I heard he was an able constabulary." Lockie had to think quickly. What he knew was more than he wished to reveal to these men.

"Then be on your way," the crass miner said. "You can go ask the sheriff over in Hopworth. If you're lookin' for a job, you got to wait till we get a new foreman."

"And hope ya don't git on Caveman's crew," a skinny guard remarked. "That's him standin' afore ya. Ya make a mistake, he'll drive ya into the ground like he drives a spike through a boulder."

Caveman sneered at Lockie and stuck out his chest. "Get along, runt, before I find a reason to nail ya to a wall."

Lockie headed to the house at a rapid walk, the smoky frost puffing from his mouth. He passed Wiltfang heading the other way. Apparently, he had been sent home. He had great relief upon his face, having been saved from an appalling death.

When Lockie reached the porch, Cratchit was standing, peering into the darkness. He had pulled his scarf up over his nose, and his hands tucked under his armpits.

"Any word of Samuel or Dimwittle?" Lockie asked.

"Nothing. And Abigail is beside herself, and Lucy too."

"I'll go in and see if I can comfort them."

Cratchit looked his young office worker up and down. "Mind you, don't embarrass yourself. Don't say anything stupid. They're worried enough."

"Yes, Master Cratchit." Lockie went inside.

When he entered, he spied Edmund and Scrooge pacing the floor in the dining room, and Lucy, perched on the edge of a settee, smiled briefly and weakly. "Hello, Lockie. Thank you for going out looking. We're so glad that Mr. Cratchit was found ... and the shopkeeper saved, as well. Mr. Scrooge told us what happened."

Lockie hastened to Lucy, bowed, took her hand, and kissed it. "All of us are worried about Samuel. Where, dear Lucy, is your cousin, Abigail?"

"Why. She's just there."

Lockie looked in the direction Lucy nodded, and his eyes came to rest on Abigail curled in a ball in a corner by the window, her head just high enough for her to peer out the bottom of the window. She was visibly distraught, trembling and sobbing. Lockie straightened. "Is there anything I can do?"

"You are so kind, Lockie," Lucy replied, "but I've tried. She's like a caged animal. I fear for her mind."

"I do, as well."

A commotion began on the porch, and, suddenly, Dimwittle rushed in wide-eyed, his cap in his hand. He looked fervently about. Cratchit was inches behind him. Dimwittle spotted a pile of papers and a pencil and grabbed them up. He made multiple guttural sounds, and soon, Mrs. Owsley, in her dressing gown, came down the stairs.

"What is it, Clarence?" she hollered.

Dimwittle was facing away from her, and she came up behind him, grabbed his arm, and turned him around. He immediately began scribbling on the page, then handed her the paper. She took the spectacles perched on her bonnet and eyed the paper.

"Oh, dear," she said. "It appears Grumbles has struck again. Dimwittle says Samuel is dead."

"No!" Abigail screamed, rising and racing across the floor. She tore the page from Dimwittle's hands and tried to read it. "This is mere gibberish."

"I know enough of his hand to understand it," Mrs. Owsley said. "I think you men best go with him and recover the body."

"No, no, no. My dear Samuel!" Abigail cried and ran upstairs. Lucy followed.

"Lockie, stay here," Scrooge commanded. "Here's my pistol. If that fiend comes here, shoot him dead. The rest of us will go with Dimwittle."

Lockie examined Dimwittle, who was walking shamefacedly out the door. Never had he seen a more contrite face on a man, his hands trembling. Lockie felt sorry for the gardener. Considering that the murderer might come to the house, he lifted the heavy pistol and aimed down its barrel.

Just then, Michael appeared at his side.

"I've been with my foster father. I'm afraid he will be appalled at this news. Family is all to him. Me, I'm just a ward. I was listening at the top of the stairs. So, I know what has happened."

"Yes, Michael," Lockie said. "I wish I could come to grips with this monster."

"I believe it is Grumbles for sure, and he won't be satisfied until everyone who might have ever wronged him is dead."

Lockie stuck the pistol in his belt. He remembered the day Grumbles rushed into Scrooge's counting-house and looked to be entirely a man falsely accused and needing to run. Now Lockie was beginning to believe Grumbles's story was a ruse, merely to obtain funds to support his escape.

"Come," Michael said. "Let's play some cards. There's nothing we can do to help anyone right now."

Lockie agreed, and they walked into the dining room, and Michael fetched a deck of cards. Mrs. Owsley came briefly from the kitchen and smiled at Michael. It was the first smile Lockie had seen her make. "Michael, what do you make of this housekeeper?"

"She's all right. Takes good care of my foster father, Mr. Tamperwind."

"Why do you think your foster father sent letters to his nieces and nephew?"

Michael studied his hand of cards. "He has moments of confusion. With his illness. He can barely rise from bed without assistance. Very ill."

"I understand."

They began their game of *blanks*.

Outside, the wind had picked up again. With their lanterns glowing, the three Londonites followed on the heels of the meek gardener. Their path twisted along through narrow passages between rocks and over some quite large boulders. Scrooge, who had the wherewithal to grab pencil and paper, took hold of Dimwittle's arm and stopped him. He wrote on the pad, "Is this the exact way you came?"

Dimwittle read it and nodded.

Scrooge wrote, "But why?"

Dimwittle took the paper and wrote, "We were following Grumbles."

They resumed their sojourn until they reached a sage-laden spot perhaps a mile from the shantytown. The lantern light revealed the pale, stiff body of Samuel, his eyes closed, his jaw twisted open. The arms were contorted at odd angles, the back arched. Edmund bent down to the body's chest and listened. "No heartbeat!" he hollered into the wind.

Dimwittle attempted to gather Samuel's arms to pick up the body.

"Wait," said Cratchit. "Let us examine it for clues." He pushed the gardener, who then released the man's arms. Edmund and Cratchit examined the surrounding area. The area was muddy with many footprints. Scrooge bent down to examine the body. He found dirty finger marks and scratches about Samuel's neck, but no wound from a bullet or knife.

"I can find all our footsteps, coming from our heading easy enough to note each one," Edmund said. "There's Bob's square-toed boot, and there's yours, Uncle, the pointed toe. Here's mine, and here are the clodhoppers of the gardener."

"Over here, the steps are all piled together, heavy, and it looks like a struggle occurred," Cratchit said. He hastened back, his own shoes making a sucking noise in the mud. "But the body lies here, away from the struggle."

"I believe," Scrooge began, "that Samuel fought with his assailant, quite a fight as I might imagine. He was strangled, then his skin torn by ragged fingernails. Then, I believe Samuel's body was thrown this distance, perhaps five yards from where he first fell."

"His assailant would have had to have great strength," Edmund added.

They all nodded their heads.

"And great cause in his mind," Scrooge concluded. He turned to the gardener and wrote again. "What were you doing during this?"

Dimwittle wrote: "I was lost. Fight happens. I run. Get lost again. I see Grumbles running away in his big black cape. The killer."

"How do you know it was Grumbles?" Scrooge wrote.

Dimwittle pointed at Samuel's body, the air puffing quickly from him.

"I know you're scared," Scrooge wrote. "Did you see Grumbles's face?"

"Yes," the gardener scribbled. "He wore mask."

"Hmm." Scrooge turned and studied the body some more. "At first light, we must send for the authorities in Lazy Eye. Three murders and no professional crime solvers. I'm not up for this. Let us get the body back to the mansion."

The four men gathered the body and struggled along the dreary paths back to the mansion. Scrooge was wondering how to explain to Abigail, and indeed to any of the others, that he had sought to save Bob, but from that effort, another man was dead. He felt completely out of his element. *Are things going to get worse*? he thought.

STAVE NINETEEN

CRATCHIT JOURNEYS FOR HELP AND A MIRACLE

When they arrived at the porch, the door sprang open, and Abigail rushed out. "My brother, my dear brother!" She hurried to the side of the body and shrank back, for she saw his distorted visage. She swooned. Lockie and Lucy were quickly there to catch her and to help her inside and set her gently on the sofa.

Michael stood smiling the whole time. Lockie looked at him in dismay.

Mrs. Owsley appeared with smelling salts and ran the foul vapour under Abigail's nose. She awakened a bit, only to see the men stretch the dead body upon the dining room table amid the strewn playing cards. Cratchit pulled shillings from his pockets and placed the shillings upon the eyelids. The man's clothing and face were crusted with frozen mud.

Lockie helped Abigail rise and take stuttering steps to the table. She wept so bitterly that everyone's eyes became wet, save the gardener who hung his head ashamedly and Mrs. Owsley with her grim expression of exasperation, and Michael, who was still smiling.

Lockie turned to him. "How dare you smile at a time like this!"

Michael shrank away, tucking his fisted hands about his face.

Mrs. Owsley stood with a proud expression and spoke. "That is how Michael has coped with tragedy. Before he came to be Mr. Tamperwind's ward, he saw too much in his life. He means no harm."

Michael tucked his head to her bosom and whimpered.

"Sorry, little friend," Lockie said to Michael. "I'm just worn out myself. I've not seen this much dyin' since the plague back in '41."

Mrs. Owsley walked away with the boy still clinging to her and sobbing like he had lost his own relative.

Abigail sat beside her brother and was picking bits of grass and mud from his clothing. Then she arose, and taking her apron, sought to remove the grime from his face. "He has such a handsome face, don't you think?" she said to no one at all and to everyone.

"Yes, yes," everyone said.

Mrs. Owsley returned alone. "Out with all of you. If I'm to clean this body, I need all of you out of the way. I've dealt with enough miners dead upon this very table. I know what to do. Miss Lucy, attend to your cousin. Take her upstairs. The rest of you be gone." She shooed them out, then turned the lantern lights to high and had Dimwittle light the chandelier over the table. She called to the retreating men. "And one of you should stand guard in case Grumbles returns."

Lucy took Abigail's arm, and they retired upstairs.

"Edmund," Cratchit said, "if you wouldn't mind taking the watch, I plan to take the fastest steed available in the morning and ride to Lazy Eye and bring back a constable."

"Fair enough," Edmund replied. "Tired as I am, I don't believe I could sleep. I'll take the watch. Mr. Scrooge, you rest. You've had a wretched day. You were almost killed, and Bob Cratchit almost killed, and now this kind gentleman dead."

Scrooge nodded, and he and Cratchit trudged upstairs to their separate bedrooms. Edmund pulled off his coat and boots, set his two pistols on a lamp table and sat, stretching out his long legs. He observed Mrs. Owsley cleaning the dead body, something he had never seen before. She removed the prone body's clothes and began ferociously scrubbing his entire body with rough, wet cloths. She bore down hardest on his face, neck, and chest.

Cratchit, when he arrived in his room, could only pull off his boots, then collapsed on his bed, and despite the harrowing events of the day, fell asleep when his head touched the pillow.

Scrooge, on the other hand, could not sleep. He pulled off his clothes and put on his nightshirt and cap, lit the logs in the simple fireplace, then sat on his bed. He concentrated on the crimes and the clues he had found. Large footprints of someone who was the cause of death of three men. He reached to his breeches and pulled out the writings of the gardener and his own scribbled notes, seeing the fingerprint ink smudges, the slant of the words. Had he asked enough questions? Did he ask the gardener the right questions? *The poor man must be beside himself with grief.* What did Marley's ghost have in mind when he insisted Scrooge go on this venture? Surely, being in hell had driven his former partner crazy.

Scrooge could not imagine accomplishing anything at this point. He had tried to fashion himself after a policeman but felt he had failed miserably. He had almost been killed, Bob had almost been killed, and now a true gentleman by every right was dead, and they were nowhere closer to catching the criminal. At length, he fell asleep.

He awoke in the burgeoning morning to Cratchit clomping down the hall. He jumped from the bed, though the air and even the floor was frigid. He tiptoed across the floor as if it were ice. He made the door, opened it, and caught sight of Cratchit at the head of the stairs. "What, ho, Cratchit! Leaving so soon? The sun's barely on the horizon."

Cratchit turned. "Look out the window, Scrooge, a blizzard has already begun. If I don't go soon, I won't be able to make it to Lazy Eye to gain a proper policeman for these crimes." He buttoned his waistcoat, threw on a lambswool sweater, wrapped two heavy scarves about his neck, and donned a wool cap. Next, he pulled on wool gloves. "The gardener is already saddling a horse for me. I hope the animal is good in snow."

Cratchit hoofed it down the stairs before Scrooge could make any further admonitions.

Hurrying back to his boudoir, he gathered his clothes, put on slippers, and went out into the hall and down the stairs. He made the front windows and watched huge snowflakes blowing amidst the austere trees across the shadowed lawn, and though the sky shone pearl glazed, the sun was not visible. The gardener appeared from around the house, bringing out a charcoal black gelding just beyond the gate, at which point Cratchit leapt to the saddle and bolted away.

Scrooge turned to see Edmund, weary but wide awake. "How was the night?" Scrooge asked.

"Quiet is all I know. I certainly am glad of it, but I'll turn in." He rose from his chair and gathered his pistols as if to go to his room, but subsided back to the chair, his eyes closed.

Scrooge looked to the dining room. The body of Samuel lay there still in the nearly opaque dining room. Then Scrooge noted a figure dressed in a black dress sitting in the far corner near the large window. Abigail had her face covered with a black veil, but he knew it was she. No movement, stiff, silent except for the gasps of sobs. She held a kerchief to her nose. Scrooge realised he was not dressed appropriately, so he strode to a corner and quickly put on his clothes. Sensing the deep cold in the room, he went to the living room fireplace, opened the flue, crumpled some old newspapers, threw them under some half-burned logs. He took the wick from the box and lit the fire.

To his satisfaction, the fire flamed up and wafted warmth into the room. He stood before it and warmed his chest and arms, then turned to warm his backside. Grabbing some more newspaper and a lit twig from the fire, he carried them to the dining room fireplace where an abundance of logs was stacked, and he repeated the process. The flames licked up and flashed odd shadows on the stagnant body on the table.

He walked to Abigail and noticed she also held a rosary in her hands, her lips trembling under the veil.

"My deepest condolences, my dear," Scrooge said to her. "He was a good man, and he was in the act of doing a most worthy deed, attempting to save someone else. No greater love than to lay down one's life for ..." He thought better of his commentary and wished he had not spoken the sentence.

Abigail nodded slightly.

Mrs. Owsley clumped into the kitchen, turned up the lamps, and waddled into the dim dining room. "You'll have to eat in the kitchen. It's just porridge this morning. I'll not be fixing bangers and eggs this day. It'll be ready soon. And the young maiden should eat first."

Abigail rose quickly, setting her rosary on a side table. "I'll eat now. For I may never eat again. Without Samuel, I shall starve."

"Let's hope that you survive, deary," Mrs. Owsley said.

Abigail sat at the kitchen table in her black dress.

"That dress you wear that belonged to Mrs. Tamperwind fits you well," Mrs. Owsley said. "I'm glad I had it for you. I know it's a bit tight. I hope it doesn't make you faint like you did yesterday."

Abigail nodded.

Mrs. Owsley dipped some porridge from a deep pot.

Scrooge walked over to the corpse and again examined it. The body was pristine clean, naked, save a cloth across his privates. Mrs. Owsley had done an admirable job. He saw some virtue in her yet, despite her grumpy nature.

He found Samuel's clothes draped neatly on a side chair. Without thinking, he began digging in the pockets of the jacket and waistcoat of the dead body, something he had not thought to do the night before and felt foolish for not having done so. Anything might be a clue. "Old Marley, when you first visited me, you were the advent of a miracle in my life. Was it only possible that God might have intervened earlier, and a miracle should have occurred for this poor man and his sister? I guess we have to take the miracles when they come."

He glanced back at Abigail, who was making a sour face at Mrs. Owsley's porridge. For any good points, Mrs. Owsley was not the best cook. He strode to the window and looked out past the lawn of the mansion to the shantytown, grey and dismal, with white ranks of snow piling on the roofs and banking against the walls.

He then heard a tinkling of bells from the town, followed by a clanging of hammers on anything metal, on pipes, on anvils, and he wondered at the clattering commotion, then more bells pealed, followed by a great bell tolling something momentous. Bells and gongs rang out, all of them hard in the winter with the wind driving like great hammers in upon them, facing out into the world, not near fires ablaze, but their sound like a gleaming conflagration of their own. What was their portent? Was there an emergency? A warning of the storm?

Then he knew. It was Sunday, the last of Advent. Christmas was coming this week. Now, *there* was a miracle. No sooner had he realised the day than he saw the people of the town, indeed every last one of the people of the town, turning out from their homes, battling against the icy snowstorm, heading to the church. It was a pitiful excuse for any structure, but no less a place of peace for these people whose lives had been torn by violence.

Scrooge whispered to himself, "And Christmas is drawing nigh! Is it not the greatest harbinger of the greatest miracle of all, a saviour of our souls born in a stable, for sure, and a true sign of hope for people to hang on to in the direst of times? Hope is on its way."

"I'm sorry, Mrs. Owsley," Abigail spoke behind Scrooge, "but this porridge is most distasteful. I'll not eat another—" She froze in her remarks and pointed.

Scrooge turned and witnessed the same unimagined event. Samuel's hands were twitching. He then moved a hand up to his head, knocked the coins from his eyes, and was wiping his brow. His other arm was waving around like the muscles had been asleep, and he was attempting to wake them.

Scrooge sprang to the table and was immediately beside the man.

Samuel opened his eyes and blinked at Scrooge, aware of the man standing beside him. He offered a weak smile. As he attempted to rise, Scrooge took hold of his shoulders. "Easy, good man, you've been through a great commotion." Scrooge was smiling.

Abigail rushed to her brother, who by virtue of some miracle of some answered prayer was *not* dead.

He was shivering. "Why am I on this table?" He looked adamantly confused.

Scrooge threw off his own jacket and placed it on the prone man's chest. "Mrs. Owsley, quickly, blankets."

Mrs. Owsley turned, grumbling, and shuffled to the blanket pantry.

Abigail was crying, but now the tears were of joy that flooded down her cheeks. She stroked his forehead. He had the most perplexed look on his face, glancing first at his sister and then at Scrooge, then back and forth. He shivered uncontrollably.

"Hurry, Mrs. Owsley," Scrooge called.

"Why are you wearing black, sister?" Samuel asked.

"My dear brother, we thought you dead."

"Dead!" Samuel coughed.

"Yes, my dear. Mr. Cratchit has gone for the authorities because someone attacked you."

"Attacked me?" His eyes glanced back and forth as he tried to remember. "I cannot recall anything short of our arrival here a few days back." He began to shiver even more violently.

"Hurry, Mrs. Owsley!" Both Abigail and Scrooge shouted.

The old woman tottered forwards and tossed a pile of blankets at Scrooge. He and Abigail spread the blankets across Samuel's body.

"Fine thing," Mrs. Owsley stated. "I spent two hours cleaning his body for burial. I'll want some payment for my time, I will."

Scrooge and Abigail ignored the woman.

"Put that down, Michael!" Mrs. Owsley screamed. "Don't touch it."

Michael had arrived at the kitchen table and lifted a spoonful of the porridge to his lips. He stopped.

"Not that," she continued. "Miss Abigail said it was horrid to taste, and I'll not have you spitting it out all over my clean kitchen. I work too hard." She turned towards Abigail. "I'm sorry, deary, my porridge is usually better, but I guess all this worry has put me in ill sorts. I'll make a fresh batch. I'm truly sorry, and I'm glad your brother lives."

"That's quite all right. This is a day of great joy," Abigail responded. "I can survive a little porridge."

"No, you are your uncle's niece and deserve better." Mrs. Owsley turned to Samuel. "Tell me, Samuel, do you have any recollection of me cleaning you last night?"

"No, I was unaware."

"Do you remember anything about being attacked?"

"Nor that. I have little memory of this day. Or the day before. How long have I been out of my mind like this?'

"Since the night previous to this morn," Scrooge replied. He pondered a long moment. "Perhaps you were *not* dead."

Michael had come to the table and stood with his mouth agape. Lockie and Lucy arrived and shared in the joy of the reawakening.

Lucy hugged her cousins. Lockie shook Samuel's weak hand.

Edmund rose from the couch in the parlour where he had fallen asleep, rubbing bleary eyes. He set down his pistols and stumbled to the dining room. "Am I dreaming?"

"No, indeed," Abigail proclaimed. "We thought my brother dead, and yet he is alive."

Edmund helped Scrooge and Lockie lift Samuel to sit and dangle his legs off the table. He was as weak as a fledgeling dove.

"I listened for your heartbeat last night," Edmund said. "Perhaps with the wind blasting, I couldn't hear it. I'm sorry, old man."

"Forgiven," Samuel whispered. He coughed. His shivering had subsided.

"I've read," Scrooge said, "of incidences of others being thought dead, especially those who have been lost in the snow or in the bitter cold, and their hearts slowed so much that many thought them dead."

"I heard a story of a man saved by the bell," Lockie said. "An Irishman was buried after a wake. The bell was hung by the grave on a pole, by tradition. They draped a string from the bell down into the grave into the dead man's coffin. Sure enough, so I was told, he woke from the dead and rang the bell. They come a runnin', dug him up, and he was fine as a fiddle."

"Lockie. What have I told you about your stories?" Scrooge scolded.

"Saved by the bell he was."

"Speaking of bells," Scrooge said, "who's up for church?"

Scrooge was joined by Lockie and Lucy to journey to the mine town Anglican church.

Edmund stayed behind with Abigail to assist Samuel, who said his back no longer hurt him.

Mrs. Owsley said she nor Michael ever joined "that" church but held their own services with Mr. Tamperwind in his bedroom. They went upstairs.

The storm buffeted Scrooge and his companions, but they made it inside the crowded establishment for God just as the service was beginning. The parson entered. Beside him, young acolytes bearing long tapers, their flames flickering near the boys' noses. On the altar, stubby candles of various sort were lit in abundance, and more candles flickered on plates on windowsills. The heavy cross on the wall was draped in purple. The grim-faced and white-haired priest turned to face the congregation and forced a smile, then began with a blessing.

The three newcomers stood against the wall by the rear doors, for no pew seats were available. The doors were not secured well, and a great crack remained between the two at the spot where Scrooge and Lucy stood. The church was already a breezy, blue-nosed, tooth-chattering place, and the raucous north wind leapt through the door at regular intervals and right up Scrooge's backside, and no sooner had the wind sallied forth to some other crevice of the building than it hastened back to stab an icy knife in Scrooge's back again. He moved left and right as best he could, but the wind would take hold of his jacket flaps and toss them up like a tent awning and run a crystal spike into his spine.

He could barely attend to the service and was soon shaking like a sail loosened from its mast. Though Scrooge was banged and worried and even lifted off his feet by the wind, Lucy and Lockie seemed undisturbed and spent more time smiling at each other than listening to the service, though they sang with gusto on the hymns, each beaming while holding the hymnal together.

Scrooge twice saw their timid hands brush slowly across the other. He worried for the young woman, for Lockie had not yet been fully gainfully employed, and his pay as an office boy was insufficient for any couple. "Youth," he said to himself. "Oh, but to be young again and believe all things are possible."

When the priest called for prayers from the congregation, several sought the blessings of peace, and one man called loudly for Mr. Grumbles to be caught and brought to justice, for which the congregation at large uttered many an "amen." Scrooge prayed quietly for Cratchit to be kept safe on his journey to Lazy Eye, for the storm had increased.

STAVE TWENTY

THE BLIZZARD, NEW REVELATIONS

As for Cratchit, his efforts against the snowy gale were becoming more confounding. The snow had piled in drifts like tall, undulating waves across the pitched road, and sometimes, the snow blew so fierce, he could not see his hand in front of his face. Still he urged his steed forwards, watching closely to ascertain some semblance of a road, for there were few signposts. At one point, he looked up and saw a wagon pulled by a team of oxen some thirty yards to his right. He realised he had completely wandered from the byway. He forced his horse through the tall mounds of snow, the horse often floundering and sinking to its chest in the white product. Cratchit made it to the road and followed behind the oxen cart. He attempted to hail the driver several times, but his voice vanished in the wind.

His bangs wore icicles, his nose was raw, and his eyes burned. The sharp wind cut through his being like every muscle had melded into ice. He began to feel his cognizance slipping. Why had he made this journey? Suddenly, he could not think, and all went black. He awoke in a snowbank, his horse's face poking at his, the great nostrils snorting vapour at him. He rose, bewildered. Nothing in his life had ever felt so cruel. Even the day before, being trapped in the cave had not felt so deadly. He felt his life slipping from him.

With the last of his strength, he pulled himself to the saddle and encouraged the horse forwards. All was white about him, a white darkness, a blindness. He was growing tired beyond his reckoning, and his fingers no longer had feeling. He could not sense his feet in the stirrups, he was totally lost, and death was on his heart.

Then, he was being dragged from his horse, the animal drawn away by unseen hands. Other hands and arms gathered around him, and he was brought towards a dim light, then a door was banged open, and he was thrust into a vast, stuffed chair before a roaring fire. The ice across his brow and bangs and eyelids began to melt and trickle down his face. He heard voices but could gather no meaning from them. Small creatures moved around him, threw blankets over his body, took off his boots, and dipped his bare feet in a pan of tepid water. Other small hands rubbed his arms. He could only see glimpses. Was that his heart pounding? Was it trying to leap from his chest? His strong chest felt stabbed with a cleaver. Was the snow his assassin? His head bobbed, and his mind went dark.

Scrooge was glad to return to the house after the church service and to warm himself by the fire. The service had been unpleasant, the sermon boring, but he felt most blessed to be alive and especially thrilled that Samuel had not died, or at least had retreated from death's doorway. Mrs. Owsley and Michael were talking in low tones and sometimes laughing in the back pantry. Lucy had joined Abigail in the sitting room, and Lockie hung at the doorway, watching the two and seeming quite content to do so. Edmund sat on a chair opposite Samuel on the sofa. Samuel had lost the blue tint to his features, and his cheeks were ruddy once more. His nose dripped from a cold he had surely caught, but he seemed in good spirits. Samuel and Edmund took occasional bold shots of brandy.

"I cannot believe that my bout with death in some way healed my aching back," Samuel said for about the fourth time.

Edmund stood and joined Scrooge by the fire. "Samuel still does not remember the events of last night, not even that we had gone looking for

Bob. But I haven't pressed him too hard. He says he remembers seeing a light and multiple white beings. Beyond that, his memory is weak. Even Mrs. Owsley sat beside him at length and tried stridently to get him to remember. To no avail."

"Yes, let us hope Bob makes it through this storm to Lazy Eye."

Lucy and Abigail came forth from the parlour, holding a wreath of greenery, red berries aplenty, and abundant red ribbon. "Look what we made," Lucy announced. "We're so proud. We'll be ready for the Yuletide. For the life of me, I cannot see why Oliver Cromwell would even think of cancelling Christmas like our saviour's coming was some law passed by man."

"Your artistry," Abigail said to Lucy, "adds so much to the décor of the house. Thank you."

"You should both be proud," Samuel said. "And now that I'm not dead, I say we have a talk with Uncle Erasmus. He beckoned us here, and it's time we found the reason." He rose unsteadily. "Let us go now."

"What if he's asleep?" Lucy asked.

"Then we'll wake him. I personally have been through enough, and I'm sure you have been too. Murders or no, we have the right to know why he called us here."

The cousins went upstairs, and Scrooge, Lockie, and Edmund followed. The door to the old man's room was opened by Michael. "Hello," he said. "I was just speaking with Father about your good fortune, Cousin Samuel."

"Good. We wish to speak to Uncle Erasmus."

"I know he wishes to speak with you as well."

The group went to the bedside. The sick man coughed and bade them come closer. "I haven't much lung strength, but I do wish to speak with you." He coughed again. "Some water, please, Michael."

The young lad gave him a drink, which he guzzled down.

He began again. "Dear Abigail, Lucy, and Samuel. Thank you for coming. Samuel, I am so glad you are alive. So pleased." He looked dismal in spite of his kind words. "I have you here because I thought I was near death, having a bad bout for which no physician could offer a reason. I beckoned you here to tell you of my will and show it to you if need be. I will die soon, and I want there to be no probate court or other sly lawyer taking the wealth I have accumulated. For a while, I thought someone was after my wealth, seeking a way to take it from me. Grumbles, the engineer. He was conniving. I know it. After I sent the letters, he must have heard about them, and to get even with me, he killed my friend, the mine manager, Mortimer Owsley."

Scrooge could not help himself. "How do you know it was Grumbles?"

"Why! We have witnesses, not least of which is my ward, Michael, and some miners. And Mrs. Owsley saw him leaving the building as well."

"Could they have been mistaken? It happened at night, did it not?"

"No mistakes, Mr. Scrooge. I believe that's your name. I don't see that's any of your business. We must keep the mine working. I have a man running the daily toil for a while, a man nicknamed 'Caveman,' but he's inexperienced. I want to give Mr. Nuckols a chance, but I've not made up my mind if he's the engineer and the manager for the job. I believe I'll have more men interested."

"My pardon, sir," Scrooge said and stepped back. He was beginning to doubt his friend's, Mr. Grumbles's, sincerity. Was there more to the entire crime than Grumbles asserted?

"I would appreciate it if the rest of you would leave and let me have some time with my nephew and nieces," Mr. Tamperwind said, pointing weakly at the door. "And Mr. Nuckols, if you do want to be my engineer and mine manager, I think you ought to be about the task. That *is* the job."

"I will get there hence," Edmund replied. The cadre left the room, leaving the man with his nieces and nephew.

When they reached below stairs, Scrooge, Edmund, and Lockie were feeling low. Scrooge remarked when they were out of earshot of the room, "I'm of the opinion that when Bob returns with the authorities that we give up on the endeavour. I know, Edmund, that I enlisted you in this, and you are missing time with your family. For all we know, the murders may never be solved, and Grumbles may well have been the perpetrator of these foul deeds, though I cannot fathom his becoming a devil of revenge. Why would he still stay here to face capture, only to exact more violence?"

"I don't know, Uncle, but I'll wager there's more to the story than we have gathered so far."

The three put on their coats and opened the door. They were astonished to see the two dead bodies that had been removed from the shopkeeper's meat locker now lying on the lawn, snow blowing across the bodies, partially hiding them.

STAVE TWENTY-ONE

NEW FRIENDS

ratchit awoke with a start. Before him, a pleasant fire glowed, and a cup of tea sat on a small stool beside his chair. His legs were covered with blankets. He turned his head and looked out a frosted window where moonlight glistened on a soft snowscape. The wind had retired to its home in the north, and the sky was hung with brilliant jewels of light. The stars.

"Ah, you're awake," came a female voice in a calm, sweet declaration.

Cratchit looked around the chair, and in a twinkling, a short woman of about a yard tall appeared before him, obviously, from the maturity in her brow, a woman, not a child. In short order, four additional short people gathered around his chair.

"We thought you might die right here in our house," she said cordially. "And you'd be a heavy burden to carry out, you would. So, you've saved us some travail. Welcome to our home."

The other members said hearty welcomes as well. Each face smiled. Several small, meaty hands patted his arms and shoulders.

"You're dwarves," Cratchit commented, not meaning to hurt feelings.

"We prefer *little people*, that's who we are."

"I've been saved from death by dwarves."

"Yes, here, drink some tea." The woman handed him a steaming cup. He drank it swiftly. "I'm ever so grateful. How's the horse?"

"He'll be fine in the morning. We have him in the barn."

"How far am I from Lazy Eye?"

"My, but you ask a lot of questions. Let me ask one. What's your name?"

"Bob Cratchit, ma'am."

The little people giggled. Cratchit could not tell why.

"Why were you out in that wild storm?"

"I was in pursuit of the constable in Lazy Eye or St. Blazy to investigate the murder of three people up at the Tamperwind Mine."

"The constable?"

"Yes." He was beginning to grow tired.

"Your error led you to the right place. My name is Cora Wheeler. These are my cousins and children."

Cratchit eyed the batch of gawking souls, and honestly appreciated their pleasant smiles. The smallest one gave Cratchit a lump of cheese, and he, being famished, quickly downed the morsel.

"That one is my son, Robert. We call him 'Bobbie.' That's why we laughed. He's named for his father, Bobbie, who is out right now, cleaning the barn and milking the cows."

"Shall I prepare supper for the family now?" a sweet voice called from another room.

"Yes, Ginny, make yourself useful, dear one."

Cratchit looked up to see a tall, shapely damsel of twenty-odd years, an apron about her twice-turned dress, made brave with ribbons. No dwarf, she walked in, hefting a large pot by its handle. She hung the pot on the swing rod in the fireplace, gathered a bellows, and pumped air from it into the fire. The flames roared up, licking the bottom of the pot. While she toiled away at stirring the contents of the great pot, Cratchit took in her appearance. Her black hair was cut short just below her ears; her skin was as white as alabaster, her cheeks rosy. He particularly noticed her dark eyes with specks of gold that seemed to dart about like sparks and hosted a sort of unbridled joy and even mischievousness.

Trim bodied, with a slight bosom, her pretty face appeared filled with a jubilant spirit.

"This is Ginny," Cora Wheeler said. "She is our adopted daughter. We found her at about age three, wanderin' through the forest, naked and crying. We took her in, and though we tried to find her parents, it was to no avail. So, we made her our own daughter. She was so pale white when she was little, we nicknamed her 'Snow.'" She pulled Ginny by the arm from tending the pot and made her stand.

"Ginny, this is Bob Cratchit."

Ginny curtsied. "Pleased to meet you, sir."

"And I am pleased to meet you, and in fact, to meet all of your kind family. You saved my life."

"Oh, I was against saving you," Ginny responded. "I wanted to let you freeze, then cover you with snow to make a proper snowman." She skipped away into a bedroom.

Cratchit's mouth flew open. The other family members guffawed.

"Pay her no mind, Master Cratchit," Cora said. "She is such a tease. She's the one who rushed out first to save you."

Cratchit attempted to rise, but Mrs. Wheeler, stronger than she looked, pushed him back down. "You'll not be risin' yet. You came close to meetin' the grim reaper, you did."

"But I must reach a constable and bring an end to the murders at the mine."

"Well, you'll have no luck in Lazy Eye nor St. Blazy. Their constables quit, and there's not been a replacement. The law is in the hands of whoever has the biggest knuckles with an arm to fling them."

"But ..."

"No 'buts.' You'll be stayin' here this night. You'll be havin' sup with us, you will. Tomorrow is another day. Besides, my son of nine years, Cornelius, needs a new chess opponent. He never loses. Do you play?"

"Well, yes, but—"

"What did I say about 'buts'? Besides, I want you to meet my family. This is Cornelius." A lad stepped forwards, her hands on his shoulders. Then Mrs. Wheeler went down the line, introducing children first. Bobbie, the lad of two hundred weeks, had his dress collar tight about his neck. Though small, he was no dwarf. He bowed like a gentleman, then stepped away. Next, Mrs. Wheeler introduced Effery, the girl twice Bobbie's age, but his same size, for she was a dwarf. She then introduced Angus and Barnabas, the adult dwarf cousins, though she explained they were not really cousins, but friends of long years. Angus, the older of the two, had great tufts of grey hair sprouting from every angle about his scalp and face. Barnabas's peppery beard was long and stringy, and his scalp was as hairless as a glass orb paperweight.

A fierce stomping sounded just outside the door.

"Ah, and here comes my husband, the intrepid Bobbie Wheeler, Esquire, finest wheelwright in three counties." Mrs. Wheeler's face shone with pride.

The stout dwarf entered, shaking snow from his clothes and brushing snow from his ample beard. He set down two pails of milk. After removing his boots, hat, comforter, and leather apron, he shook hands with Cratchit. "Pleased to make your acquaintance, sir," he said, his tone brusque.

"And yours as well."

Mr. Wheeler strode into the washhouse, and the two cousins went outside and bore in more wood for the hearths.

While the pot's lid clacked atop the pot of bubbling, spicy soup, the enticing aroma swelled up into Cratchit's nose, and he felt intense hunger. Scented candles stood in holders around the room. Holly and pine boughs hung from the rafters. He was conscious of a thousand odours floating throughout the home, each one a reminder of a thousand hopes and joys. His cares, for a time, were forgotten.

Cornelius, or *Corny*, as he preferred to be called, brought out the chessboard, and Cratchit and he played the game with the board perched on Cratchit's knees. In short order, the intrepid man found his king cornered by the astute, young chess enthusiast. Cratchit observed the boy's furrowed brow, intent upon his strategy.

When the announcement for supper arrived, Cratchit was pleased when Corny offered a draw for the game and was abundantly gratified for a sumptuous potato and wheat soup, laden with carrots and chunks of sausage. For dessert, the mother served a delightful plum pudding, coated with sugar. During the repast, the entire family chattered like magpies at a bird convention. Cratchit hardly noticed how cramped his legs were, sitting at the low table and low chairs. Ginny sat at the end of the table in a larger chair but bent over to eat. She frequently smiled at Cratchit, and she lent her lilting voice often in the conversation.

After the dining was done, and the plates were cleared, and the women went about their washing and scrubbing and giggling in the washhouse, Bobbie Wheeler senior placed a Welch wig on his head, banked up the fire, and lit a long pipe for himself. His bearded cousins took pipes as well.

Cratchit turned around his comfortable chair, inhaled the sweet plum and molasses-flavoured tobacco scent, and joined in lively joke-telling. Though some of the cousins' jokes bordered on the ribald, he found himself laughing more than he had in a long while. When the womenfolk came inside from their chores, all rosy-cheeked and smiling, old Bobbie rubbed his hands together, adjusted his sleeves, and laughed all over himself from his shoes to his bearded laugh chamber. "Yo ho! Come now, family, no more work tonight. 'Tis the season for celebrating, for the Lord is born soon."

Barnabas and Angus stood like soldiers at attention.

"Hilli-ho, Barnabas!" old Bobbie cried while skipping around the floor. "Clear away, me lads, and let's have plentiful room. Chirrup, Angus and Barnabas!"

The two cousins made mock, and even hilarious salutes, and set about pushing chairs, tables, and whatnots against the walls and into corners. Soon, a small dance area emerged, surrounded by chairs.

Each family member, save the mother, drew out an instrument from various cupboards and eaves, and they began playing the liveliest tunes. Bobbie strummed a lute-like instrument, Barnabas stroked a fiddle, Angus clacked two spoons, Corny bent a concertina, and the younger Bobbie tapped a drum. The two Miss Wheelers, Effery and Ginny, blew on recorders. When they were not tootling their instruments, the daughters and Mrs. Wheeler sang with able voice, with Ginny's being the most engaging. They sang, "Good Christian Men, Rejoice," "Hark,

The Herald Angels Sing," "Deck the Halls," "We Wish You a Merry Christmas," and more songs.

Cratchit thought it charming that the family did not wait until the Yuletide arrived to celebrate.

Then, the mother, all smiles, brought in a great, hammered silver bowl, brimming with a brew with a pungent, spicy effluvium, and oranges slices floating atop. She set it on a small table and fetched pewter goblets. While the mother shook her finger at each child who drew close to the beverage, each man, including Cratchit, plunged a goblet into the bowl, gaining inordinate quantities of the brew. Cratchit found himself imbibing again and again until the room seemed to him a tad blurry.

When the dancing began, the entirety of the family began gambolling, prancing, cutting, bouncing, and promenading, either with partners or without, until all were panting and fanning their faces.

Then cousin Barnabas stuck up a slow waltz. Ginny appeared before the seated Cratchit and curtsied. "A dance, please, kind sir."

At first, Cratchit waved off the offer, but when he saw Ginny indicating the only other much shorter dance partners in the room, he relented. Though his mind was muddled by the excellent beverage, he figured, "One dance with a fair maiden would do no harm."

By the end of the festive evening, he found he had danced more than one dance with Ginny, one with Mrs. Wheeler, and one sort of circumnavigation around the room with all the children clasping hands. When at last he sank back into the comfortable chair, he fell quickly asleep. In his drowsing, he felt a caress, supple and tender as a baby's hand, brushing softly across his lips, and he smelled the breath of the sweetest sort.

Cratchit dreamed of his wife that evening, her sweet face, her lovely eyes, her fiery temper, born of her Irish heritage. He admired her so, for she ran the household like a profitable business, with heart and rigour. She had often offered him sage advice on the new company he and Scrooge had forged, and he regularly mused about how accomplished she would be at the head of an industry. The sweet lips that brushed his had set a fire in his dreams, and he yearned for his dear wife.

When he awoke, the sun was shining bright through the window, the snow melting and pouring off the roof in sheets. He did not have to ask that the weather had warmed, for it had done so considerably. He wondered if the family's celebrating had stirred up so much heat that it had warmed the weather on this shortest day of the year. His mind turned to what to do now that there was no constable to be had. His brow creased.

STAVE TWENTY-TWO
A BURIAL AND TWO UNEXPECTED VISITORS

Back at the Tamperwind mansion, Scrooge and the others had raced outside in the blowing storm to the dead bodies lying in the yard, dishevelled in their death throes, the skin turning black from the cold.

"What's this?" Edmund remarked. He bent over and pulled a scribbled note from the waistcoat of Smyth's corpse. "It reads: 'These bodies must be buried before the end of the winter solstice, or the dark eye will be upon us all.'"

"The dark eye? What does that mean?" Lockie asked.

"I have no idea," Scrooge said.

"I do." Mrs. Owsley toddled up to the group. "There's a belief here among the miners that a dark eye causes all the calamitous events that ever occur. There be a load of stories about it, some of it mere poppycock, but I am inclined to believe it myself, especially of late with the death of my poor husband."

Scrooge noted that that was the first time the woman had mentioned the loss of her husband in any manner. She wiped her eyes with her apron, snuffled her nose, and hung her head. She bent down and lightly stroked the coat of the body whose face was mangled. She straightened and sighed.

"But why bring the bodies here and lay them in plain sight?" Edmund seemed confounded.

"Because." Mrs. Owsley stomped her foot. "Up here on this hill is the only soil deep enough to bury a body. Down the hill and all around, and all the way out to the ocean, two inches past the topsoil is nothing but rock. That's why the cemetery is at the side of the house." She pointed.

Scrooge and the others looked. Scrooge had not noticed the vine-covered gravestones lined up under some trees to the far right of the mansion. He wondered why he had not detected it. Perhaps if he searched the mansion grounds, there would be clues he had not considered. Striding a short distance towards the graveyard and rounding the corner of the house, he saw the stable and carriage house beyond. The two shaggy Shetlands and a grey plough-horse trotted about an enclosure. Past the stable stood the simple groundskeeper's cabin.

"I say we bury them now!" Mrs. Owsley exclaimed. "Put all this death behind us."

Scrooge wanted to ask, "But why now, after the bodies have been stowed in Hopworth, then stolen away?" He did not ask the question but remained puzzled. *If the constable returns with Bob Cratchit and wishes to exhume the bodies, that will be his call.*

Edmund went straightaway to gain coffins from the carpenters at the mine. He did not have to ask for any to be built, for several coffins had already been prepared because death regularly hung its dark cloak around the mine. Edmund imagined the grim reaper regularly leaned his scythe against a mine tunnel wall and waited for any opportunity.

When the coffins were loaded on the cart at the carpenter shed, Edmund was approached by the same large man with the dark eyes and bushy eyebrows who had accosted Lockie the night before.

"See here," the brute exclaimed, positioning himself squarely in front of Edmund. "Your comin' 'ere ain't give any 'o us any rest. We'd rather fix things ourselves and run the mine our own way without a fancy city dweller tellin' us wha' to do." The man's broad chest heaved, and the dust flew from it in a cloud, and he stuck his scowling face within an inch of Edmund's. "Got it?"

Edmund tipped his hat and then swept past the man, "I'll take your concerns into consideration." He hurried to the two men who were pulling the cart of coffins and bade them pull the load up the hill in haste. He glanced back to see Caveman holding a bludgeoning stick in one hand and pounding it into the opposite palm. He was surrounded by a throng of mine workers, all scowling at Edmund while he retreated up to the graveyard.

Scrooge had sent Lockie to obtain the services of the parson of the church. The priest came, prayer book in hand, and after a short ceremony in the blowing storm, the two men's coffins were lowered into shallow graves.

When the rite concluded, and the mineworkers were tasked with tossing soil on the grave, Scrooge could stand the cold and sadness and disappointment no longer, and so trudged ahead of the others into the house and slowly up the stairs. His companions and Mrs. Owsley and the priest came in behind him and without Scrooge in attendance, sat and commiserated in the parlour and discussed proper headstones for the deceased.

In his room, Scrooge flinched at the snowstorm's wind howling like a wild animal. He sat at the small writing desk and tried to put his thoughts on paper. After thumbing through the notes from the gardener regarding Samuel's near demise, and his own notes he had jotted down during their sojourn there, he gazed out the window where Dimwittle and the two men from the mines finished piling soil onto the graves. "I am at a loss. I hope Bob Cratchit will find a capable constable to bring some order to all this." The next day was the winter solstice. He longed for summer. The storm howling outside, and weariness overtaking him, he laid down on his bed.

Suddenly he was being shaken. It seemed the whole room was trembling. He tumbled from the bed and found himself looking at enormous bare feet below a fur-lined, green robe.

"What ho!" came a booming voice, "Why, if it isn't Ebenezer Scrooge!"

Scrooge worked his way to standing and peered up at a giant, his jovial face wrung round with a deep, dark beard. He was holding a torch, the flame touching the ceiling of the room, but not igniting it. A holly wreath crusted with a tiny bit of ice sat tilted in a jaunty fashion on his brow. He looked similar in appearance to the Ghost of Christmas Present who visited Scrooge two years ago, but he was altogether different. He was leaner, his cheeks rosier, his nostrils more flared.

When the ghost saw Scrooge's expression, he belly-laughed, and his entire frame shook.

"How good to see you, Ebenezer Scrooge. How good indeed!"

Scrooge put a finger to his lips to shush the inordinately loud giant ghost.

"Pooh! I say," the ghost said. "Or what did you used to say? Humbug? Yes, humbug to your shushing. Not a soul can hear me, save you. Come closer, man, and know me better."

Scrooge approached and peered up at the remarkable entity. The ghost seemed to fill the room.

"You've not seen anyone like me before, have you?" the ghost announced.

"Well, I did meet one of your brothers two years ago on Christmas Eve." Scrooge's voice fairly squeaked, for he was not sure if the rest of the household could hear the goings-on.

"That you did, Ebenezer. A fine brother, 1843. Fine indeed. And although you don't know it, you almost caught sight of my brother of last year—1844. You were celebrating Christmas at your cheery nephew's home, and you almost had a glimpse of true Christmas joy then."

"I think perhaps I did feel a presence." Scrooge chuckled at the fond remembrance. "We were playing a game of blind man's bluff." Then, his demeanour sank. "However, now I am at a loss, and feign I would continue in this endeavour, for my coming here has almost had me killed, and the good man, Samuel, was almost killed as well. And Bob Cratchit, had it not been for Lockie's fortuitous discovery of the hidden cave door, he might have died as well."

Scrooge almost detected a frown from the great ghost. "Now, see here, Scrooge. Shortly after our Lord Jesus was born, did not Joseph have to hide the family away in Egypt, else the child be killed by Herod's soldiers? Life is not always easy. That's the point. Yet we celebrate those good particulars of life anyway. Mankind finds a way to overcome." The Christmas spirit trounced around the room, making the whole room shake. He seemed so heavy, yet he moved with the elegant grace of royalty. "I cannot stay, Ebenezer, this is not truly my time. I was allowed to come a few days early to give you a hint."

"And what might that hint be?"

No sooner had the words left Scrooge's mouth than a loud rapping sounded at his bedroom door. He blinked his eyes and found himself lying in his bed, a blanket over his feet. The ghost was nowhere to be seen. Scrooge rubbed his eyes. Indeed, the ghost had vanished, not unlike the similar one of two years previous.

He rose and stumbled to the door. Lockie was standing there. "Beggin' your pardon, Master Scrooge, but did you feel the house shakin' just now?"

Scrooge caught himself before he said a word about the ghost. "No. I guess I slept through it." He looked back into his room as if expecting the huge ghost to jump out and say, "Boo!"

"Well, the rest of us felt it. 'Twas an earthquake like the ones I've read about in Arabia. The floor was shakin', the walls too."

Scrooge nodded. "They've had them here in England occasionally too. Most often in Scotland."

"The other reason I sought to break you from your sleep is that there's a … lady, I would say." He dropped his voice to a whisper, putting a palm near his lips. "A lady of the evenin'. The one from the other night in Hopworth. On the front steps. Insists she needs to talk to one of the engineer gents, and since Master Cratchit is off to Lazy Eye and Master Nuckols is down at the mine, and Master Samuel and Mistress Abigail are kneelin' in church givin' thanks that he ain't dead, you're the only one here that's able to speak to her."

"Did she say what she wants?"

"No, sir. But she's at the door. The poor gardener, Dimwittle, tried to take her by the arm and lead her away, and she belted him in the face so hard, she bloodied 'im. She's skinny, but strong."

Scrooge hastened downstairs and to the door. He first peered out the door's frosted window and beheld a scantily clad woman in her thirties, just a shawl about her shoulders. Mrs. Owsley arrived at the same moment. "You are not letting that creature into this house, are you?"

"We shall see." Scrooge cautiously opened the door, expecting a rush of frigid air, but instead, the weather had warmed under a clear sky and bright sun. Icicles were melting off the porch roof. Rivulets of melted snow slid through the snowdrifts down the hill.

Standing on the porch, the woman of the evening shivered in her shawl. Behind her, Dimwittle held a bloody handkerchief to his nose and a forlorn look on his face.

"I must speak to you," the woman announced. "I have information on the murders."

Scrooge hesitantly pointed for her to enter, which she did.

"That is indeed good news." Mrs. Owsley, who had previously sought to forbid the woman's entrance, now took her by the arm and led her to a comfortable chair by the fire. "Poor dear, you must be freezing. Let me get you some tea. But don't say a word until I return. I want to hear the news." She bustled to the kitchen. She met Michael there, peering out of the doorway. She pushed him back into the kitchen. "You'll not be lookin' at a woman of that sort, Michael. No, you won't. You're too young."

Scrooge turned to Lockie. "Go fetch Samuel and Abigail."

The office boy raced out and down the hill to the church.

The woman sat, rubbing her shoulders. Her skin was more blue than white. Her pupils were dilated wide.

"Do you have a name, miss?" Scrooge asked.

"I don't likely know if I should tell you, but I guess it will do no harm. The men all call me 'Beebe.' Will that suffice for your lordship?"

"Far be it for me to denigrate a name, and I am no lord. Pray tell, do you not have a heavier bolster against the cold? That shawl is hardly equal to this wretched weather."

"I did, but I gave it to a man what had nothin' but a thin shirt."

"You gave a man your coat?" Scrooge was incredulous.

"Well, ain't that wha' we supposed to do? Take care o' our brothers and sisters of this world, be they Christian or not?"

"I agree, but not to the detriment of our own welfare."

"Well, I don't know what that word means, but I'm doin' all right." She smiled, a molar on one side missing.

"I see." Scrooge sat in a ladderback chair across from her. The warmth of the room seemed to be doing her good. Scrooge noticed her complexion was somewhat scarred from smallpox. Her colour was returning, and her cheeks were turning rosier. He smelled a rosewater perfume emanating from her hair.

"I am sure," he continued, "that when Mister Cratchit returns with a constable, the officer will be pleased to hear what you have to share."

"I ain't sharin' it for free. I got ends to meet. Values. Food. Coal for me stove."

"I see." Scrooge crossed his arms. "What is this information that you have that I might determine its worth?"

"I'll tell ya for 'alf a crown." Beebe crossed her arms.

"First of all, tell me why you need the money. Are you in such dire straits that you need to get paid for information that might bring justice?"

"Well, I don't know what them dire and straits are, but I 'elp the men what's got no wife to comfort 'em and make 'em feel at home. They's lots of 'em up 'ere. Come up 'ere to get work in the mines. Young men, ain't got no fortune but needs a job. So, they come 'ere to Tamperwind and Hopworth. This last week, folks is 'fraid to take a stroll at night. They gots the willies. So, me business is down."

"I see." Scrooge was altogether ready to send the woman away when Mrs. Owsley arrived with a teapot and cups and a bowl of soup on a tray. "Here you are, deary. Have you some word about the dastard, Grumbles? How to find him? More evidence?" She poured Beebe a cup of tea.

Beebe took the sugar bowl from the tray and ladled four heaping teaspoons of sugar into her tea. She slurped on it.

"Mrs. Owsley," Scrooge said, "have you an extra coat, one no longer used, that we might give this woman?"

"I believe we do. Belonged to a small miner what was crushed in the mine when a wall caved in." She nodded and put a finger to her chin.

"Would you fetch it, please?"

Walking away, she said over her shoulder, "Eat that broth, too, deary. I don't want any more deaths in Tamperwind or Hopworth, especially not to starvation."

Scrooge remembered he had still not located his lost keys to his office, and he considered that the money he carried with him might be all the funds he owned if someone found and used his lost key to ransack his stores of money. Sighing, he fumbled out his coin purse, untied the ribbons, released the latch, and fingered the inside. "Very well, Miss Beebe. I have a half a crown here that I am loathe to part with, so let's hear your information."

"Gi' me the coin first."

Scrooge, in as slow a fashion as he could, relinquished the coin into her dirty hand.

She bit it and looked at it. "All right. Here's what you need to know or to tell the constable. They's men what works in the mines that know things. They know a lot, but no one's asked 'em yet."

"What are their names?"

"John."

"John who?"

She shrugged her shoulders.

Exasperated, Scrooge asked, "What's another name?"

"John. They're all John to me."

"Can you point them out to us? If not, I'll have my money back."

"That I can." She slurped down the rest of her tea, then began shovelling the rich potato soup into her mouth, portions of it dribbling from her chin. "Mm, mm. Tastes nutty too."

"Where can we find you when the constable arrives?"

"Just ask anyone in Hopworth. Someone will know where I am. And just so ya know. I want the murderers imprisoned too. It ain't safe for a lady."

Mrs. Owsley returned, bearing a worn but heavy miner's coat. "Here's a comforter for you, my dear. Wear it in good health."

Beebe put the coat on, though it was overlarge and fairly swallowed her. "I'll be goin' now. Ain't one for socializin'." She rose and headed for the door.

Scrooge interceded and took hold of her wrist, then wrested the coin from her hand. "When you point out the men, you'll get the money. Not until then."

Beebe raised her arm to throw a blow at Scrooge, but Lockie burst through the door like a whirlwind. Before she could send her blow, he pinched her neck, causing her to fold to the floor. "Naw, ya won't be assaultin' my master." Lockie's voice was fierce.

Samuel and Abigail followed after Lockie. Beebe, seeing she was so outnumbered, rose sheepishly. "Find me in Hopworth. I know all the men. I'll show ya the ones what knows things." She exited like she was being blown away by a gale wind.

"Thank you, Lockie," Scrooge said, placing the half-crown once again in his coin purse.

"You're welcome, sir." He swept off his cap and made a little bow.

Mrs. Owsley closed the door after Beebe. "Were it not for the good Mr. Owsley, that would have been my fate." A tear formed on her eyelid. Wiping the tear, she waddled to the kitchen.

STAVE TWENTY-THREE
CRATCHIT RETURNS, MORE BAD NEWS, A PLAN

The sun was leaning on the horizon when Bob Cratchit rode back into the Tamperwind yard on his stout, black horse. Dimwittle met him at the gate, and after Cratchit dismounted, the humble gardener took the horse to the stable. Cratchit trudged slowly up the porch steps and into the house. Scrooge, Edmund, Lucy, Abigail, Mrs. Owsley, and Lockie met him at the door.

"'Tis no use," Cratchit said. "There's no constable in Lazy Eye, nor in St. Blazy, nor any other town in the entire two counties. Seems the locals are entirely happy to handle their own justice. I was saved from dying in that wretched storm by a family, and they told me some horrid stories of how justice gets meted out in the various villages. Boiling a poor soul in a big cauldron, smashing the toes of another, tying a man to a tree for the birds to peck at him. I'm glad I live in London." He took off his scarf, hat, and comforter and sat wearily in a chair near the fireplace.

Each man and woman gathered around the disconsolate man, save Mrs. Owsley who had gone to the kitchen and began humming and banging pots, preparing the evening meal. Lucy knelt beside his chair, rubbed his arm, and smiled broadly. "Take heart, brave Bob Cratchit. Mr. Scrooge has what you will surely think is some favourable news."

Cratchit looked up. "Pray tell, Ebenezer. What news?"

"Samuel is alive!"

"What?" Cratchit leapt to his feet, surprise all over his face.

"Or perhaps he was never dead, just a frozen heart. He's upstairs resting now."

"That is wonderful news! I am a better man for that news." He sat back down.

Just then, Samuel ambled down the stairs, dressed in a robe, and looking very much alive. Cratchit jumped up once more, rushed to Samuel, and clasped the man in a bear hug. "So glad to see you, old man," Cratchit said.

"And I, you," Samuel responded.

They both smiled, giving each other hearty claps on the back.

"But I am famished, my appetite has returned," Samuel said, rubbing his stomach.

Abigail took her brother's arm and escorted him from the group to the kitchen. "Let's see if Mrs. Owsley has a morsel for you before the meal," she said.

Lucy followed her cousins into the kitchen.

"And there is more good news." Scrooge waited until the three cousins were out of earshot, shoved his thumbs under his lapel, and then spoke to Cratchit, Edmund, and Lockie in a tight circle.

Cratchit turned with surprise again on his face. "More news. Do not make me wait."

"It seems we have ..." Scrooge paused to select his words, "... A woman who says she knows particular miners who know what has been going on. Valuable information that may expose the villain. We were waiting for your return with a constable. But that not being the case, I guess we shall proceed on our own."

"What about Mr. Tamperwind growing suspicious in that we're not attending to the workings of the mine?" Cratchit said. "I fear he may already be."

"We cannot worry about that now," Edmund enjoined. "This has gone on too long as it is. And we pretend mining engineers shall venture together, gather the woman, and go to the mine. When I saw how far the mine was behind on its quota, I set up a night shift to keep the ore coming out of the ground. The woman Mr. Scrooge alluded to, Beebe by name, can see a great number of the miners this evening and point out the ones who have information."

Cratchit motioned for his companions to come closer. "Oh, I have one more piece of news. Bad news." He extracted a newspaper from his hip pocket and opened it. "This news story is in the London paper of yesterday. Somehow, it made it out by coach to St. Blazy even in the storm. The story tells that our gallant Mr. Grumbles has been detained in Normandy."

"He's been found!" Scrooge held his hand to his brow. "So soon?" His thoughts flew to the probability that he would lose the loan he had given Grumbles, never to be repaid.

"Yes, apparently this story made its way to the front page and has all of London in a dither. Our policemen, the well-trained Peelers, are crossing the channel to extradite him back for trial."

"That means," said Edmund, "that another man is perpetrating these foul deeds and almost killed Samuel. Perhaps our Mr. Grumbles is truly innocent of the first murder."

The whole group's words then flew furiously, so no one could understand the others.

"What's going on?" Mrs. Owsley called from the kitchen.

"Nothing, Mrs. Owsley!" Edmund called in response. The men quieted.

Cratchit lowered his voice. "The story goes on further to state the police's belief that he had an accomplice. I fully expect a reporter or two to be here tomorrow on the evening coach."

"Then we had better hurry to speak to this woman," Edmund said. "Else there will be so much hubbub around here that no one will tell us a word. Time is of the essence."

"Lockie," said Scrooge, "go out to Mr. Dimwittle's cabin and tell him we need as many lanterns as he can bring. And here, take this pad and pencil in case you need to write it out for him."

"Yes, Master Scrooge." Lockie took the pad and pencil and raced outside to the gardener's abode.

Michael traipsed in from the kitchen, a slate and chalk in his hand. "Look, I've just solved the most amazing math puzzle. He held up the slate, laden with numbers and formulaic signs.

Mrs. Owsley pattered along after him. Seeing the three men donning their outerwear, she remarked, "Where you be a-goin' with the sun going down? 'Tis cold and dangerous."

"We're going to the mine, Mrs. Owsley," Edmund said, shoving a woolen cap onto his head. "I've put on an evening work-shift at the mine. The man named Caveman is in charge, but the three of us should see that the shift is working efficiently. We must get more ore out of the mine. We will return for a late supper. Feed everyone else and yourself, and keep it warm for us. Please let Mr. Tamperwind know we are endeavoring to bring him more profit."

"All right, gentlemen. Be safe. Be wary. Mr. Grumbles may still be about."

The three men nodded, but none would dare tell her what they knew from the news article. Before exiting the front door, each one stopped and kindly took on an amazed look at little Michael's slate.

"Good work," Edmund said.

Cratchit tousled the boy's hair.

The young fellow smiled and said, "Do be careful down at Hopworth."

Lucy and Abigail came from the kitchen. They took a knee beside Michael, admired his math scribbles, and complimented him on his astuteness. Samuel, munching on a muffin, strolled in from the kitchen to the sofa, sat, took a large pistol from under his robe, and cocked it, laying it within easy reach on a side table. "I'll keep an eye on things here while you're at work."

Once the gardener had returned to his abode, Scrooge said, "Lockie, you stay here and help protect the women. Samuel has a pistol and knows how to use it."

"Are you not taking any guns with you, Master Scrooge?"

"No, we don't want to draw attention to the fact there might be danger. We will mostly be at the mine entrance and in the village of Hopworth."

"Be careful. The criminal is fast and strong."

"We will be the soul of caution," Cratchit said.

Lockie returned inside and joined Samuel who had taken a position looking out a front window. Cratchit, Edmund, and Scrooge headed down the hill, passed the mine, its entrance and yard lit by lanterns hung on staffs, and then out into the dark night towards Hopworth, their lanterns glaring in broad strokes across the melting snow and mud.

Samuel and Lockie watched the lantern lights grow smaller and dimmer. Abigail and Lucy came up beside them. Abigail announced, "I'm not sure we so much need your protection, Samuel. I believe I am quite capable of caring for myself. I was not the one almost killed." She turned and was up the stairs like an ocean squall.

"Well, Miss Lucy, do you think you might need my caring assistance?" Lockie asked.

"I most assuredly would like your company, Lockie. Let's go see if Mrs. Owsley requires help in the kitchen."

When Lucy and Lockie went to the kitchen, Samuel stepped out onto the dark porch and was met there by the gardener, snow all about his boots and clothes. He and Dimwittle turned to look out into the craggy hills where a starlit sky dwelt. Samuel listened to the clanging of the pumps in the mine. He turned to Dimwittle. "Even the noise of industry at night out here in the country."

The man turned to Samuel with a look of wonder on his face, batted at his ears, and shrugged his shoulders.

Samuel thought the gardener an unfortunate being, indeed, totally reliant on the beneficent Mr. Tamperwind who lay gravely ill upstairs. What would happen to the man when his benefactor passed on? What would happen to the ward, Michael? He knew Edmund Nuckols knew enough about the economic plight of the mine to order a night shift to begin. If Samuel's uncle had left plans that, upon his death, dictated that Samuel take over the running of the mine, he was not sure he would be up to the task.

In his mind, he could think only of a huge, black-cloaked, faceless form taking him down to the ground and strangling him. He worried further that though Scrooge, Cratchit, and Edmund Nuckols numbered three, they did not know the strength of the one man who had almost killed him.

STAVE TWENTY-FOUR

BEEBE, MISSUS GRAVE,
A PLAN FOR LUCY AND ABIGAIL

Walking towards Hopworth, Scrooge was trembling. He considered himself a gentleman, and as an English gentleman, he was required to be brave, if need be. Keeping a stiff upper lip was part of the heritage. However, he had never seen himself as a man of adventure, one who throws caution to the wind and embarks on one astounding exploit after another. He had, for so many years, grown cautious and more vigilant in protecting so many aspects of his life, especially his money. The half-crown in his pocket purse was growing hot, in that he felt he did not want to handle it, lest it burn his fingers. He was all for turning back, not for fear of the night or the appearance of the villain bent on killing them all, but for the necessity to avoid parting with his hard-earned coin of the realm. He was troubled, too, that Grumbles had been captured; thus his loan would most likely never be repaid.

He trembled with each step. Perhaps this murderer is a collaborator with Grumbles.

After the three had gone a portion of the distance, Edmund turned back to the mine, telling Scrooge and Cratchit to go on without him. "It will take a while to gather all the workers from their duties in the mine. Once you gain the woman, hurry to the mine where I hope to have them all gathered, so she might see them all at once."

Cratchit and Scrooge made their way to Hopworth, and once again got lost on the path, losing valuable time. Upon arriving in Hopworth, they found the lamplighter heading for his home; a heavy handbell hung on his belt and clanging while he walked. He told them that Beebe lived with her mother in the very last house of the village, which stood a healthy distance from the last house before it. The two Londonites walked timorously into the patchy darkness where only occasional streaks of light from the town slipped through the trees and rocks that guarded the path.

At last, they saw the humble dwelling, a candle in the window, and a lantern on the porch.

When they came up, an older woman with grey sprigs of hair spilling out from under a bonnet of sorts greeted them. She wore a dress and blouse with multiple mends and a tattered shawl. She had a sheep-like face and her voice fairly bleated like a forlorn lamb. "You must be the gents that want to speak to my darling daughter, Beverly."

"That we are," said Bob.

"Well, I've a story to tell you before ya goes inside. You see, my little, darlin' daughter works to keep food in our pantry and such. Ain't much I can ever do to hepp our finances 'cept take in laundry. So ..."

"Go on, Missus ..." Cratchit admonished.

"Oh, we ain't got a last name, not in our business. Harder for the law to accuse us, ya know. Just call me Missus Grave. That'll do."

"Very well, Missus Grave."

"Well, in my story, Beverly comes home in a tither, feelin' puny after visitin' with you gents up on the hill. I asks her what's wrong and she won't say, but goes and lies down." The mother twisted her skirt around and patted down the front of it. "Then later I'm in the back room, my hands in folks' laundry in my tub when a gentleman caller arrives. Beverly gets up and goes to the door. I can't leave my work, so I lean around the door frame, and I can't see the man, 'cause where Beverly's standin'. Him what wants some time spent with her, 'cept I can see he looks like a small man, for I can only see his legs. And he has a small voice. You can tell if a man's big or small without seein' the whole man, you know."

"Yes," Scrooge said. "Do you have a point?"

"Here's the rest o' my story. She goes outside with the man, and I don't know where she goes, and she stays only a short while. After she comes back, she don't say nothin' but goes straight to her room. After a time, I hear her wailin' to beat the band. I goes to see her, and she's awful ill, holdin' her stomach, and green as a cucumber."

Scrooge looked at Cratchit.

"May we see her?" Cratchit said.

"Why, o' course ya can, but I doubt she'll be much service to ya. Sick as she is."

Beebe's mother showed the men into the dishevelled hovel and to a back bedroom where the prostitute lay, drool dripping from her lips, vomit on the floor. The stench was overwhelming.

Scrooge and Cratchit approached the bed, hat in one hand, the other hand at their nose.

"Miss Beebe, or Beverly, as you see fit to be called," Cratchit said in a soft tone, "are you able to come with us to the mine to point out any worker that you know who could help us solve the murders?"

The woman only choked distorted breaths, her lungs heaving.

Cratchit tried again. "I say, Miss Beebe …"

The woman sat up forcefully and grabbed Cratchit's arm. "They're tryin' to kill me," she blurted. "They are. They're not just after the men, but the women too. Be it the dark eye, or some demon. The short one. He's poisoned me, for sure. They're after the women too. The big one and the short one." She fell back on her bed, out cold.

"Two men!" Scrooge exclaimed, then held a hand over his lips. The business partners stared a long while at each other. Stares of worry. They finally trudged from the room. Beebe was curled in a foetal position.

Knowing there was little else they could do, Scrooge and Cratchit went out on the porch. Missus Grave followed them. "I'm deeply worried over my little Beverly. I've no medicine."

"Perhaps on the morrow," Cratchit said, "we can send Mrs. Owsley here. She seems to know a little of the healing arts."

"That would be very nice. Thank you kindly, gents. Oh, but don't tell Mr. Tamperwind. He would be much aggrieved."

The two Londonites gathered their lanterns and headed back through Hopworth. Scrooge finally spoke after they had passed beyond the town. "This is too big for us, Bob."

"I'm inclined to agree, Ebenezer. My main concern now is for the women, not only those living in Hopworth and at the Tamperwind Mine town, but Miss Abigail and Miss Lucy."

"I concur. We must get those two young women away from here."

After they had informed Edmund of the situation, the three men climbed up to the house. Mrs. Owsley set out a big pot of beef and potatoes stew, then went up to bed, pushing little Michael before her. "'Tis way too late for a young scamp like you."

"But I want to play with Lockie."

"Never you mind," she said and pinched his ear.

During the supper, the three men shared their latest revelation about Beebe and her mother with Lockie, Lucy, Samuel, and Abigail, and their desire to escort the female cousins to a safer locale in the morning, to an inn in either Lazy Eye or St. Blazy.

Before they adjourned their discussion, Scrooge rapped the table with his knuckles. "I believe this is all too much for me. Death at every corner, no progress made at all. I think I may join the ladies in a safer locale. I am filled with dread. My spirit is altered."

All of them looked at Scrooge aghast, the most perplexed being Edmund and Cratchit.

"We'll speak of it in the morning, Uncle." Edmund let the secret slip.

"Uncle?" Abigail exclaimed. "Is this man your relative?"

The three Londonites lowered their eyes. Finally, Bob Cratchit said, "Yes, Ebenezer Scrooge is Edmund's uncle. I am his business partner. Lockie is our office boy. None of us is here to serve as engineers or engineer interns. We are here to hopefully solve the murder of Mr. Owsley and even Mr. Smyth, for we wholeheartedly believe Hiram Hezikiah Grumbles did not commit it. He has gone to France, we know."

Now, Lucy, Samuel, and Abigail looked astounded. After a moment, a new sense of understanding shone in their eyes.

"You would actually put your own lives in danger for a friend?" Lucy stated, admiration shining in her eyes. "You are indeed sterling individuals. Perhaps we can help."

"Yes," Samuel said, "if you truly believe Grumbles did not commit the murder, is in France, and that another is responsible, then that explains the other man or men who are doing these villainous deeds. Count on us to help."

Abigail and Lucy nodded approval.

"Now the best help you can give us, Lucy and Abigail," Cratchit said, "is to hide yourselves away from this place, so we needn't worry."

Abigail was poised to object when Samuel clenched her hand. "Dear sister, you must look after our cousin. Who better than you?"

She dropped her eyes and gave a slight nod.

Scrooge stood abruptly. "That's all well and good for you, gentlemen. Tomorrow, I travel on the coach to Lazy Eye, either with these fine ladies or without. Pray, don't be hard on me. Don't be flowery either. Just know I am a man of business, not detective work." He turned and fled up the stairs to his room. There, he stoked up the fire in the fireplace, took off his shoes and socks, and sat on the edge of his bed in total dejection. "I am afraid," he whispered, "to go to sleep lest another ghost appears, and since the last ghost I saw was the Christmas Present, then I fear my future is short."

After a long while, he heard his friends wind their way to their bedrooms. He figured Cratchit, being the conscientious sort, would spend some time pouring over the mine's books, despite all he had been through. He did not hear Edmund's footsteps. He knew his nephew would be sitting guard in the downstairs parlour. He lay back on his pillow, too anxious to sleep.

STAVE TWENTY-FIVE

TWO GHOSTS

Scrooge heard the big clock downstairs peel one o'clock. Then he heard the unmistakable clanging and scraping of chains and lockboxes on the stairs. He sat up and swung his feet over the side of the bed. He felt the bitter chill of the hardwood floor. In a twinkling, his locked door sprang open and in sauntered Jacob Marley's ghost.

Scrooge's mouth dropped open, and his heart pounded. Had Jacob's ghost come to seize him and drag him to hell?

The ghost, no longer sauntering, floated across the room to Scrooge and bent down to touch his nose to Scrooge's nose. Scrooge suffered such an ice-like chill in his face, he felt faint. The ghost exhaled rancid, grave-fetid breath at Scrooge.

"Do I know you?" Jacob's ghost said.

Taken aback, Scrooge whispered, "Yes, I was your partner in life." He rubbed his near-frozen nose.

"Oh, yes." The ghost leaned back and float-walked behind a chair. His voice was like an unoiled door scraping on a hard floor. "The old Scrooge. I remember now. When last I saw your visage, you were a *new* Scrooge. One with hope, one with an initiative for good." He frowned horridly at Scrooge.

"How is it," Scrooge attempted to change the subject, "that you make so much noise with your chains and such, and no one else in the house hears it?"

"What noise?" the ghost said. "Oh, that noise. I can only tell you that one other in this house hears that noise and wonders about it, but that one can only speculate at its cause. That noise is not your concern, but your soul's welfare *is*."

"Yes, yes. I know I am acting afraid."

"Acting? Hardly! You *are* afraid, and well you should be. All mortals fear for their lives. What you need to do now is to be *brave*."

"Brave? Me? I've never been brave in my whole life. How can I—"

The ghost grabbed at his own throat with both hands as if being choked, in fact, his entire body, fainter than a shear cheesecloth, was being dragged from the room. Before he departed, still clutching his throat, the ghost gagged out, "Expect a ghost when the clock tolls …" Then he was gone.

Scrooge sat dejected on his bed and suddenly felt again the icy chill of the floor on his bare feet, so he pulled his feet up and slid them under the blankets. He vowed to stay awake until the next ghost appeared.

The clock chimed two, and Scrooge sat up quickly. He realised he had fallen asleep. He was fully aware a ghost was coming. Was it at this time? At another hour? He was prepared for almost anything but was not altogether ready for nothing. No shape appeared. Five minutes passed, then ten, yet no spirit came. Then, through the crack beneath his door, light flooded in, a warm, glowing light, followed by what he surmised to be a hundred bells, tiny to large, tinkling, clanging, and tolling.

"Make haste, Scrooge!" a booming voice called from below stairs. Scrooge hit the floor at the best run he could muster, unlocked the door, flung it open, and raced down the stairs, pausing on the last step. Lo and behold, standing in the front parlour, his green robe inches from the sleeping Edmund, stood the Ghost of Christmas Present, the same one he had seen earlier that had made such a commotion, but now, he was even larger. The parlour, the ceiling of which was twice as high as any normal room, barely held his stature.

He was seated on a great stack of gift boxes, some wrapped in colourful paper, some in brown paper, some open and shining with glittery treasures. A hobby horse rocked while he tapped it with his foot. Enormous stockings were brim-full of nuts and fruits and assorted candies, all of which were piled neatly about each other in a sort of pyramid. The giant leaned an elbow upon a side table, and Scrooge thought for sure that his great weight must definitely break it asunder, but it did not. Atop a vast dining table, lit by three tall candelabras, all manner of food was heaped—turkeys, geese, bread, sizeable joints of wild game, sausages wrung round a great stack of pies, plum puddings, chestnuts in a roaster, and bowls brim full of punch. The feast seemed to extend on forever, and the abundant smells made Scrooge's every tastebud tang, his mouth water, and every olfactory node yearn to smell and capture it all.

Scrooge ultimately crept down the last step, unsure that his footsteps would wake Edmund. "Might all this awaken my nephew?" Scrooge whispered.

"Not a chance," the ghost rumbled. "I sprinkled all the merry folks and the not-so-merry ones with a dusting of pleasant dreams. They won't waken now, but when they do in the morning, they will feel so refreshed." He placed his familiar torch in a long, empty stocking and stood erect.

"You are much bigger than before," Scrooge said.

"That is because this Christmas is growing bigger. The world is mostly at peace, and the good news of the Lord's coming is spreading far and wide. It is an amicable time, so I grow larger with it."

"I see. Might I sample one of the pies, perhaps a turkey leg?"

"Of course, you may. Help yourself. Partake of the abundance of Christmas joy."

Scrooge did not hesitate but tore off a turkey leg and began munching on it, then, forgoing a spoon or fork, dove his hand into a mincemeat pie. In short order, he was stuffing his gullet, and smiling ear to ear.

After a few moments, the giant said, "Scrooge. You've come a long way."

"I hope so. I'm trying to be a better man."

"Not that, Scrooge. I mean you have travelled to this locale a long distance for the welfare of another man whose innocence has been proclaimed to you. Do you know who I mean?"

"Why, yes. Mr. Grumbles."

"Precisely. You see me here before you—the pinnacle of earthly joy—the delight and promise of Christmas! Do you not?"

"Indeed, you are." Scrooge grabbed a goblet and dipped it in a red punch, then gulped the liquid down. He felt immediately giddy and began laughing, slapping his thigh, and spinning around like a top.

"Straighten up, Scrooge. My time here is very short. I should not be here at all, but in that so much depends on your progress here. In a few days, Christmas will come, and I will be gone, though a new brother will be born on the first day of the new year. Do you follow?"

"Yes, more brothers." He drank another draught and tilted a little, his eyes crossing.

"Listen carefully, Scrooge, for I know you have seen the poverty and want that my brother two years previously showed you, hidden in his mantle, the malice of *ignorance* and *want*. Your task here is great, in fact, enormous. You must not fail."

"Must not fail." Scrooge's eyes were glazing, his words mumbling. He stuck his finger in a plum pudding and licked the sweetness.

"Scrooge, here are the hints I had intended to tell you earlier."

"Yes, shints, I mean stints, rent. Rent is due." He wobbled to the sofa and sat.

"Listen carefully. The hints are these. Do you need a pencil and paper?"

Scrooge waggled his finger and then tapped his skull, indicating he could remember. He drained the cup.

"First," said the giant ghost, "is the cave. Second, the grave. Third, something you have saved. And, last, something only Lockie would know. The way the gardener behaved."

"Cave, grave, saved, behaved. Got it." Scrooge tilted his head back and was soon snoring.

In the pitch-dark early morning, Scrooge awakened barely from his inebriated snooze and seemed to see a broad figure wearing a long sock cap enter the front door and pass as if on rabbit's feet. Was the figure carrying something? He could not tell the size, for the creature seemed to bulge in and out. Was it one of the Ghost of Christmas Present's minions bringing gifts? He mumbled, "Edmund," and tried to snap tired fingers, but his nephew did not stir and was snoring, the pistol on his lap.

STAVE TWENTY-SIX
LUCY AND ABIGAIL DEPART, THE INHERITANCE

When Scrooge awoke again, Edmund was shaking him, and the bright sun speared through the frosted windows. Scrooge stirred, his head throbbing, the sunlight piercing his swollen eyes. He used his thumb and a finger to pry one eye open.

"Uncle," Edmund said. "Have you been drinking?"

"I don't think so." Scrooge raised his hand and saw the red-tinted goblet still in his hand, a dribble of liquid sloshing in the bottom. "Well, I guess I have." He set the cup down and put both hands to his aching head. He wondered why his hands were sticky, then remembered the food from the feast.

"Uncle, this is no time to be drinking. Or to be drunk."

"Oh, I'm not drunk now. I feel horrible."

"You had better hurry and pack. It appears you are already dressed, save your shoes and socks. The coach will arrive soon, and if you plan to be on it with Abigail and Lucy to—"

"I'm not going."

"What? You said last night that—"

"I know what I said. A man can change his mind, can't he?" He stood and took a few feeble steps. "I must see what remedies for a headache Mrs. Owsley has." He stumbled towards the kitchen.

"Bob is escorting the ladies to Lazy Eye or St. Blazy, whichever has accommodations," Edmund called. "The stagecoach awaits. He will rent a carriage once they are safe and return."

"Yes, yes. Thank you, Edmund. We have much to do here, with Bob or without. Where is Lockie?" Not waiting for a reply, he waded into the kitchen and found Mrs. Owsley and Michael eating a porridge. She got up before he could even say a word, drew down a bottle from the cupboard where several bottles of herbs, spices, and medicinals perched. She took the blue bottle, gathered a spoon, and poured Scrooge a spoonful of the sour concoction.

"That'll help your head. If there's anything I know, it's a man with a headache that's drunk too much."

Scrooge drained the spoon, then slumped down at the table.

"I'm sorry you don't feel well, Master Scrooge," Michael said. "Perhaps a brisk walk will do you good."

"Thank you, Michael, I will in a while. Much to do at … the mine. Do you happen to know where Lockie is?"

"No, sir, I don't. I should like to know also, so I can challenge him to either a game of chess or to a swordfight. Wooden swords, of course."

While Mrs. Owsley and Michael finished eating, Scrooge sat pondering the odd pronouncement of the Ghost of Christmas Present. What did it mean? He felt he had let down the ghost by falling asleep. "I didn't get him to explain," he said aloud.

"Get who to explain what?" Mrs. Owsley asked, surprised.

"Oh, nothing. I think I will take the air." He strode from the kitchen and met Lucy and Abigail coming down the stairs, each holding a bag. Lockie came behind them, carrying two more bags.

"Lockie, I need your assistance, but, as yet I don't know why."

Lockie gave him a look of confusion.

"Never mind for now. I've got an allocation of considerations on my mind." He turned towards the door, oblivious of the forlorn looks on the two maidens' faces. He mumbled, "Cave, grave, saved, behaved."

Samuel came in the back door. Edmund, Mrs. Owsley, and Michael joined them to say goodbye.

"We've taken our goodbyes from Uncle Erasmus," Abigail said. "We gave him a kiss on the cheek. He cried and wished us a safe passage." She turned to Edmund. "He wants to speak to you, Mr. Nuckols. He wishes to know the on-goings in the mine, whether the night shift is working out."

"I'll see to his concerns."

With Lockie carrying their extra bags, the two ladies joined Bob Cratchit and they walked to the coach. Lockie had the most forlorn look on his face as he bade the ladies farewell, and they boarded the coach. In a few minutes, the coach whisked them away. Lockie turned, head down, kicking the snow. The gardener stood waving his gentle goodbye, then turned, a sad expression on his face.

Scrooge joined Edmund to go talk to Mr. Tamperwind.

Upon entering the room, the old man looked wearier and paler than previously. A grisly beard covered his face; the rims of his eyes were red. He had a towel tied around his head from chin to scalp and smelled of liniment. "Come closer," he croaked. "I've little strength left, and I wish to leave the mine in good order before I pass."

Edmund and Scrooge walked to his bedside and listened to his whispered questions about the mine. While Edmund endeavoured to answer each question, Scrooge noted the blue veins of the man showing through his skin. He noticed his rough hands, and the nails torn down to the quick. His face looked raw, though, as if he had been long in the sun. The disease had surely taken its toll.

Scrooge could not keep up with the intricate questions and answers, and his mind raced to his encounter with the Ghost of Christmas Present. "Cave, grave, saved, behaved," he said aloud, then caught himself just as Tamperwind and Edmund turned in wonder at him.

"Nothing. Nothing," Scrooge said. He backed away, and the engineer and mine owner continued their discussion.

The old man took a fit of coughing. He spit into a kerchief. Edmund straightened and waited for him to finish. Finally, the old man took a laboured breath. "I want you to know when I die, the wealth is to go to my three heirs: Lucy, Abigail, and Samuel." He heaved another wheeze. "If they should not be able to receive the inheritance, then the mine and whatever I have put aside was to go to Mr. and Mrs. Owsley, though Mr. Owsley is now dead. I also have bequeathed a small amount to my ward, Michael."

"I see," Edmund said.

"There. Take a look at the will. It's on top of the papers on my desk. I may be asking you to be the executor of it." Scrooge walked to the desk and retrieved a faded page. "That's it," the old man said.

The two faux engineers read it, terse as it was, some smeared ink spots, smudges, and the like, but signed by two witnesses—a lawyer named Mr. Cragle, and the Hopworth shopkeeper, Wiltfang.

Edmund handed the will to the old man. "It's just as you say."

"So, please make the mine profitable for my heirs. Focus all your efforts on the mine. I will make it worth your while. And here ..." He reached in a lampstand drawer and pulled out a metal box. He took a key from around his neck and unlocked the box. He took out a thick handful of bills, then counted each one. "Take this money. This is the miners' pay and some back pay. Be sure ..." He hacked a cough. "That each man gets his wages." He closed the box and locked it, then slumped against his pillow.

"Thank you, Mr. Tamperwind. We shall dole the money to the miners."

Edmund said, "Mr. Scrooge, Mr. Cratchit, and I will do our best to improve the output of the mine."

When they turned to go, they almost ran into Lockie, standing with his cap in his hands near the door.

"Lockie," Scrooge said, "have you been here the whole time?"

"Just about, Master Scrooge. You told me you needed me."

"Yes, but let us return downstairs. My headache is getting better. Mrs. Owsley's remedy is working."

When the two men reached for the doorknob at the same time, Scrooge noticed Edmund's hands were covered with grime, black and grey, his fingers raw and hangnails were torn. "Edmund," he said while they trundled down the stairs with Lockie following. "Has your work in the mine done such a chore on your hands?"

"I'm afraid so, Uncle Ebenezer," he said looking at his hands, "The constant handling of the ore for examination, assisting the miners with a load, one thing and another, is wearing on the skin. Hazards of the job, I suppose."

"Edmund, I suppose we must go to the mine, and go we shall, but when Bob returns, Lockie, he, and I will return to the Hopworth Cave. I have a feeling we will find something there that may help solve this case."

At the mine, Edmund set about checking on the ore samples as an engineer might do and giving orders as a mine manager might give. One cart driver brought one of the mine ponies to Edmund, wanting to know what to do if the pony would not pull.

"Try riding him," Edmund said.

The cart driver shrugged and agreed.

Scrooge kept an eye on the pumps and the pump workers. He realised quickly which ones were capable workers and which ones were shirkers. Still, he felt completely out of his domain. When one of the pumps ceased working, he made a point of watching the men repair the pins and bolts, then nodded approval when the men got it functioning again.

Michael arrived and desired for Lockie to go on an adventure with him. Scrooge nodded for Lockie to go with him, and the two galloped through the mine town, down a long series of uneven steps, and then out onto the rocks that led down to a small beach of no more than thirty yards in length beside the crashing sea. Lockie saw the small wharf that Scrooge had noticed earlier.

They took off their shoes, built a small sandcastle, threw rocks and shells into the waves, and laughed a great deal.

At noon, a worker clanged a bell, and all the workers stopped for their meal. While Edmund was going around wishing the workers well, handing them their wages and back pay, and complimenting them where he could, the big miner called Caveman approached.

"So, what are yer plans," Caveman growled, "for loadin' the ship when it arrives 'ere tomorrow? We needs to know."

Edmund did not flinch, though the man was intimidating in stature and demeanour. "I shall have a plan tomorrow."

"A plan. What does that mean? Why ain't we doin' like we always done it?"

"That is essentially it, with some variations."

Caveman snarled and went on his way, chomping off big bites of dried meat he had impaled with a sharp stick. Michael and Lockie strolled up barefooted, holding their shoes and socks.

"I'm not sure about that big miner," Michael said to Edmund. "Do you know anything about him? He gives me the jitters."

"No, I don't," Edmund said. "Is there something I should know?"

"I've just seen him sneaking around outside the fence of the house like he's up to something."

"I'll keep an eye out." Edmund turned to Lockie. "You watch for him, too, Lockie."

"I will, sir."

"Well, I've got to be getting home." Michael began loosening the laces of his shoes. "I want to visit with my ailing foster father. I so wish he would get better." Michael dashed away, pausing only long enough to put on his socks and shoes before ascending to the big mansion.

"I wonder," said Lockie, "that they don't worry more about the boy. He's fun to play with, sure, but what has he been doin' before I arrived. He seems to take many chances. I'm not sure Mrs. Owsley knows how to watch him."

"Yes," Edmund replied. "I would hate for some accident to befall him."

Cratchit returned from St. Blazy as twilight was drawing near, and the night mine shift was starting work. He informed his friends that the two ladies had been secured with a kindly innkeeper. Scrooge told him of the plan to check out the old Hopworth mine. While Edmund organised the night shift workers, Scrooge, Cratchit, and Lockie took lanterns from the Tamperwind mine itself, rather than cause suspicion by having the gardener get them. Bob placed a hammer and chisel in a burlap sack.

On the way to the mine, with brilliant stars beginning to twinkle in the firmament, Scrooge asked, "Lockie, have you noticed anything unusual about how the gardener behaves?"

Lockie reflected a moment. "Not that I can think of. He seems awfully timid. Do you think he knows something?"

"He may, but with his being deaf and dumb, he doesn't know how to tell us. He may know something. We should try to talk to him on the morrow." He snapped his finger. "Oh, I forgot to have Mrs. Owsley to attend to the ailing Beebe woman. I hope she has fared well."

STAVE TWENTY-SEVEN
INTO THE DARK, DARK CAVERN

When the three Londonites arrived at the Hopworth Vittles store that covered the entrance to the abandoned mine, the plump shopkeeper, Harold Wiltfang, stepped outside and started to close up. "Not much you can buy this evenin', gents," he said. "Been a busy day what with the dole made today. Lots o' men got their backpay this day. Outta barley, outta fruit, sugar's gone, cinnamon's gone. Hay for the horses has all been loaded and taken to the mine. Even out of the axes I carry. Been a good day."

"May we visit the mine?" Scrooge asked. "We are interested in seeing more about it, and this may be our only chance to gather some ore samples with the new evening shifts beginning and the rush to get the ore loaded to take down to the wharf for the ships."

"Well, I doubt you'll find much in that pit. It's a dry hole, it be. I think I'll have to say no tonight. I'll be closed for several days until the next cargo comes up from Cornwall. Come back then. Go on now. I'll not have you ruinin' me night." He locked the door with a large padlock and stuck the key in his waistcoat. He stood rocking on his heels until Scrooge and his companions walked away.

They trod up the trail a short distance; then, almost in unison, the three darted behind a rock and peered out around it. They could see the store in the dimming light. "We're going in that cave," Scrooge announced.

"Indeed, we are," Cratchit said.

"Indeed," Lockie echoed.

In short order, they sneaked to the door. Cratchit bashed the lock off the hasp with the hammer, and the three entered. Lanterns lit low, they made their way through the store, down the stairs, and to the office area and the wall that held the hidden door. While Scrooge and Lockie searched the office and surrounding area, Cratchit sat at the top of the slide that ended in the cavern. "I'm going down. I know how to find my way out to the secret door." Before Scrooge could respond, holding his lantern high, Cratchit slid down the slide. "Yoodle hoo!" The call echoed several times.

When Scrooge peered over the edge, he saw Cratchit on his feet, the lantern spreading an ample glow about him. "Do be careful down there, Bob."

"Cautious as a lamplighter."

For an hour, Scrooge checked crevices of the office and the shelves hung on the walls, ran his hand along the slabs where the two corpses had laid. He found a button but did not know what to do with it. Lockie looked high and low outside the office to no avail. He opened the secret door and searched several yards down the tunnel.

"Ebenezer! Lockie!" Cratchit suddenly called from the deep hole in the ground. "I think I've found the cause for the killings. Come quick."

Lockie immediately jumped on the slide and barrelled down, holding his lantern up. "The queen's underwear!" he hollered all the way down.

Scrooge was terrified of the slide. Trembling like a leaf, he stepped gingerly onto it. Before he knew it, he was gliding down, screaming like a child, and he landed in a heap at the bottom of the slide atop the old mattresses. He stood, straightened his jacket, and then saw the rats on the mattress. He leapt back and clutched his heart. Gathering his wits and brushing the dust from his clothes, he said, "Humbug." He kicked at the rats, and they scampered away.

"Come here quickly." Cratchit stood in a narrow tunnel that extended out from the central cavern, angling down. His lantern light bounced off the walls, and the shadows ran like fantastical creatures along them. When Scrooge made his way to Cratchit's side, Lockie was already there, his mouth agape, his eyes wide in wonder. "Look!" Cratchit demanded, shining his lantern directly next to the wall.

Scrooge and Lockie had no trouble detecting in the lantern light fine filaments; two feet long, spidery veins in the red and black crystalline rock wall, crooked pencil lines of grey with some black and some astonishing metallic tone, but most evidentially like tarnished silver spoons turned on edge. The three explorers stood entranced.

"And here." Cratchit moved a few feet farther and showed a palm-size smudge sprinkled with red splotches, and of a metallic tone in the grey and black rock. The light brought forth the sparkles of elements of quartz crystals, like thousands of stars in the wall.

"What are we looking at?" Lockie asked.

"Before he died," Cratchit said, "my father was a miner in a silver mine. He often brought home samples he had slipped out in secret. I saw the ore so many times, I know this is silver, in raw form, but still silver. I would stake my life on it. My father often said if he could get a hold of a small amalgamation pan and enough bottled mercury and salt, then he would refine the silver from the rest of the rock and treat us to some real wealth. Of course, that never happened." He hung his head as if the memory of his father gave him ill feelings.

"This mine," he finally continued, "which contains considerable lead and quartz, as far as I can tell, must have played out for tin. When I was going over Tamperwind's books, I came across a document of sale and some other letters and notes. The former owners, the Hopworths, abandoned it and sold it to Mr. Tamperwind, who was more interested in the land adjacent, and in the tin found in early digs in what is now the Tamperwind mine. The Hopworth mine was mostly forgotten except for the children who played here, and the shop owner, Wiltfang, who uses the old cave manager's office for cold storage for his meat."

"And here too." Cratchit squatted down to let the lantern gleam on a chisel and hammer, several burlap sacks, each one laden with chunks of ore, and a small one-wheel barrow. "Here is why Owsley was killed.

Someone has discovered silver in this mine. Perhaps Owsley did too. Then there was a falling out. And—"

"Yes." Scrooge held his hand to his chin. "The killer had a motive, and Smyth must have been in on it too."

"And someone has been working at it a little at a time, perhaps not to draw attention to it," Lockie said, "as evidenced by the few tools. And look here!" He held the lantern beside the hammer. In the wood handle was etched the name "Smyth."

"So, our conjecture about Smyth was correct. But I had no idea you knew so much about metallurgy, Bob," Scrooge said. "Why have you kept that a secret?"

"When one's father dies in a mine cave-in, one prefers to forget what he knows about rocks."

"I am still amazed."

"Amazed you can be, but the silver is in raw form and must be amalgamated and purified. Otherwise, it is just a peculiar rock. The silver does not shine until polished."

"Meaning?" Scrooge proffered.

"Meaning, if these surreptitious silver miners are extracting the ore, where are they taking it to have it assayed and smelted?"

"I see. That is one more missing element in this growing mystery. Still. We have reason, a motive, we can say, for the murders. Cave." Scrooge made a checkmark in the air. "Now grave."

"What do ya mean, sir?" Lockie looked hard at his employer.

"More to learn in the morning, Lockie."

Before exiting the cavern with its multiple tunnels leading off it, the three searched for the stream that ran through the cavern. In short order, they found the quiet, black water, running along a back wall of the huge cavern. They followed it several hundred feet into a narrow crevice that shrunk in size every few feet. They had to turn sideways to walk through it, their shoes in the narrow, shallow stream. They ducked their heads. The roof of the crevice grew lower and lower until they came to where the stream widened and deepened into a pool, and then ducked under a cave wall. Bending down, they could hear the crash of waves, distant but still tellable. They made their way back to the exit tunnel and left out the secret doorway.

The three came out the door of the shop. Cratchit rehung the padlock on the hasp and turned it to appear locked. They then walked up to the Tamperwind mine where Edmund was speaking to a group of miners and helping them secure their candle stubs on their tunnel hats.

Scrooge invited his nephew away from the miners. After Scrooge and Cratchit had appraised Edmund, the four decided to keep their knowledge a secret from Mr. Tamperwind for the time being. The winter solstice wound quickly away. Before retiring, Scrooge told Lockie to be ready to do some digging in the early morning.

In his trundle bed in the wood room, Lockie could not sleep. When he deemed that everyone was asleep, he flung on his coat and boots and ventured out the rear entrance of the mansion. He crept to the gardener's hut and found that the light shone through one curtained window. He slipped closer and peeked through a bare opening between the curtains which allowed him a scant view of some of the interior.

A fire glowed in the hearth, the flames dying upon red, charred wood, and a dark shape sat, wedged against the hearth. He saw Dimwittle asleep on a bed in a back room, still wearing his heavy coat and shoes, one leg dangling off the bed. He barely managed to see, on a table nearer the window, a small hammer, a mortar and pestle, a few burlap bags, and some ore samples.

Lockie stepped back and looked up at the vault of stars spread like diamonds on a dark blanket. The quarter moon sailed behind a light cloud and looked like a single, ephemeral galleon on a jewel-tossed sea. Thinking of the wealth a few, select gems could bring him, he considered going back to the cave and carving out some of the silver ore for himself. "Just a little, not much," he whispered.

Just then, the moon slipped from behind the cloud, and its light shone straight at the window. Lockie looked again through the curtains and was amazed and mystified at what he saw beside the hearth.

"Just a little of what?" the voice behind him caught him off guard. He jumped. Turning, he beheld little Michael with a small pistol trained on him. "Oh, 'tis you, Lockie."

Lockie looked down at the gun, concern racing through his mind. "You can lower your firearm, Michael. Just me out for a stroll."

Michael did not lower the pistol but stepped closer. "What're you doing out here on this cold night, Lockie?"

"Taking a stroll, as I said. I might ask you the same question." Trying to throw off his young friend, he searched his mind for a way to change the subject. He felt his underarms beginning to sweat. "You can put the pistol away."

"I know I can, but it feels good in my hand." Michael made a mischievous grin.

For a long minute, the two stood facing each other, Michael's flintlock pistol a mere foot from Lockie's chest. Finally, Michael lowered the gun. "I was just fooling with you, Lockie. Here, you take the gun. It's not loaded." He handed the small gun to Lockie who took it with measured caution and shoved it in his pocket.

Michael, though considerably smaller in stature, threw his arm around Lockie's back. "My dear friend, I meant you no harm. I just love an adventure, and you helped me make an adventure."

"You had me worried for a moment, but let's get away from here before we waken the poor gardener."

"Yes, the poor, poor gardener. We don't want to talk too loudly and wake him. He works so hard and needs his sleep. Anyway, I calculated you would be out tonight and be spying on the gardener. I knew I'd find you here at about this time. It's all mathematical, you see."

They trod arm in arm up to the back door. Before entering, Lockie said, "How is it mathematical? How did you know I would be checking on the gardener?"

"Oh, I know you've been spying and carrying on. You think you can solve who killed Mr. Owsley and Mr. Smyth all by yourself. Anyway, I just figured this was your next move. May I have my pistol back, please? Mr. Tamperwind gave it to me. No shot, no powder. Just the little gun."

Lockie drew the weapon from his pocket and handed it to Michael. They entered.

"I hope you find the killer, Mr. Grumbles. Best of dreams, Lockie."

"And to you, Michael. Try not to scare me like that again."

Michael smiled and crept up the stairs to his room. Lockie settled himself once more on his bed in the wood locker. Edmund never stirred from his chair in the parlour.

STAVE TWENTY-EIGHT

TWO GRAVES

When Lockie was shaken awake roughly, he was sure a pistol was in his face. Opening his eyes more fixedly, he saw it was only Scrooge's index finger pointing at his nose.

"Get up, Lockie. We must work fast. We have to be done before Mrs. Owsley awakens. Quickly now. Go wake up the gardener and have him join us at the graves with shovels."

Lockie rose quickly, put on his coat and shoes, and raced out the back door. When he got to the gardener's hut, the curtains were pulled back, and enough light from the early sun shone through the windows to reveal the man was not at home. He joined Scrooge and Cratchit at the still fresh soil of the gravesites.

"The gardener's not home. He may have gone to market or is caring for the horses. Where's Mr. Nuckols?"

"He's at the mine, organising the shift change," Scrooge whispered. "The miners are also bringing up all the pit ponies to pull the ore carts to the wharf. It's shipping day. Edmund's challenge is to oversee the effort to ensure all the ore gets down to the ships. Now, did you find any shovels about the gardener's cabin?"

"I found none, not in the shed. The gardener must keep them hidden. Shall I look further for them?"

"No, we'll have to make do. We concentrate on Owsley's grave."

Using only thick branches, they shovelled and scooped at the soil for a good while. Lockie left to hunt for buckets. He found three pails, but digging in the frozen soil with them was tedious and onerous for all three of the labourers.

In an hour, the sun was up in a grey, dismal sky.

"So much for working quickly," Cratchit said.

At that moment, Edmund approached with two stout men, each carrying shovels. "I thought you might need some help," Edmund said.

In short order, the two burly miners had removed the soil atop the grave and were lifting the wooden casket out of the grave.

"Open it, please," Scrooge said.

"There'll be a stench," one of the miners said.

"Open it. I won't take long."

"What in the world are ya men doin'?" Mrs. Owsley screeched, waddling like a goose towards the gravesite. "Why're ya disrespectin' my husband's grave?" Her face was beet red.

Cratchit stepped in front of her. "We've got business to attend to here."

She tried to force past him, but he restrained her. The miners pried open the box, and a noxious odour swelled up. Scrooge, a kerchief over his nose, drew close to the dead man's arm. He lifted it, pulled the jacket and shirt back as far as the elbow, examined the hand and arm, then did the same for the other. Next, he opened the buttons of the shirt and looked at the alabaster white neck and chest.

"You may close the lid and rebury the deceased. Thank you, gentlemen."

The men replaced the lid and hammered the coffin shut, then lowered it back in the hole.

"What was that all about?" Mrs. Owsley screamed. "I'll have the meanin'. I shall."

"Yes, you shall," Scrooge said, "but not at this moment."

Mrs. Owsley waited until the men began pitching the soil atop the coffin before she hurried back to the rear entrance of the mansion. Scrooge, Cratchit, and Lockie stood together like a wall, their backs to the grave. They watched the outraged woman tread heavily up to the porch steps. Michael was waiting there, a forlorn look on his face. When she reached the steps, she called, "I'll have the law on ya, ya heathens."

"We must truly act quickly. Time is of the essence in this game." Scrooge walked so fast it was almost a run. Leaving the miners to finish the burial, Edmund, Cratchit, and Lockie hurried after him.

"Where are we going?" Edmund was panting, trying to keep pace with Scrooge, Lockie, and Cratchit.

"I want to speak to Missus Grave, the old woman," Scrooge said. "Something she said is remarkable."

"You'll have to go without me," Edmund said. "I must attend to the loading of the carts and see that all the ore gets delivered to the wharf. If I don't, Mr. Tamperwind will surely think something is amiss."

"Go, Edmund, but be out in the open. The killer is at large and may try to slay any of us. Go back to the house and take your pistol with you. And tell Samuel to be alert."

Edmund departed to gain his pistol and to warn Samuel.

When Scrooge, Cratchit, and Lockie arrived at the harlot's home on the edge of Hopworth, and after they knocked, the old woman called from inside, inviting them in. They made their way to the back bedroom and found Missus Grave sitting by the bedside of her daughter, Beebe, whose skin shone lucent and bore a green tone; her eyes were red-rimmed. Beebe turned away from the men. The room smelled of vile vomitus.

"She threw up all night," Missus Grave said. "Ain't nothin' left in her. She may have beaten the sickness, but the dark eye was upon her, for certain."

"'T'weren't no dark eye, Mama," Beebe called over her shoulder. "'Twas the wee man what poisoned me. Put poison in ma tea."

Cratchit took it upon himself to stroke the ratted hair of the sick woman. "Dear lady, do you know who tried to poison you?"

"I told ya, 'twas the little one. Told me he just wanted to have tea with me. I thought that odd, but if he was payin' for ma time, I was good for it. Then, at the café, somethin' caught ma attention, and I turned ma head, and when I wasn't lookin', he put somethin' in ma tea, I'm sure of it."

"Can you point him out if you saw him?"

"She probably cannot," Missus Grave said. "Her eyes ain't never been too good. That's how she can be with almost any man, 'cause she can't tell what they look like."

"Can too." Beebe sat up. "I can tell 'em by their body odours, their breath, the size of their muscles, the moles on their faces, the width of their chests, and how much hair on those chests, and by how they lean, and how they walk, and even how they stand. You bring me close to a man, I'll tell ya if I know 'im." She lay back down. "Unless I die first." She made a retching sound, but she did not vomit.

Scrooge turned now to the mother. "Missus Grave, when we left the other day, you said for us not to tell Mr. Tamperwind about Beebe or about you, for he would be much aggrieved. Why?"

Missus Grave hemmed and hawed and stamped her foot, then walked away. After a moment, she returned with her head bowed. "Don't tell Master Tamperwind because ... Beebe is his progeny, his daughter. There. I've said it."

"Mama, ya wasn't s'posed to tell." Beebe's voice trailed off.

The two men and Lockie had difficulty not showing their surprise.

Finally, Scrooge broke the silence. "Missus Grave, I know that took a great deal of courage. Thank you for your honesty. You're saying Mr. Tamperwind is Beverly's father, and yet he has allowed you, the child's mother, to live in this squalor, you and his daughter."

"What could he do?" Missus Grave said. "He loved his wife, and one night of drunken misbehavin' is hardly a reason to lose his entire way. He only got lost for a while but found his way back. Loved his wife dearly, he did, till she died. She was a darlin', she was. She took such good care of the miners and their families. I don't blame 'im. 'Twas really my fault. He's been good to me and Beebe all this time. From time to time, a pouch of money has showed up on the stoop, just like St. Nick would do. That's been enough. Ain't been any money for a time now, since he's been ill for most a year."

"That long?" Cratchit said.

"Goes not to the mine. Only ones ever get to see him were Mr. Owsley, a'fore he died, and Mr. Grumbles, and, o'course, the housekeeper, Mrs. Owsley, and his ward. That's all."

"I guess you know him as well as anyone in these parts," Cratchit said. "Better than some."

Missus Grave nodded.

"Missus Grave, we may need to impose on you for help again. May we?"

"Yes. And if you're about catchin' who murdered Mr. Owsley and Mr. Smyth, could ya catch the dastard what tried to kill my Beverly?"

"Yes, ma'am. Be ready. We may call at any time," Scrooge said.

The three left the home, each deep in thought. Cratchit finally said, "So now we have to be on the lookout for a small man. One of the miners, perhaps?"

"Yes. It could be a miner," Scrooge said, "or someone who stays hidden in one of the caves around here. There are plenty of hiding places. I'm sure of it. What it tells us is there is more than one killer in what must be a gang of murderers. Oh, dear."

The sun was leaning on noon when they trod back towards the mine. Passing through Hopworth, they noted the store was still closed though the padlock lay on the steps. The snow that had covered the ground was melting quickly, turning the path into sludge that made walking difficult.

Almost to the Tamperwind mine entrance, Lockie said, "Master Scrooge, I been thinkin' about what you asked me about the gardener behavin' in any odd way. I can't say he's done anything mean, acts meek as a mouse. But the other day, when I went to get him to get lanterns for us, I knocked on the door, he jumped like he was startled by the noise. He got up and came to the door. Then, the other night, I'm beggin' your pardon first, before I tell you. The other night when I thought everyone was asleep, I slipped out to the gardener's hut. He was asleep, but Michael showed up. I guess he weren't asleep like I thought. We talked, and I said we didn't need to make so much noise to wake Mr. Dimwittle, and Michael agreed with me. If he's deaf, why would Michael agree with what I said?"

"Thank you, Lockie," Scrooge said. "That may explain a great deal more of what's going on."

"And there's one more thing."

"Later, Lockie. We must speak to Edmund. And there he is." Scrooge pointed and quickened his pace.

STAVE TWENTY-NINE
THE CLUES COME TOGETHER,
MICHAEL HEADED FOR DANGER

The three arrived at the mine entrance where the clamour of horses, carts, and busy miners made quite the racket. Edmund stood on a boulder near the mine entrance, yelling orders to the miners. The engines pumped, making a fearsome sound, more pronounced than usual. The three walked up beside Edmund.

"How's it going, Edmund?" Scrooge asked.

"Not well, Uncle. I mean, the loading of the ore is moving along as good as I can expect. The men generally know what to do. But an hour ago, two of the men drilled too deep into the rock wall in one of the cavern portions of the mine, between the cavern wall and the ocean. A slab of rock fell away, and a seam opened, letting the ocean in with every wave. It's a narrow crack so far, about two inches across, but it's still allowing the water into the cavern. Fortunately, it's in a wide cave, way below any of the tunnels, and its ceiling is quite high, so everyone is safe right now. I've got men working to seal off that crack with a blend of plaster and rock. I hope they can get it sealed. And I've got all the pumps working. I hope we stay ahead of it."

"Edmund," Cratchit said, "is there real danger?"

"I wish I knew more. Caveman, the big man who calls himself the 'foreman,' doesn't seem too worried. I wish I knew for sure."

"Is 'Caveman,'" Lockie interjected, "the name that all the miners call him? He strikes me as a man with a penchant for violence."

"I hadn't thought of him, Lockie," Scrooge said. "Maybe we should keep an eye on him."

Scrooge motioned for Edmund to come closer. He stepped down from the rock and leaned in so Scrooge could whisper in his ear. His face showed amazement, then understanding.

Cratchit stayed with Edmund to assist and monitor the efforts to seal the water leak.

Scrooge and Lockie went up the hill.

When Scrooge arrived at the Tamperwind mansion, he went straight to his room, opened the little desk, and pulled out all the notes he had made, plus the notes from the gardener reporting the attack on Samuel, and lastly, the pouch of coins and silver dollops he had found on Smyth's dead body.

He looked carefully at his notes, then at Dimwittle's note, then, ignoring the coins, he examined the silver dollops, one by one, each of them *not* perfectly round, but misshapen. He noticed the dollops had flecks of other ores in them, generally red ones. He heard a creak on the floor behind him. He turned and found Lockie standing on his tiptoes, watching what Scrooge was doing.

"Lockie, why are you here?"

"Beggin' your pardon, Master Scrooge. I had to watch. I want to learn what you're thinkin'."

"Well, that is hardly the way to do it, and another thing—"

"Beggin' your pardon again, but did you notice that one silvery blob, there on the right, has a finger smudge blended into the silver?"

Scrooge turned to look at the silvery blob. He held it up to the light. On the flat dollop, plain as day, was the indelible, imbedded mark of a thumbprint, definite curved lines of a singular print. The realisation arrived in Scrooge's mind. This print could match a specific person's thumb.

He lowered the marked, coin-sized metal, and then pulled out the note written by Dimwittle telling of Samuel's death. He laid the thumb-printed metal side by side with the ink-dirty thumbprint on the foolscap page. The thumb markings on each matched exactly. "Precisely as I conjectured."

"On our way here," Lockie interrupted, "I tried to tell you what else I saw in Dimwittle's cabin."

"Yes." Scrooge was distracted, thinking of his premise regarding fingerprints.

"Next to Dimwittle's hearth was an odd contraption with various levels of copper and lead pans. There was a sort of caldron at the bottom where a man who wants to could shove wood for burnin'. Burned charcoal covered the floor around it. It had a large pipe that extended into the hearth and then up the chimney. Like an odd rum distillery, but not. On the shelf above it, clearly marked, were two huge bottles, one marked *Mercury*, the other *Salts*."

Together, Lockie and Scrooge stated the awareness. "Dimwittle is amalgamating the silver and trying to make counterfeit coins."

"But he's not very good at it," Scrooge said. "These blobs of impure silver could never be taken for coins."

"There's somethin' else," Lockie said. "I almost forgot. In addition, I saw on a table in his hut, plain as day, an assay scale, a pile of silver filings like they'd been shaved off a silver crown, and a metal object that looked like a coin mould."

Scrooge looked hard at the young man.

"Don't be too mad at me, Master Scrooge, I just forgot to tell you earlier."

Scrooge's glare softened. "That is all right. I have one more thing to do. I believe I have solved this case. I've been to the *cave* and found a motive. I've been to the *grave* of the murdered man and discovered a clue and to Missus *Grave* and gathered further evidence. I've found out from you the way the gardener *behaved*. And more, besides. And through careful analysis of the notes and coin dollops that I've *saved*, the answer is quite clear."

"I believe I have solved it, too, sir."

"Oh, really? Are your skills at observation that acute? Never mind. Hurry, and get Edmund and Cratchit. Tell them to come here at once. The mine be damned."

"Yes, sir." Lockie was a lightning streak out the front door.

Scrooge said to himself, "Cave, grave, saved, behaved. Thank you, dear ghost." He went downstairs and waited on the front porch for Edmund, Cratchit, and Lockie. At the corner of his eye, he observed Mrs. Owsley often peering out the curtain at him with a concerned expression on her face. He pretended not to see her. Presently, Cratchit, Edmund, and Lockie appeared, labouring up the long hill. At that moment, Michael came around the side of the house, a heavy satchel on his shoulder, leading a Shetland pony and whistling a jaunty tune.

"Hello, Mr. Scrooge," he said, "I'm heading down to the mine. It's too boring here. I have a chemistry experiment I want to try there." He stopped. "I say, is that Mr. Nuckols and Mr. Cratchit coming up the hill? Are they taking a stoppage at the mine? I should hope not. Why! The miners are still loading the ore, are they not?" He turned and looked an inquisitive eye at Scrooge.

Scrooge hunched his shoulders as if indicating he had no knowledge.

Michael hunched his shoulders as well. He turned again to watch the men trudging up the snowy hill. "Wonderful. There's Lockie. Perhaps he'll join me at the mine to watch my experiment. I hope he does."

Edmund and Cratchit came in the gate first; the gardener was nowhere around to open it for them, so they had to unlatch the contraption latch themselves. When Lockie entered after them, he was immediately accosted by Michael begging him to join him at the mine. He even tugged on his coat sleeve.

Lockie, at last, jerked free. "Not now, Michael. Perhaps later."

Michael's face was downtrodden.

"I wish you wouldn't go to the mine, Michael, but I know you've done it before. Do be careful. Don't get in the miners' way."

"I shall be cautious. I always plan ahead." With that, he mounted his little stallion, and trotted down the hill, guiding his mount to leap small logs, and tossing stones from his pocket at nothing in particular.

When Lockie arrived beside the three men, Edmund asked, "What's this about, Uncle?"

Scrooge beckoned them to the far end of the wide porch and spoke in hushed tones. "I believe I have solved the murder."

"Details, Scrooge, details," Cratchit whispered.

In short order, Scrooge explained all the clues he had gathered, plus those Lockie had observed. He still needed a witness to verify his deductions. He bade Edmund return to the mine and continue overseeing the ore-loading efforts and the tunnel leak.

"Do you have your pistol, Edmund?"

"I do."

"Then go and stay alert. I don't know how many cohorts in this murder ring are involved. If the unlucky Smyth was one, then there may be others."

Edmund departed swiftly.

"Cratchit," Scrooge said, "I want you to bring Missus Grave up here. Be sure she understands why we need her here. She may help us catch the murderer. And take your musket with you."

"I shall bring her." Cratchit took his gun from a corner of the parlour, then paced quickly down the hill.

"Lockie," Scrooge said, "you go keep an eye on little Michael. He needs to be safe too. And be a runner for Edmund. Stay alert."

Lockie nodded and headed to the mine.

Scrooge entered the mansion and found Samuel and appraised him of the situation. Scrooge sat by a window, watching for Cratchit. In his pocket, he kept the notes he had obtained and the silver plug with the thumbprint. Samuel stealthily slipped outside and took a position on the side of the house, gun in hand.

At last, Scrooge saw Cratchit, accompanied not only by Missus Grave, but Beebe struggled along with them.

When they arrived at the porch, Scrooge stepped out the door and spoke in whispers to the women. He opened the door and let them inside. Closing the door, he turned to face Mrs. Owsley, her eyes squinted like a serpent's.

"I'll not have their type in me home. Not ever."

"But," Scrooge said, "you let Beebe in just recently and gave her tea. How is this any different?"

"It's different, is all. Get 'em out of here."

Scrooge beckoned to the ladies of the evening and Cratchit. "Come with me." He swept past Mrs. Owsley, but she raced to block the stairway, stretching her arms from bannister to wall.

"You'll not bother the poor, sick Mr. Tamperwind."

"Get out of the way, Agatha," Missus Grave broke in. "Mr. Tamperwind won't mind a visit from an old friend. You may be ma sister, but you won't stop us. Ya hear?" With that, she forced past Mrs. Owsley. Scrooge and Cratchit looked astonished at the revelation.

"Missus Grave and Mrs. Owsley are sisters!" Scrooge pronounced. The men followed the woman up the stairs, Cratchit shouldering his musket and supporting Beebe with his other arm.

Mrs. Owsley stormed away to the kitchen.

STAVE THIRTY

THE VILLAINS REVEALED, THE DANGER INCREASED

The four entered Mr. Tamperwind's room without knocking. The man sat at his enormous desk, attempting to pry open a drawer with a letter opener. He looked up, astonished, then almost fled to his bed, but gave up the effort and stood before them, his nightgown tucked into trousers.

"I believe your charade is up, Mr. Tamperwind," Scrooge said offhandedly.

"Hello, Mort," Missus Grave said. "You don't make a very good Mr. Tamperwind. But you do make a suitable Mr. Mortimer Owsley, husband of my not-so-dear sister."

Owsley sank into his chair. Scrooge drew his pistol and aimed it at Owsley. Cratchit aimed his long gun and cocked the hammer.

Suddenly, Mrs. Owsley rushed into the room, a pistol in her hand. Cocking it, she prepared to shoot, but Cratchit, who was standing nearest the door, knocked her arm up and the gun discharged into the ceiling. He grabbed the pistol from her and pushed her by the shoulder to the floor. She began to howl.

"Aw, shaddup, ya old crone," Beebe said, "or I'll smack ya, like I did that worthless gardener."

Mrs. Owsley quieted. When she attempted to rise, Cratchit held the pistol barrel first and threatened to beat her with the handle. She settled back to the floor.

His gun still trained on Owsley, Scrooge said, "So, Owsley, you had quite a plan. Kill Mr. Tamperwind, whom no one has seen for over a year, bash his face in so no one could recognise who it was that was dead, dress him in your clothes, then blame the only other man who could identify Erasmus Tamperwind—Hezikiah Hiram Grumbles—for the murder. All you had to do was pretend to *be* Mr. Tamperwind, stay up here in the house, and take in the fortune from the mine."

Owsley, his head down, managed an affirmative nod. He then raised his gaze with a haughty stare at his captors.

"Then you found out the real Mr. Tamperwind sent letters to Samuel, Abigail, and Lucy." Scrooge stepped closer to Owsley. "And you knew they were to inherit the mine, that is unless they were dead. You knew they had not seen their uncle since their youth and would easily believe you were their uncle. You planned to kill them, leaving you and your wife as the only heirs. You only had to keep them around long enough to carry out your plans. You almost succeeded in eliminating Samuel, sneaking out your balcony staircase to attack him, but your own wife rubbed his chest so hard, trying to erase any potential clues, she brought him back to life."

"You old crank!" Owsley screamed at his wife. She stared back at him.

"Also, I observed your hands, still raw and crusty like the hands of a mine manager, not like the softer hands of a *mine owner*. The hands of the man buried in yon graveyard who had his face bashed in, whose hands and arms were soft as a woman's, are none other than the hands of Erasmus Tamperwind, cordial gentleman, whom you savagely murdered. And more importantly, somehow you found the vein of silver in the old Hopworth mine."

"Yes, there it was, under Tamperwind's nose all these years," Owsley complained. "That confounded sheriff found it by accident. We were going to be rich."

"Yes, you had your gardener and Smyth already taking out the ore, then you were skipping the assay office, and were having your gardener experiment with finding a way to amalgamate the silver, and then produce counterfeit coins. Poor effort, I must say." He held up the smudged dollop.

"It wasn't the gardener doing the mining of the silver, it was only Smyth," Owsley said. He began wiping makeup off his face with a kerchief. He took a comb from the bureau and combed his hair. Though his hair was silver, he looked younger and not ill at all.

Scrooge continued, "But Smyth got as greedy as you, so you killed him. You dressed in a black cloak and mask and attacked him with a knife exactly when a single witness would see you, thus perpetuating the fabrication that Grumbles was the killer. You didn't expect Smyth to have a gun. Unfortunately for him, in the struggle, the gun shot him, but not before he yanked some of your grey hair. I found it clutched in his dead fingers."

Owsley rolled his eyes and showed a bored expression.

"What is more, the gardener is your counterfeiter. Lockie saw the coin mould and the other apparatus in his cabin. But he's not too good at the occupation. You see, this print smudge on the coin matches the smudge on this note he wrote about Samuel being attacked. And he's no more deaf than the Lord Mayor of London is a unicorn. By pretending to be deaf, he could keep an eye on things and an ear on things and keep any miner who wants to see you away. An insidious plan."

"You've got it all figured out, haven't you!" Owsley suddenly growled. "You just missed some important parts." He stood up and advanced to a coat hanging on a hook, Scrooge following him with the gun the entire time. Owsley put on the coat, buttoned it, and then put on a hat.

"I don't know where you think you're going." Cratchit now trained the musket on the criminal.

Just then, Samuel rushed into the room. "You best come take a look. There's something really big going on at the mine. Everyone's running."

"Edmund! Lockie and Michael!" Scrooge yelled.

"Oh, I wouldn't worry any about Michael," Owsley said. "He's way ahead of you and has everything well in hand."

"What do you mean by that?" Scrooge scowled.

Owsley hunched his shoulders, smiling deviously. "You'll see."

"We *shall* go and see," Cratchit motioned for Owsley and his wife to proceed them out of the room and down the stairs. Missus Grave and Beebe came last. Beebe made a point of stepping close to Owsley and sniffed him vigorously and clamped her hands for a moment on his biceps.

When the group reached the front door, Samuel opened it, and they stepped out onto the porch. Below the hill, the miners and the women ore scrubbers were running from the mine, then they formed in little groups, yards away. Wives and children from the town came forth from their homes and joined the men, all staring at the mine entrance.

Scrooge and his companions were so busy watching the hubbub that they failed to see Edmund sprinting up the hill, leaping the fence, and coming to the porch. Panting, he attempted to speak.

"Let me say it for you," Owsley interjected. "Everyone has fled the mine, for someone is about to blow a hole in that already-weak wall by the sea, thus flooding the lower mine and anyone still down there."

"Yes," Edmund gasped.

"And there are two lovely ladies tied up down there," Owsley continued. "A Miss Abigail and a Miss Lucy. Correct?"

Edmund nodded. "How did you know?"

"Michael told us the plan. You never suspected. Last evening, our gardener, a true cousin of Samuel and Abigail, went to Lazy Eye and convinced the young ladies of the urgent need to travel back here with him. He then took them into the mine through a hidden passage. I believe they are tied up in the flooding cavern now."

"Yes, he's right," Edmund panted. "We have to save them."

"And you shan't save them if you don't let my wife and me be on our way. We already have a schooner at the dock for our escape, courtesy of our little ward, Michael."

"Wait a minute!" Beebe's voice rang out. "I been with you of an evening or two, Mort Owsley. You got a certain smell and a tilt in your walk, and a feelin' in your sinews. I had to figure it out." She shook her finger at him.

"And what of it?"

"And now, I knows who the little man was that poisoned me. He's your ward. The villain." She gasped. "He's naught but a boy. But so mature. Fooled me, he did. His smell matched yours, Mr. Owsley. That's how I know."

"Well, he might have done that, but you have no proof."

"Don't we, though?" Missus Grave said. "Agatha Owsley, with all the arsenic off-castings in these mines, and your knowledge of herbs and medicinals, I'll wager you found a way to concoct quite a poison."

"Ah, but you're wrong," Mrs. Owsley announced, a smug look on her face. "Our little chemist, Michael, worked it out. He gave us the whole plan, to counterfeit the silver, to kill old Tamperwind so that no one would know who was killed, put the blame on Grumbles, and—"

"That'll be enough, Agatha," Owsley commanded. "Let them do their conjecturing. We'll be on our way to America soon enough, enough bags of silver ore stored in the sloop's hold to make us a fine, high life." He turned to Scrooge, Cratchit, and Samuel. "Put down your guns, gentlemen. If you want to see Abigail and Lucy alive, you must let us depart unobstructed."

Scrooge, Samuel, and Cratchit lowered their gun hammers. Scrooge and Samuel stuck the pistols in their belts. Mrs. Owsley went inside to the kitchen, returning with a heavy bag of coins, then gathered a coat from the coat rack by the door, and she and Mr. Owsley strolled leisurely down the hill and out the gate.

Edmund stepped up beside his friends and his uncle. "Lockie came running up from the lower tunnel, the one that runs through the old cavern, and warned me. He had followed Michael into the mine, to the cavern area of the mine as far as where the crack in the wall is. He said when he started down the last stairs, he saw the explosives—a small, open keg with black powder. Michael was right beside it with a fuse, one of those William Bickford safety fuses, and a torch to light it. Then he saw Lucy and Abigail, tied up back to back on a rock just above the water already flooding the cave floor. That's all I know. Before I could stop him, Lockie ran back down to try to talk Michael out of whatever he's planning. I ordered everyone out of the mine. The pumps will continue to work for a while longer, but without the men shovelling coal to fire the engines, they'll stop pumping the water out. And—"

"Well, I'm not going to stand here!" Samuel exclaimed. "I've got to save my sister!"

"We're all going with you." Scrooge was already heading down the steps.

STAVE THIRTY-ONE
DEATH AWAITS IN THE CAVERN

L eaving Missus Grave and Beebe on the porch, the men ran down the steep incline. Scrooge was soon far behind the younger men. In front of the tiny church, he paused to catch his breath. In the corner of his eye, he saw the two Owsleys slipping down an alley alongside the church. He turned and watched the unscrupulous couple. He surmised that was their path to the escape vessel moored at the small dock. He looked at the shabby appearance of the house of God.

"If I survive, I'll do something to rebuild this church." He marked their escape avenue in his mind, then hastened past the crowd of miners and their families.

Upon arriving at the mine entrance, Scrooge found his companions facing the huge mountain of a miner, a pickaxe in his hand. Caveman set down the pick and placed his fists on his hips and grimaced at them.

Edmund appeared to be trying to reason with the man, though Scrooge could not hear him because of the racket of the pumps.

When he got close enough, the huge man smiled and leaned down. "I be thinkin' you gents need some help to rescue the dames."

Edmund was the most surprised of them all. "Yes, please."

"Follow me, gents. I know a secret, faster way."

Before they started, Cratchit turned to Scrooge. "Ebenezer, I'm only forty-nine percent of our firm, but I'm ordering you to stay here above ground. If none of us comes back alive, you're the one who can tell the story. You have all the proof."

Scrooge nodded. "Do be careful, Bob. You're my best friend."

"Cautious as a mouse near a sleeping cat, dear friend."

Caveman held a torch in one hand. He handed a lantern to Edmund. "Mr. Mine Manager, keep these gents close. There's no time to lose."

While Scrooge watched them go, the four men hastened down a narrow tunnel and were soon out of his sight. He closed his eyes and began praying aloud. In that flash of a moment, he knew the Ghost of Christmas Future was nearby, pointing and shaking his head.

Led by Caveman, the four men soon entered a narrow but cavernous room in the mine. The human mountain led the three to a steep slide that headed down into a dark chasm. He sat in the lead and handed the torch to Samuel. He then grasped thick, well-oiled ropes that ran along the sides the distance of the slide. "Climb on behind, men."

The three sat straddled behind him, tandem style. When all were seated, Caveman lessened his grip on the oiled ropes, and they slid like a coach blown by a whirlwind into deep blackness. Caveman used the ropes to slow their downwards progress by increasing his grip on them, thus bringing them to a smooth stop. Landing gently at a wooden platform, they climbed onto another slide, and again shot down, down, down into darkness.

The four men suddenly arrived at the tail of the tunnel at a rock outcropping at the upper edge of the lower cavern. Looking out, they saw the cavern floor filling with water. Beyond the cave portion, the opposite tunnel extended into abject opaqueness. Torches burned in several sconces on the wall of the cavern and partially illuminated it and the wave-driven water below. A few bats flitted at the cavern ceiling.

Large, rusty iron pipes that sucked out the water protruded from the surface, the dark water sloshing higher with each wave spilling through the opening. Then, they saw Lucy and Abigail in the shadows on a boulder, tied back to back, barely above the water's edge. The water lapped near their feet.

Perhaps thirty yards beyond them, holding a small torch was Michael, kneeling. He held a long twine fuse in his other hand. The fuse led to a satchel sitting on a small keg marked *explosive* in white lettering. His torch flickered brightly, revealing *black powder* in the open keg. He knelt directly above the crack in the wall on a ledge where miners used to pause and eat their meagre meals. He looked to be delighted by every ocean wave that drove more seawater into the cavern, chuckling and smiling at each wave.

Michael glanced up and saw the four men on the outcropping above and behind him by thirty yards. He smiled and gestured at them, then pointed at the keg of powder. "I was wondering when you'd arrive!" he hollered, his squeaky voice bouncing from wall to wall. His speech sounded so puny, yet maniacal.

"No, Michael! For the hundredth time, no!" Lockie was kneeling on a ledge by a stair thirty yards opposite where Michael perched across the wide cavern. He clenched his hands together in a pleading motion.

Michael gave a delightfully proud smile. "Hello, Lockie. I's so glad you sneaked in over there. You're good at sneaking around, aren't you? You may be seven years my senior, but I count you as a good friend. Look! The water must be ten feet deep. Good for swimming … or drowning!"

"Yes, Michael. Perhaps we could go for a swim in the ocean later. We've had fun playing, haven't we?"

"Yes, we have. I value every minute. I only wish I had killed you that night at Dimwittle's cabin. Though I told you it was not, the gun *actually was loaded*, after all. That would have been a fine game. You wounded and dying, and I, the heroic champion trying, though in vain, to save you. Me, crying over your corpse." His tone had turned sarcastic and cruel.

Lockie gulped. "But it's not play now. No one needs to get hurt. How about you step away from that explosive?"

"No, I don't think so. I believe our pretend gardener has had enough time by now to join the Owsleys at the schooner. I have my own plan of escape."

"Well, how about we go for a play first, rather than killing these fine ladies?"

"No, I don't think so. Since you and your companions are here, when you try to save them, you'll die too. What an adventure!"

All this while, Caveman, utilising the shadows along an upper wall, had been slipping around the outer edge of the cavern wall, inching ever so quietly closer to Michael on a narrow ledge. While Lockie was making his last entreaty to the boy, he arrived directly above Michael by just a few feet. He was preparing to jump at Michael when his foot nudged a few pebbles that tumbled down. The young lad turned and saw him, pulled his pistol from his pocket, and shot the man in the chest. He plummeted into the water and did not come up. The gunshot echoed around the cavern a half-dozen times.

"Tsk, tsk," Michael said. "Interesting how one little bullet can bring down a giant."

Cratchit, Edmund, Samuel, and Lockie began calling to the boy in echoing sorrowful pleadings.

"Goodbye, Lockie. I've got to go." Michael lit the fuse and darted through a narrow and constricted crack in the wall a few feet from where he had knelt. He was immediately gone from sight.

Lockie tossed off his shoes and jacket and jumped first into the water and swam towards the women who had begun to scream. Samuel dove in next. Cratchit almost dove in, too, but stopped when he eyed coils of rope a few feet away. *We can use that rope to help them get out of the water.* He held the torch, and Edmund the lantern, the light glimmering and casting vast, gloomy silhouettes that chased each other along the walls like the drawings of ancient men hunting a prey.

Cratchit drug the rope to the edge of the outcropping and looped one end to a large rock, securing it with knots. He watched Lockie and Samuel valiantly stroking their way through the seawater towards the burning fuse and the keg of powder.

Then the bomb blew.

The noise echoed like a hundred cannons throughout the cavern. A wide slab of rock slid from the wall beside the crack, crashing into the water. Pebbles and rocks spun through the air, clacking and smacking against the walls. Bob and Edmund ducked. The two women could not dodge the missiles and were pelted head to foot, tearing their clothes and their skin.

Samuel and Lockie vanished under the surface, the shockwave billowing across the water. The two women were almost shaken from their perilous position on the rock.

Cratchit and Edmund held their ears to the reverberating echo that went on for some long moments. Smoke like that from Hephaestus' furnace consumed the cavern. Finally, the smoke dissipated, flowing out the tunnels, and Cratchit and Edmund saw the bloodied faces of the women, still alive but terrified.

The two men scanned the sloshing waves for their friends. Then they beheld the water was rising rapidly, mounting up the rock where the women were tied.

Edmund handed the lantern to Cratchit, flung off his coat, and tore off his shoes. He jumped into the murky, sloshing water, now almost at the women's bound feet. Cratchit could see the terror and hopelessness on their faces. He watched in despair at the water, no sign of either Lockie or Samuel. The women screamed when a wave sloshed up to their knees.

Then, in the water, two heads appeared. Edmund drug a bewildered Lockie up to cling to the rock just where the two young ladies perched, the waves now sloshing at his neck. Lockie shook his head a few times, then began clambering up the rock, slipping again and again.

Cratchit still watched the water for almost a full minute.

At last, Edmund brought up Samuel, sputtering and gasping. The two swam to the boulder on which the women perched and barely had time to gulp air. Lockie had attained the boulder top beside the women. He drew a knife from his pocket and began carving away at the rope that bound them around their waists.

Samuel climbed the slippery boulder to assist. He set to untying the women's feet that were underneath the churning water.

Suddenly, an immense wave washed through the hole, sending the water above all their waists. Lockie bent down under the water, continuing to saw at the ropes. Edmund was driven up by the wave to the boulder beside them. He motioned for Cratchit to throw the rope.

With one rope end secured, Cratchit tossed the other end. The water rose to the women's chins, then sloshed over their heads.

At last, Lockie sliced through the rope, and they were free. All of them swam towards the rope that Cratchit had lowered. The water had risen so high that they did not have to climb far. Cratchit reached over to help Lucy, who was supported by Lockie, to climb up first. When he looked again, dozens of miners' hands were extended, helping the swimmers up onto the outcropping. The miners, many with lanterns, gathered the drenched ladies and men up to the now-crowded rock platform. Two miners immediately began swabbing the women's bloodied faces with dry cloths. Others flung heavy coats over the wet survivors' bodies.

"To the stairs!" one of the miners called.

Cratchit was already dashing ahead of them along a narrow ledge to the stairs, then sprinting like a mountain goat up them. At the top of the stairs, he found the ladder to the next level, traversed it like a cat, and in short order, was racing out to the entrance of the cave. He bounded up to Scrooge. "Do you know where the Owsleys have gone? We're not going to let them get away, leaving poor Grumbles to face the courts."

"I believe I do know where they went," Scrooge said. "Follow me."

Scrooge leading the way, Cratchit and he sped to the alley beside the church and followed through the narrow passageway. They reached a fork in their path.

"They took the path on the left," a voice called from behind them.

Looking back, they saw the good priest who had been working in his garden, a hoe in his hand.

"Hurry on, now," he called. "They'll get away."

Soon, Cratchit and Scrooge were negotiating down uneven rock steps towards the small, hidden wharf they had seen days before. It extended out some two hundred feet from the rocky shore, beside which was anchored a short two-mast schooner.

Cratchit soon outdistanced his partner, and Scrooge, already weary, could not keep up. He stumbled and landed hard on his knees. Rolling around in agony on the steps, all he could do was watch Cratchit sprint down the stairs straight to the ship, rocking in heavy waves.

Foam spewed up around the ship with each wave. Scrooge could see the deckhands were making final preparations to set sail. Several men were at the windlass, drawing up the anchor.

Cratchit raced to the wharf, the gangplank already pulled into the ship, which seemed to be teetering, battered by the strong waves. The captain was calling hurried orders. Cratchit sprang from the wharf, grasping the gunnel and hauling himself up into the vessel. The sailors came towards him, but he pulled out Mrs. Owsley's pistol, and they backed away. "Where are the Owsleys?" he barked.

"They're below deck." A black-caped man approached from Cratchit's rear. Cratchit wheeled around and saw the hulk of a man before him. He wore a black ribbon mask over his face, save slits for his eyes. He wrested the gun from the surprised Cratchit, then slowly peeled off his mask. The gardener—Clarence Dimwittle—gave a humble, pleasant smile.

"Well, how now, Mr. Cratchit." Mort Owsley emerged from below deck. "Looks like our intrepid thespian, Mr. Dimwittle, will have to dispatch you like he did Erasmus Tamperwind and almost did Samuel Tamperwind. Shoot him, Clarence."

The gardener pulled the trigger. It did not discharge. He cocked it and pulled the trigger again. Cratchit remembered Agatha Owsley had fired the gun in the bedroom when he knocked her arm.

Cratchit, having well-honed muscles working in perfect rhythm, sprang on the huge man and drove him to the deck and began pummelling him with his strong arms and rock-like fists. At last, the man lay still, a frightened expression on his face, blood pouring from his nose and mouth.

"Ah ha!" Cratchit exclaimed, pinning the man's shoulders with his knees. "Not such a tough scoundrel, after all."

"Oh, I wouldn't be so sure, Mr. Cratchit," Mort Owsley said, unsympathetically. "You see, Clarence Dimwittle is the stepbrother to Abigail's father, her mother's second husband. He suffers, or perhaps excels, from the same malady that she lives with—humble and kind one moment, then a fearsome terror the next. That's how he could easily smash in Tamperwind's face and choke Samuel almost to death. Oh, and it was he who killed Creaker Smyth, not me. His hair is black now because he dyed it. It was grey when he killed Smyth. He's quite the actor, is he not?"

Cratchit looked at Owsley incredulously, then at Dimwittle.

"We have only to say the right words, for we have trained him so," Owsley said. "And he will reduce you to a pulp."

Mrs. Owsley arrived from below deck to stand beside her husband. "Oh, goody," she said. "I've always wanted to watch him do his work."

"Clarence," Owsley growled, "wild dogs! Wild dogs!"

Cratchit found himself flying through the air, hurled by the demented man. He landed on a group of sailors who were extending the gangplank out to the wharf once more, causing them all to fall in a heap. The huge adversary was on his feet and stomped like a madman towards prone Cratchit. His teeth were gritted, his eyes like a hungry wolf. He grabbed Cratchit by the lapels with his right hand and began pounding Cratchit's head with his left. Cratchit collapsed, and the man took him by the throat and began squeezing. Cratchit, as strong as he was, could not fend off the man. His face turned purple, his veins popping, his lungs vacant.

Then Dimwittle stopped choking Cratchit.

Ebenezer Scrooge, a good man of business, had strode across the newly replaced gangplank and had positioned his pistol flush against the temple of Dimwittle. "That's right, you violent man, this pistol *will fire*. The powder's dry, and I have no compunction against pulling the trigger."

Dimwittle rose, a contrite expression on his face, his hands in the air. Cratchit struggled to his feet.

"Wild dog! Clarence. Wild dogs!" Owsley called.

Dimwittle lunged at Scrooge, but the former miser, now brave warrior, at least for the moment, fired his weapon into the man's shoulder, blood spurting from the wound. The man crumpled to the deck.

Scrooge chuckled. "I've never fired a gun before. It's quite the article."

Cratchit took the gun from Scrooge's shaking hand and began reloading it with his own powder and shot. In ten seconds, it was ready to fire.

"Captain," Scrooge called, "these three people are murderers. You heard them admit it, and they need to be taken into custody. You, as a captain, can do that."

"Indeed, I shall." The captain drew his own pistol and aimed it at the Owsleys. His crew grabbed short swords or cudgels. The Owsleys held up their hands.

Cratchit and Scrooge bent to Dimwittle and used scarves and kerchiefs to staunch his wound. The sailors picked him up. "We'll take him to the ship's surgeon," one of the sailors said. They drug him below.

Cratchit, with a newly loaded pistol, and Scrooge, weary but satisfied, and the captain, with a guard of sailors, took the manacled Owsleys and their stolen bags of silver ore up the ragged rock stairway and into the mine where the murderous couple were imprisoned in a pump-engine room. Two sailors with muskets and swords were posted as guards.

Cratchit took the bags of silver, planning to give them to the Jiggins and Lucy so they could have them melted down, assayed, and the true silver sold honestly.

Edmund stepped down from the boulder from which he was monitoring the loading of the tin ore and made his way to Scrooge and Cratchit. "Good job, Uncle, and you, my fine friend, Bob Cratchit. How in the world did you manage to capture the villains?"

"We'll explain later," Cratchit replied. "How are our two ladies and Samuel and Lockie?"

"They're all fine, up at the mansion, getting warm. I've stood long enough by those big coal fires of the steam-pump engines that I've dried out entirely."

"How's the flooding in the mine?"

"Well, the water can only rise as high as the level of the sea. I've already ordered careful placement of explosives to seal that shaft in the morning. That one will be lost, but there are other tunnels. We will seal it and dig elsewhere in this crag. And besides, there may be a greater fortune in the silver of the old Hopworth mine. Fortunately, at the large wharf, the ore ship's captain has agreed to stay over until the next day, so we can finish the loading."

"What about the big miner who helped us?" Cratchit asked.

"We searched for the body, but it may have been swept out to sea through the break in the wall. Several miners swam about in the flooded cave but found nothing. We may never find it. He was a brave man and a loss to the mining operation. The miners are passing a hat for his widow."

"I shall contribute twenty pounds," Scrooge said, without a second thought. "And what about the conniving Michael?"

"No idea. He's apparently made an escape unless he's hiding in some hidden part of the mine." Edmund hunched his shoulders. "Several miners have muskets or pistols and are continuing to search for him. And for now, I am done here. I've called a halt to the work. It's soon Christmas Eve."

With the sun sinking behind the craggy hills by the sea, Edmund, Cratchit, and Scrooge walked arm in arm up to the mansion.

"Surely," Scrooge said, "nothing else can go wrong."

STAVE THIRTY-TWO

A JOYOUS REUNION, A TEMPORARY
RESPITE FROM THE DANGER TO COME

That evening, Lockie and Lucy stepped out onto the porch to survey the stars. They held hands. Lockie looked with deep admiration at the smiling, demure young woman. His heart pounded. Finally, sighing deeply, he said, "I shall miss London at Christmas."

"We shall have to make a joyous Yuletide here," Lucy said. "Look there, the miners have lit the yule log." She pointed where a vast tree stump was already blazing in a deep pit just beyond the mansion grounds. The pit had a small picket fence around it. While the flames licked the sky, bright sparks flitted higher and higher into the heavens. The families were hugging, drinking wassail from great mugs, and singing carols in such a raucous fashion, they sounded loud enough to wake the dead. He saw Missus Grave in the crowd, swaying, and her mouth open in song. He saw, too, Beebe, leaning into the arms of a miner, both of them smiling.

Lockie put his arm around the fair woman. Watching the miners and their families gathered around the bonfire, he smiled. When he paused and looked beyond the gathered families, he saw, at some thirty yards past them, a shadowy covered hansom carriage. Michael stood at the open door of the carriage, a lantern in his hand. A grey figure sat in the driver's seat.

Before Lockie could respond, Michael waved, blew out the lantern, and ducked inside the carriage, and the driver snapped his whip. In three seconds, the carriage vanished into the darkness.

Lucy saw the surprise, then frown, on Lockie's face. She took his hand in hers. "What is wrong, my dear Lockie?"

Lockie sighed. "Nothing, my angel. It's a good day to be alive." He drew her close and kissed her lips passionately.

⁓⤳⤳⤳

Christmas Eve morning broke bright and cool, the wet ground dried, the snow still crisp and even, and the yule log—attended by a single, inebriated, yet awake soul—blazed away.

When Scrooge, Edmund, and Cratchit gathered at the mansion's table for breakfast, it was Abigail who did the cooking. She fried eggs and bangers and found some marmalade for the toast. "I was careful to ensure nothing used in the cooking was of a poisonous nature. I didn't mind getting up early, especially after all that you brave men did for us." She poured tea for each one.

Lockie heard his friends' conversation and stumbled up from the sofa where he had slept all night, pulling his clothes back in order. He managed to bank up the fire in the fireplace and warm himself. He and Lucy had stayed up, talking into the wee hours, long past everyone else who had gone to bed. Lucy came down the stairs last, yawning. When she saw Lockie, she could not stop smiling.

Scrooge remarked, "Ah, to be young again." He had a winsome memory of Isabelle, his intended bride of long ago. They had been but seventeen years of age when they became betrothed. After two years, she left him because he had become so hard and flintlike, caring more for financial gain than anything else in the world, including the woman he loved.

Lockie and Lucy sat next to each other at the breakfast table, primarily staring into each other's eyes, barely touching the hot meal. When Lucy gave Lockie a peck on the cheek, Scrooge smiled, for he saw the love that had blossomed between the two and was glad for it. He leaned towards Cratchit who was munching on toast. "I think we will have to raise young Lockie's salary."

The group were in gladsome revelling, chatting and laughing.

Edmund rose. "When we gather for the Christmas dinner on the morrow, we shall have to make a great number of toasts. I happen to know that Mr. Tamperwind, may he rest in the arms of our Lord, has a well-stocked wine cellar."

All applauded.

"Yet, with me having to attend to the final loading of the ore on the ship today, I'm saddened that I won't be home for Christmas in London."

No sooner had the words escaped his mouth than an early coach pulled in at the weigh station down by the mine. The group stood from the table and rushed to the windows to look out.

When the travellers stepped out of the carriage, Cratchit exclaimed, "I can't believe my eyes!" He raced to the door.

"Nor can I!" Edmund followed on Cratchit's heels. The two men sprinted down the yard, leapt the short fence and bounded down to the coach. Edmund met his wife descending from the coach and swept her into his arms, then, lowering her, he bent down and hugged his two young boys, kissing them on the cheeks.

"Well, Freddie," Bernice said. "Frederick Edmund Nuckols, you didn't really think we could let you be alone for Christmas. And there are presents for you and the boys atop the coach." She pointed to where the driver and guard were handing down suitcases and a crate of silver and gold paper-wrapped gifts.

Edmund grabbed her by the waist and gave her a long kiss. He stepped back, his arms around hers, smiling broadly. "It is a miracle you are here. As for your gifts, I'm sorry. The work here has been taxing, and I've not had time to shop for a gift for you, not that I could find much in this locale."

"Pish, posh. And what is more. Look there!" Bernice pointed.

A second coach drove up at a great speed and shuddered to a stop. When the coach doors sprang open, out bounded the entire Cratchit family. First came Peter, his long legs churning, then Belinda, the younger children, Cratchit's wife, and last of all, Tim without a crutch and making a steady pace. The gleeful children, save Tim, took hold of their father before he could say, "Hello, dear family," and brought him bundled in their arms down into a bank of snow. Such laughing and tickling. Such genuine merriment was not to be equalled.

Then Tim joined them, but to their side. He landed back first into the snow beside them and began making a snow angel. Soon all the children and Cratchit himself were making angels in the drifts. Such a delightful hubbub and screams of delight. Cratchit stopped long enough to reach up and gently take the hand of his wife and slowly pulled her down atop him and kissed her face abundantly until she was giggling like a schoolgirl. "Oh, my dear, dear wife," he said. "I love you so."

"And I love you, Bob," she said. "I trust everything has gone smoothly here. Well, has it?"

Cratchit, somewhat taken aback by her direct question, replied, "Yes, yes. Smooth as silk. 'Twas no task at all to bring the ne'er-do-wells to justice. We can all sleep easy now."

"Just being with you, Bob," Alvina kissed him again, "is Christmas enough for me and for all of us, especially for Tim. It was the goodwill of Bernice Nuckols who insisted we come with her, and she paid for the coach, as well. And look, here comes your good friend and partner." The two stood, and Alvina raced to Scrooge and gave him a hug, then a kiss on the cheek. He blushed as he always did. They walked arm in arm down the snowy incline.

Scrooge, with Alvina on his arm, and the others from the house arrived beside the coach. Lockie bounded atop the coach and helped bring down the abundant parcels and bags. "Isn't Lockie so brave and thoughtful!" Lucy exclaimed.

Scrooge gave his niece, Bernice, and her boys hugs, then introduced all the Tamperwind relatives.

After shaking hands with them, Bernice turned and saw Cratchit by the coach talking to a dwarf. She said, "And there is good Bob Cratchit talking with our new friend, Mr. Bobbie Wheeler, who rode with us on the last miles of our journey."

Cratchit spun about and made a grand gesture towards the dwarf. "Ladies and gentlemen, may I introduce the man who, with his family, saved my life. He is a friend, a good joke-teller, and a lifesaver. I give you Bobbie Wheeler, Esquire."

"Glad to meet all of you," Mr. Wheeler said through his bushy beard. He stood tall as he could, then pulled back the lapel of his jacket. On his chest shone a copper star. "That's right. I'm the new constable in Lazy Eye, and I may take on the job of sheriff of the county now because, as Bob explained, the pretend sheriff is no longer here." He gave a proud look. "I can still build and repair wheels and find a little time to enforce the law too. When Bob told us the other night about the need to solve a series of murders here, I decided to take the job. Pays well."

The group applauded, and each person shook his hand. The happy group started to head to the mansion when a wagon appeared, pulled by six horses and laden with bags and bags in the bed. The driver, one Ginny Wheeler, with Angus and Barnabas sitting in the seat beside her, drew the team to a halt. Ginny stood up, pulling hard on the reins. "The gifts are here, Papa!"

When the wagon came to a complete stop, Mrs. Wheeler and the dwarf family boys and little girl emerged from the pile of bags. They climbed down. Bobbie Wheeler ran to them, helped them from the wagon, and the entire family began singing a rousing carol—"God Rest Ye Merry, Gentlemen."

They had finished but one stanza when another short cart arrived, pulling up beside the other wagons and coaches. The driver, a baker's apron sticking out from under his coat, looked as weary a man as Scrooge had ever seen, and upon stopping, appeared to nod to sleep.

"Finally," Bernice announced. "We stopped at the inn in Lazy Eye last night and knowing that you probably had not had time to prepare a proper Christmas feast, I located the grocer in the village who happened to have two geese hung and ready for roasting. I begged the cook at the inn to prepare the meal for today. And I believe he stayed up all night." She walked up to the man, nudged him, and thrust coins into his gloved palm.

He awoke with goggled eyes. "Thank 'e, mum."

"Come, everyone!" Bernice exclaimed. "We need help unloading the roast geese, the fruit, the stuffing, the potatoes, and puddings and pies. We'll need help, too, with handing out all these gifts to the miners' families."

"I'll get the hearth started," Abigail hollered above the joyous uproar. "So that we can warm the food."

Peter and the other Cratchit children helped carry in the food. Tim stayed with his father and mother in order to hand out gifts.

There was an abundance of gifts. Edmund and Cratchit jogged to the mine and mine town and called the men from their loading of the ore, and the women and families from their homes to come up to the blazing yule log. When the miners and families arrived in one extended half-circle around the package-filled wagon, at once, the Wheeler family; the Cratchit family; Edmund, his wife, his boys; Lucy Tamperwind; Samuel; and Abigail Jiggins all handed out gifts to the poor families. Christmas gift-giving was celebrated a day early.

Each family member shook their gifts, then tore off the twine and paper wrappings. The Wheelers had categorised the gifts so that little girls received gifts such as dolls and such things that girls would like, and boys received balls and toy swords and more. Women discovered in their boxes and bags some aromatic soaps, shawls, and linen hankies, and the men got new boots or hand tools.

Such screams of delight, Scrooge had never heard. He stood back, giggling, pointing, and smiling. He could not remember feeling such joy, and for a moment, though his eyes were watering from laughing so hard, he could have sworn he saw the deep green robe of the Ghost of Christmas Present sweep past behind the throng of happy, smiling, and boisterous families. And was that a late-morning quarter moon smiling through the barren trees on the hill, or was it the grin of the Christmas giant?

When the gifts were all given, Wheeler jumped from the bed of the wagon and strode to where Scrooge and Cratchit stood. "If you're wondering where I had the money to pay for all this. Well, besides being the best wheelwright in the entire three counties," he said, then whispered, "I also have a little silver mine behind my house. Dwarves are good at mining, you know. So, I may be the richest man in three counties as well."

Cratchit and Scrooge chortled, holding their bellies.

Once Tim had thrown the first snowball, the entirety of the youngsters—Cratchit's children, Edmund's children, Wheeler's young ones, and all the miners' children—joined in the jubilant fray. A few adults entered in, and Cratchit and Edmund soon found themselves bombarded by a flurry of snowballs in an all-out assault by the children. They retreated in happy defeat.

When the revelries slowed, Edmund led the miners back to the mine to complete the last of heaping the ore on the carts, then saw to their loading the ore on the ship. Scrooge and Cratchit took Wheeler aside and explained the entire series of events, leading to the capture of the criminals.

"You be makin' my job too easy," Wheeler said and shook their hands.

Before the ship sailed, Bobbie Wheeler, the new constable, ne Sheriff Wheeler, met with the sloop's captain and took the Owsleys and Dimwittle into custody and interrogated them. He manacled each of them to the wheels of his wagon, and, leaving Barnabas guarding the trio who sat on the hard, cold, wet ground, he then strode up the hill to the mansion.

After the ore ship sailed, Edmund had a handful of his most trusted miners set the explosives for sealing the cavern and adjacent tunnels. About three o'clock, they blew the black powder and successfully sealed it all.

As dusk was settling around the mine and the environs, the four families and Scrooge celebrated with food and drink in the mansion, the merriment escalating.

STAVE THIRTY-THREE
AMAZING REVELATIONS OF THE CRIMINAL GANG AND TWO PROPITIOUS ANNOUNCEMENTS

Bobbie Wheeler located Cratchit in the parlour, talking ebulliently with the Jiggins brother and sister and sloshing wine from his glass as he swung his arms around in large gyrations. Cratchit stopped his spirited activity and poured a glass of wine for Wheeler.

He took the glass. "Bob," Wheeler said, "I found out a few things. Turns out, the Owsleys have a history of crime that goes back about a decade. Dimwittle told a great deal that the Owsleys did not want me to know. When Mort Owsley took the job of mine manager under false pretences here two years back and obtained the employ of his wife as housekeeper, they had it in mind to rewrite the old man's will, kill him, and take over the mine. Mrs. Owsley was using small amounts of arsenic, the by-product of the mining, by adding it to his food, in order to slowly poison Tamperwind. He got sick all right, but he was tough and wouldn't die."

Cratchit nodded and bade Wheeler sit with him at the dining room table. "Further." Wheeler pulled his long pipe from a deep pocket, stuffed it with tobacco, lit it, and puffed away contentedly. "Since Tamperwind was not dying fast enough, and the miner that went by the name of Smyth was getting too mouthy, they killed them both."

"I see." Cratchit stood and in his somewhat inebriated state, toddled over to Scrooge who was speaking to Ginny and Alvina and took his sleeve. "Ebenezer, come listen to this."

Scrooge joined them, and Lockie followed to the group.

Wheeler related to Scrooge and Lockie all he had told Cratchit, then he continued, "The gang had the former sheriff in cahoots with them. He faked his death in the mine so that Wiltfang fellow could tell the tale, and the sheriff slipped into hiding. Pickens was the name he went by. Supposedly, he and Dimwittle are cousins of the Tamperwinds, through Abigail's mother's marriage to their father who had two more wives before her. Abigail's mother was wife number three that we know of."

The three listeners nodded with their mouths agape.

"I think I saw the fake sheriff last night," Lockie interjected. "Yes, it must have been him driving the carriage that Michael escaped in. It had to be him."

"Well, that bogus sheriff has been involved in petty larceny for some time, according to his stepbrother, Dimwittle. The Owsleys tried to get the thespian-turned-deaf-mute gardener to shut his mouth, but he continued to spill his story. Turns out, the phoney sheriff's real name is Mordecai Moriarty. Be assured, I will send alerts to the surrounding towns and to London to be on the lookout for him."

"Moriarty. Interesting name," Scrooge remarked.

"And Moriarty has a son," Wheeler declared. "He's the little math genius you've called 'Michael.' Turns out, his real name is James. That's it. James Moriarty. I'll be on the lookout for him too. Starting out in crime at such a young age. 'Tis a shame. I hope we can find him and turn him from his ways, lest he becomes a worse criminal. Dimwittle said he didn't trust the lad. 'He's devious,' he said."

"That is incredible news," Scrooge said. "It seems you found out more in a few hours than we did in days. Bravo, Bobbie Wheeler."

Scrooge, Cratchit, and Lockie toasted the dwarf.

"Be that as it may," Wheeler smiled. "I need to get these criminals back to Lazy Eye and lock them up for the judge to hold court. Should be quite a trial."

"If you would like," Scrooge offered, "I have some evidence that might help. Matching fingerprints of Dimwittle and Owsley on incriminating documents and on a counterfeit coin, and I have a theory on fingerprints in general that might solve a number of future crimes."

Each of his companions looked at Scrooge incredulously.

"Truly," Scrooge continued, "I think it might be a boon to solving crimes."

"Fingerprints?" Wheeler asked, "Sounds a bit far-fetched, but I'll think about it."

Cratchit gave a doubtful look to Scrooge's pronouncement, but Lockie pondered the concept. Scrooge's face fell. He was so sure of his theories.

When Wheeler rose to leave to gather the criminals and take them to the jail with Angus and Barnabas as guards, Lockie hailed the entire party. "I have an important declaration!" He tapped his glass with a spoon. "Come here, dear Lucy."

Lucy skipped away from the couch where she had been sitting and stood next to Lockie and held his empty hand in both of hers. Lockie cleared his throat while all turned to hear his announcement. "As you know, Samuel, Abigail, and my dear Lucy are inheriting the mine, including the Hopworth mine, as soon as we have the papers read by a lawyer." He cleared his throat again. "Therefore, I ask you to raise your glasses because Miss Lucy Tamperwind, who is both brilliant and lovely beyond compare," he turned to her and gave an admiring look, "has consented to marry me in one year hence." He drew Lucy to him and kissed her, and she kissed back ardently.

The entire assembly toasted and broke into cheers. Lucy blushed, and Abigail and Ginny and Mrs. Wheeler all gathered around her, and they swept her away into the kitchen, chatting and laughing.

Though only Scrooge heard him, Lockie said under his breath, "Of course, I'll have to find a second job in the meantime so that I can be worthy of her hand."

"You'll do no such thing." Scrooge elbowed him in the ribs. "Bob, come here." Cratchit arrived beside them. "Bob, do you not think that this young man has proven himself of abundant resources and deserves to be raised in salary and position to junior partner in our firm?"

"Indeed. I agree," Cratchit said.

"Then so it shall be."

"Thank you so much, Master Scrooge and Master Cratchit." Lockie vigorously shook their hands.

"Therefore," Scrooge said, "I believe we will draw up a contract first thing upon our return to the office in London and make you a full junior partner. And for the purpose of the paperwork, Lockie, I know your last name is Holmes, but what is your real first name?"

"Why it's Sherlock, Master Scrooge. My name is Sherlock."

"Very good, Sherlock Holmes."

"Yes, it's a fine name. When Lucy and I have a boy, we will name him Sherlock, the second. Although she's *set on* our first boy being named *Mycroft*. I believe it's an old family name."

"Congratulations, my good man. I hope that Sherlock junior can have at least half the talents you have," Cratchit said. "But there's something you should know before you totally agree." Cratchit turned to the group once more, poured himself some more wine, and raised it. "Please listen to what my partner, Mr. Ebenezer Scrooge, has to say. We have another toast."

The wine bottles were gathered, and all had the glasses filled.

Scrooge took a proud stance, hands behind his back, chin out. "As you all know, or some of you know, I have always been a good man of business, more recently, *the business of mankind*. And as my partner, Mr. Cratchit, and now, junior partner, Mr. Holmes, are part of this business which is of unequalled calibre for both lending money and for taking care of those less fortunate, even those distraught because of crimes perpetrated upon them." He paused.

Everyone leaned forwards.

"Henceforth, besides being Scrooge and Cratchit—money lenders— our business shall also be ... Scrooge and Cratchit—private detectives."

STAVE THIRTY-FOUR

A BRIGHT CHRISTMAS, DISCOVERY OF A TREASURE MAP, AND AN EXCELLENT CHURCH SERVICE

Christmas rang in softly and quietly. But Bobbie Wheeler, who was returning to the mansion, was worried. After taking the murderers to jail in Lazy Eye the night before, he drove a small cart back to Tamperwind mansion. The hairs on the back of his neck had risen. He felt something was not right. Though the criminals were behind bars, and though he left Angus and Barnabas to guard them, he felt uneasy that something dastardly was going to happen. His wife often teased him about his "premonitions."

He halted the cart almost to the steps of the little church, got out, and took a deep inhalation of the crisp air and smiled. "Ah, 'tis a fine Christmas." With the burgeoning light of the sun's slow appearance, he observed the holly greens decorating the church doorway.

Down at the mine town, candles were beginning to flicker in the windows of the homes. Suddenly, four small boys raced pell-mell out of two homes and up to the flimsy excuse for the church's rectory. They rapped on the pitiful door. A new light broke through the window, and the old, white-headed priest opened the door.

"What, ho, boys," the man chuckled. "Today, you wear the red cassocks, for 'tis Christmas, a great celebration. Alleluia, Christ is born!"

Wheeler marvelled at the priest's exuberance. Slowly, he made his way up to the mansion, ruminating all the while about the criminals who got away—Mordecai Moriarty and his son, James.

He had written several letters to constabularies in London and Lancaster and given strict directions to Barnabas and Angus to ensure a post rider took them as soon as he was able, but he knew the letters would not be delivered until days after Christmas, and the father and son would likely make good their escape. He was glad that at least three of the murderous gang were imprisoned.

Still, he could not shake a foreboding sense that something was awry. Something dreadful lay just ahead. "Fine thing," he said to himself. "Worryin' on Christmas Day."

Approaching the mansion, he walked through the open gate. He saw lights beginning to radiate in various upstairs windows, then, through the front windows, a lamp in the parlour, and two in the kitchen. "Folks are waking up on this glorious day." He was excited about seeing his wife and family who had stayed the night at the house, and he clapped his small, rough hands together.

When he knocked, Edmund answered the door. "Oh, hello, Bobbie Wheeler." He put a finger to his lips. When Wheeler entered, he saw the menfolk had bedded down in the parlour. Scrooge snored on a couch. Cratchit curled under blankets on the floor by the hearth. Samuel was just waking from his snooze on a deep chair. He shook his head, ran his fingers through his black hair, and made his way out the back door to the washhouse.

"Your children are upstairs," Edmund said, and "the youngest boys of all three families in one room. The girls in another. The married womenfolk in one room. Tim and Peter Cratchit in a room, then the young ladies, including Ginny, in a separate room."

"Where might I find my wife?"

"She's already awake, my fine fellow, preparing the Christmas breakfast with Abigail Jiggins and my wife, Bernice."

In a half an hour, the sleepy, yawning people, save Samuel who had gone upstairs, found their way to the dining table. The children ate first, then the adults. By late morning, the Wheeler children, and the Nuckols children, and the Cratchit children had disappeared, out to play, and the adults, young ones and older, sat sharing stories and laughing at the breakfast table, sipping tea.

Scrooge was relating a story he had almost forgotten of his childhood, carrying wood for the family hearth, when Samuel announced from atop the stairs, "I found a most interesting prize."

The group watched him trounce jauntily down the stairs. He arrived, panting in his excitement. "I cannot believe it. I found it!"

"Found what, good sir?" Edmund asked.

"Let me begin at the beginning. When I was a tiny child, my sister and I would be left here in the care of Uncle Erasmus and his wife, a sort of vacation. That is before our parents were murdered. One time, I came upon our dear uncle at work at his desk in his bedroom, and he held open a small drawer. When he saw me, he quickly shoved something inside the drawer and closed it, and the drawer magically disappeared."

"You never told me about that," Abigail said.

"It must have slipped my mind. I was quite small. At any rate, since we are to inherit this business, I felt it incumbent upon me to examine some of the pertinent paperwork and books, all of which Owsley had stacked in disarray on top of the desk. I was there, deep in study, when the remembrance of the vanishing drawer occurred to me. I began to seek it. And ..." He paused dramatically.

"Tell us, dear brother!" Abigail's cheeks were flushing.

"Yes, then. Lo, and behold! I found the hidden latch, and the secret drawer that hid within a drawer popped out as by a spring. Inside the drawer, I found this peculiar little box. Yet no key. The box having a flimsy latch, I popped it open with a letter opener. Inside the box, I found this one item."

He held up a brown foolscap with lines and writings marked on it. Samuel could barely contain his excitement. "It's a treasure map!"

The exclamations of surprise and delight were abundant, and every adult was up and crowding around the soon-to-be rightful owner, one of the three, of the Tamperwind and Hopworth mines. Samuel was pointing and shouting. Every one of the eager participants was commenting in boisterous fashion. Abigail began dancing a jig. Lucy, for her part, pulled her fiancé, Lockie, to her. They smiled abundantly.

Wheeler stepped aside, his hand on his bearded chin, deep in thought. His earlier misgivings about the status of the imprisoned Owsleys returned. He could not put his finger on why he worried so, but his sense that something was amiss was apparent. He stared out the window.

"Apparently," Samuel said, "more than tin ore and arsenic came from the mine. I believe it indicates a goodly number or rubies are stored in a hidden location in the Hopworth mine. All we need do is follow these directions and see what Uncle Erasmus had concealed. It does note here that he had hidden the gems for his future children that he hoped he would have. Sadly, Uncle Erasmus left no children as heirs." Samuel realised the melancholy of his commentary and stopped speaking.

All were quiet.

When Samuel finally folded the map and stuck it in his inside jacket pocket, it was like the quick flight of a sparrow for Lockie's hand to retrieve it from the jacket and hand it to Lucy to peruse.

"I say," Samuel said. "How did you do that so quickly?"

"'Tis a knack. Served me well in the past," Lockie replied. "Oh, and Master Scrooge. It just occurred to me." He reached in his trouser pocket and pulled out the keys he had heisted from Scrooge when they embarked on their journey from London to western England. "I found these right after you left the office," he lied, "lying in the snow at the door. I've been carrying them around, meaning to give them to you. My apologies for the delay." He made a low bow and looked up, expecting Scrooge to wallop his head for his tardiness in returning them.

Scrooge did not strike him, but hugged him, clutching his newly returned keys in his fist. "Thank you, dear sir. And I cannot call you a boy anymore since you are to be married and are now a junior partner in the firm. We must be on the morrow's stage and return to the office. I hope the workplace has not been ransacked. Besides, there are bills to collect, and—" He stopped when he saw Cratchit's look of disapproval. With a contrite look, he shoved the keys deep in his inside coat pocket.

Lockie blew a sigh of relief that his transgression had transpired unpunished. He drew Lucy close, and they kissed.

"You are such an upright man, Sherlock Holmes," she said.

"Yes, well." In his heart, Lockie felt guilt, but the feeling passed, for he was bound up in Christmas joy.

"Tomorrow," Samuel said, "you're all invited on the treasure hunt."

The announcement was met with, "Here! Here!"

At that moment, the bells of the church began chiming.

Not wishing to be late to the service, the entire group flung on their coats and shoes and dashed out into the bracing morning. They gathered the children from their play, and they trouped their way to the church. Wheeler came last, deep in thought.

Tiny as the church was, with all the mineworkers' families, and all the families from Hopworth, even Beebe and her mother, and with the eighteen persons who came from the mansion in attendance, people lined the entire walls of the church, and the smallest children perched under the altar table itself.

When the tiny organ squeaked out the hymns, the rafters echoed with the voices singing in one accord the praises to the new-born king. The Wheelers, sitting at the front, sang the loudest. The sweet voices melded with those bellowing and it seemed that all the air in the place would have been taken up, were it not for the draft at the rear doors where Scrooge once more was positioned. Yet, he complained not about his cold backside, but smiled and sang a parsimonious, trembling tenor to all the carols.

The good parson kept his sermon short and remembered to announce a memorial service in two days for the man who had been shot by the young Moriarty. "Caveman was a big man by all rights, with fists big enough to crush a man's noggin," he said, "but it was his big heart that helped save the day." His words were not dour but hopeful. Scrooge was amazed at the humble priest blending such earnestness about a man whom he hardly knew. Scrooge felt a tear trickle down his cheek.

The walls of the minor church in the backwaters of Cornwall seemed to expand in the glow of the sermon of love and forgiveness. Then when the organ struck up "Silent Night," and the whole congregation sang out, Scrooge felt a rapidity in his heart that he had not felt since childhood, not from fear, but from sheer joy.

When the offertory came, Scrooge laid a pound coin in the basket. When the collection baskets were brought forwards, Tim reached in a corner and drew out his two crutches, one small and one longer, that he had brought from home and had stored in the church in secret. He took the crutches to the altar and laid them beside the offertory pittance the poor families had sacrificed. He turned to the congregation. "These two crutches are a gift should someone in the congregation need them. They served me well. I hope they remind us all of the one who made blind men see and the lame to walk." He strode back confidently to stand beside Scrooge.

At the end of the service, the congregation retired to their homes with the tower bells clanging out good news for several minutes. Scrooge noticed the altar servers who were swinging on the rugged ropes in the bottom of the tower like they were holding jungle vines. He remembered his favourite story of his youth—that of the shipwrecked Robinson Crusoe, and he imagined briefly that he strode through a teaming jungle with monkeys and birds chittering. He inhaled a deep gulp of the Christmas air.

Surely, all was right with the world. Surely?

STAVE THIRTY-FIVE

THE VILLAINS ESCAPE, A GUN BATTLE, A TOWN FIRE

Returning to the mansion, the women brought out a sumptuous meal, and all dined, the children sitting on the floor. Afterwards, the men took over the washing and drying of the dishes. Then all retired to the parlour to share Christmas tales. Scrooge was inclined to tell of his own encounter with the Christmas ghosts, but relented, not wishing to frighten the small children.

"I wish old Angus were here," Wheeler said as evening was drawing nigh. "He can tell some amazing stories." He stole a look out the window, whence surprise and anger stole across his face. "What in the name of heaven?" He rushed outside. The other men followed on his heels.

His coat covered with snow and slurry, Angus drove up in a small cart, the two horses sweating, for he had driven them hard. He jumped down and met Bobbie Wheeler at the gate.

"They've escaped!" Angus grabbed his cousin's arms.

"How is that possible, Angus?" Wheeler demanded. "Did you not have the musket?"

"Indeed, we did, but Barnabas took it with him when he went to post your letters with the postman. We didn't see a need to keep the gun on the Owsleys and Dimwittle since they were behind bars. I stayed behind, keepin' warm." He blubbered through his beard.

"What happened? Stop your weepin', man."

The rest of the men arrived beside the pair, and Angus looked up at them, a man defeated.

"I fought them best I could. It was a man that called himself 'Sheriff of Hopworth' and his wee lad he called 'James.' Well, I knew he was not the sheriff. You explained that well enough earlier to me, Bobbie."

"Yes."

"He said he came for the prisoner. He went for my keys, and we took to fisticuffs, and I had beat him pretty badly when another man appeared. I couldn't take 'em both. The man who called himself 'Sheriff Moriarty' called the other man 'Wiltfang.' They tied me up and took the keys. When they opened the cell, the Owsleys came out like mercurial light. But Dimwittle stayed in, sayin' he was done. He t'weren't doin' no more crime. Said he heard the clanging of chains in the mansion and in the yard one night, sure it was a demon ghost come to take him to hell. They harangued him quite a while. There he was with the wounded shoulder, and they kept yellin' 'wild dogs' over and over. Strangest thing. He got red in the face, but he refused to budge."

"So, they escaped before Barnabas returned?" Bobbie Wheeler said.

"The Owsleys did. Went out with Moriarty and Wiltfang. Dimwittle stayed sittin' on the bunk, hands on his ears. Then, the strangest thing, the boy turned at the door, drew a pistol, and shot Dimwittle in the other shoulder. After that, they took off. I ain't never seen a viler look on a child's face."

"Michael, or rather, James Moriarty shot and killed Caveman," Lockie said, "and tried to blow up Lucy and Abigail and all of us. I hate the lad."

"Anyways, Barnabas heard the shot and came runnin'," Angus continued. "He untied me, and we staunched Dimwittle's wound."

"Will he survive?" Edmund asked.

"I'm not sure if he'll survive to stand trial." Angus stood straight, wiped his red eyes. "Barnabas has the gun and is guardin' him, keepin' the jailhouse door locked until we return. I'm sorry, Bobbie."

"There was nothing more you could do."

"Just so ya knows. Dimwittle kept babblin' on that Wiltfang, the grocer, was always in on the caper, and he was the one lookin' for a chest of treasure in the Hopworth mine. I had no idea what he meant. Does it mean somethin' to you?"

Scrooge stepped to the front of the group. "Now we know their plans. They intend to search for the treasure. I have a feeling that Mort Owsley was looking at the map when we caught him at the desk, and he may have committed it to memory. We barely intervened before he could relay his knowledge to Wiltfang and Moriarty and his boy. It also means they may be searching for it this very Christmas day in the Hopworth mine, taking advantage that no one is working and everyone is at home."

"Gentlemen," Wheeler sternly announced, "if you've got weapons, get them now. We've got the Jiggins' and Lucy Tamperwind wealth to save, and five transgressors to seize."

Lockie went to Dimwittle's old cabin and gathered four bullseye lanterns. Edmund had a pistol; Scrooge had his nephew's other gun; Samuel had his pistol; Cratchit, his musket; and the Wheeler dwarves bore hefty cudgels. Lockie, though he had no weapon, was selected to remain behind and help guard the women.

Wheeler gave the men the plan. While he and Angus slipped around the side of the store entrance to the mine, Edmund, Cratchit, and Samuel would stealthily approach the front. Scrooge was to bring up the rear, him being the least familiar with a gun, and his assignment was to alert the others with a gunshot should any of the villains arrive from behind.

"With the lantern shinin'," Wheeler said, "they'll know we are comin'. So, be cautious."

On the porch of the mansion, Lockie and the women watched the lanterns grow smaller and smaller. And the land grew darker like it was sucking in shadows, no moon in sight. Lockie turned and encouraged the women to go inside.

"I believe," Abigail said commandingly, "that I can quite take care of myself." She remained on the porch, sitting on a chair in the shadows.

Lockie went to the kitchen and retrieved a butcher knife.

"Lockie," Lucy said, "I'm so scared. When will this all end? Last evening, I was so glad for us to be alive, and again in church. But now, my cousin, Samuel, is walking into danger, as are my friends, Mr. Scrooge, Mr. Cratchit, Mr. Nuckols, and the Wheelers."

Lockie hugged her, then bade the children and women go to the kitchen. He told the women to find a weapon of their own choosing. Lucy, Bernice, and Alvina each took a knife; Ginny grabbed an empty wine bottle; and Mrs. Wheeler held a cleaver. Peter and Tim chose stout logs from the woodpile. They stood in front of the wood room with the remaining children behind them, seated on the logs. Lockie turned down the lamps in the dining room, leaving only the lamps in the kitchen and parlour lit. He locked the back door and sat in a chair in the parlour and watched out a window. He hoped his own quickness and agility would serve him if the need arose.

The night fell like an anvil, heavy and cold.

On their trek to the Hopworth mine entrance, the five men in the front kept silent. Only Samuel held a lantern. "I've never shot anyone," he said.

"Me neither," said Edmund.

"Nor I," Cratchit said.

Scrooge, walking behind them, said, "Seems as I'm the only one to have shot a man with a gun."

"I hope we can muster the provident courage to shoot if we must." Cratchit gulped on his words and gripped his musket tighter.

Scrooge listened to the footsteps of the men in front of him on the crunching snow, counted their measured breaths, and he watched the single lantern dance its glow on the white surface. The wind had increased.

Then he heard the bells of the church in the distance behind him— Christmas evening vespers. Scrooge considered himself a simple man, and he characterized the bells as mysterious, for bells had rung in high towers for eons before he was even born. High and far off, like they may as well have been in a mountain cavern. He felt that he personally was being beckoned by the faraway chiming. Their ring was haunting like delirious ghosts lost in the bells themselves and ranging from one bell to the other. Were they calling to him, as the ghosts had before? Was the Ghost of Christmas Future abroad, foretelling the end of lives? Was he accompanied by the angel of death? He forbade himself to think further on it.

Distracted as he was, Scrooge fell far behind the others and even lost sight of the lantern in the twisting path. He stopped and listened. First, he heard rough voices shouting threats. Then gunshots.

He froze, not from the weather, but from sheer trepidation.

At the grocer's mine entrance, Owsley and his wife had taken positions just inside the store. They yelled epithets at the stalwart men from the mansion. Owsley fired several pistols, one after another, the shots pinging off the rocks, one time only inches from Samuel's head. While the Wheeler dwarves darted to the right and up into the boulders that ranged far beyond the store, the other three men dove down, the lantern crashing from Samuel's hand and landing some feet ahead of them, spearing its light straight at the entrance of the store. Owsley was partially visible behind a large barrel. Cratchit could see Mrs. Owsley's springy curls and bonnet poking above a heavy crate.

Samuel rose. "They've fired all their weapons. Let's rush them." He started forwards, and a bullet tore through the fabric of his jacket at the collar. He ducked behind a rock.

"They have more weapons!" Edmund shouted. He fired his pistol into the store. Whatever the pellet hit ignited some straw and wadding behind Owsley, and a fire, fanned by the stiff wind, broke out.

No sooner had he fired than two more shots from the store rang out, chipping the boulders behind which Edmund and Samuel hid.

Cratchit peered out from his hiding place, wedged between two tall boulders. He knew the lantern light shone directly in the criminals' eyes, and they were firing blind. He rose. While Mrs. Owsley was handing another musket to her husband, Cratchit took careful aim with his musket. He thought about his hours of practice at inanimate targets. He knew he had to make the shot count. He let his breath out slowly, did not clinch the gun, but held it snug to his shoulder. He fired. Owsley went down, howling and writhing in pain.

Agatha Owsley, instead of rushing to the aid of her fallen husband, sped out the front door into the Hopworth street. She did not get far. She found herself grasped by the arm and a knife stuck at her throat.

"I don't think you'll be goin' any further, Aunt Agatha." Beebe, her skinny frame, white and bold in the town's lamplight, held the knife to the old woman's throat. "You're murderin' days are o'er."

While Edmund was reloading his pistol, and Cratchit reloading his musket, Samuel raced to the aid of Beebe. He shoved his gun into Agatha's side. "Thank you, Miss Grave. I'll take it from here."

Two more shots resonated among the boulders. Chubby Harold Wiltfang struggled to run out the front door. He tossed the two pistols he had fired, and grabbed two more from his belt, aiming them squarely at Cratchit and Edmund. Both men's thoughts rushed to their families, and why had they taken this chance. Before they could dive for cover, Bobbie Wheeler leapt from the roof of the store and stuck his wooden cudgel between Wiltfang's legs. The man tumbled, splayed like an elk's hide. Before he could rise, Angus whacked the villain's cognomen hard with his own cudgel. The man was out cold.

Edmund and Cratchit sprinted to the store and dragged the wounded Mort Owsley out. The fire was spreading. While Samuel stood guard over the wounded Mort, the cowering Agatha and the out-cold grocer, the other men took off their jackets and went into the store to beat out the flames. Beebe raced to the town's fire alarm bell and rang it.

STAVE THIRTY-SIX

MORE GHOSTS, AND JAMES MORIARTY RETURNS

Directly after the first rounds were fired, Scrooge was leaning against a boulder, fingering his pistol and shaking. The old Scrooge had taken up residence in his mind. The brave one had run away. He was standing there, idling and thinking when he looked up and saw, as plain as the long nose on his face, Jacob Marley's ghost striding towards him with pain written across his face. He seemed to be hastening, and the heavy cash boxes and chains were tearing at his spirit. At last, he came face-to-face with Scrooge; his cold, fetid breath was almost enough to cause Scrooge to swoon.

"Now, Jacob. Do not reprimand me. Have you not seen how brave I have been? Do not ask me to be brave once more."

Marley's ghost turned from Scrooge. "Very well. I won't ask you to be brave."

Scrooge was baffled. He watched the ghost walk away and vanish in a fog. "Oh," Scrooge said, "perhaps it was just a figment of my imagination, a dream in my current state of dread I am in. Yes, it was …"

Marley's ghost and several other coarse and sorrowful spirits sprang on Scrooge from above, and were it not that they were spirits, they would have knocked him to the ground. Marley plopped in a heap beside Scrooge, then stood. The other spirits backed away, moaning and wailing, tugging in vain at the chains binding their necks, remorse in their vacant eyes. With as much pride as Marley's ghost could muster, he glared at Scrooge. "Old partner, your friends at the mansion are in *danger.*" His spirit and the others with him dissipated like mist.

Scrooge could not believe his ears. Why had they not thought to leave a gun for Lockie?

Despite his feeling feeble in his exhausted and frightened state, he charged up the long hill, slush and ice flying up and pelting him as high as his chest. The wind whipped his face.

જ્જ

At the mansion, Lockie stared out the window, surveying the land, wary of any approaching figure.

He was surprised when he heard Lucy call, "Lockie, I think you better come in here."

He passed through the dining room and into the kitchen. At the rear of the kitchen, Mordecai Moriarty stood with two pistols in his hands. A few feet in front of him stood young James Moriarty, but ten years old, a small pistol of his own punched into Lucy's side. Lockie almost lunged at the dastard boy but stopped when the young Moriarty pushed the gun harder into Lucy's ribs.

All the women and children huddled together in a group to the side, save Tim, who had collapsed on the floor at James' feet. He appeared out cold. The young ones were whimpering and crying.

"Sorry about your friend, Tim," James said. "That's what the ladies called him. He tried to make a go at me. I had to knock him back a bit. You should have remembered that I still had a key to the back door. Weren't you silly?"

"Michael, or James," Lockie placed his knife on the counter. "Surely you don't intend to kill us all."

"Oh, no. I don't intend to kill any of you. My father, the sheriff, and I just came back to retrieve something from Mr. Tamperwind's room."

"If you're lookin' for the map, you're too late. Samuel already found it. He has it in his possession."

"Go check, Father," James said. "You know Lockie's sort lies a lot. Pickpocket, ne'er-do-well. Sleeps with prostitutes." He shoved his pistol into Lucy's side.

Mordecai left and raced up the stairs.

Tears flowed down Lucy's cheeks. "Is that true, Sherlock?" she sobbed.

"Sherlock? Is that your real name?" James said. "That's a sorry excuse for a name. I'd never claim it."

Lockie's face turned red. He wanted to throttle the little beast.

"Making you mad, am I, Sherlock?"

Mordecai returned, both pistols out and aimed at Peter and Ginny. "He's tellin' the truth. The map is gone. I say let's kill 'em all. Startin' with the oldest. The young ones can't testify in court anyway."

"Let me think, Father," James said.

"Oh, you wouldn't want to kill me." Ginny was smiling and making eyes at Mordecai. "I think I might like to get away from the likes of these people. They're so boring, not like you." She sauntered up to Mordecai. "My, you look so strong." She stroked her hair and batted her eyes.

Lockie saw Tim, on the floor, wink at him, then pretend to still be knocked out.

Mordecai had his full attention on Ginny. That is when Lockie noticed Abigail slip up behind the man. Abigail raised a heavy skillet and clouted his head, and he collapsed, his pistols landing near his hands. Abigail smiled down at the unconscious man. "I told you I could take care of myself," Abigail said. "Thanks for the distraction, Ginny."

When James turned to see what had happened, Tim was up like lightning, knocking James's firearm from his hand, sending it flying into the dining room.

James Moriarty flew past Lockie into the dining room and dove for his gun. Lockie leapt on top of him, both struggling for the gun. Then Lockie stopped, holding up his hands, then standing and retreating.

James held the pistol, aiming at Lockie. He began backing away towards the front door.

"I guess before I go, I should dispatch my worrisome friend. I don't want anyone named Sherlock to have children. What a horrid thought!" He cocked the pistol.

"Oh, I wouldn't do that," came a scratchy old voice.

James turned to see a pistol an inch from his head. Ebenezer Scrooge, sometimes a coward, sometimes brave, reached out and lifted the pistol from the boy's limp hand.

Momentarily, the young Moriarty looked up at the former miser. "I cannot believe it—all my plans. Oh, well. Goodbye."

He ducked past Scrooge so quickly that Scrooge could only watch him race away, out the door, leaping off the porch and into the dark.

Lockie started to give chase, but he noticed Mordecai was waking up. He sped to the criminal on the floor and took up both pistols. Mordecai looked up, bleary-eyed. Lockie handed one gun to Abigail. "Don't be afraid to use it."

"Oh, I won't." Abigail cocked the pistol and aimed it at Mordecai. "I'm glad I remained sitting in the dark on the porch. I watched you two criminals wind your way around the house. I simply followed you through the back door."

When Lockie reached the porch, neither Scrooge nor he could see anything in the vast panoply of darkness, though they did hear a horse galloping away.

With the help of the townsfolk of Hopworth, the fire in the grocer's store was put out quickly. Several men volunteered to stand watch in case the fire started up again. The townsfolk crowded around Beebe, calling her a hero for saving the town.

Bobbie and Angus Wheeler marched the Owsleys and Wiltfang to the church. The pastor had just the place—a wine cellar built under the church long ago by some enterprising monks. Lockie and Scrooge brought Mordecai Moriarty to be held in the dank basement as well. Lucy tended Mort Owsley's arm wound before he was stowed away with the other criminals. Then the Wheeler men tied the criminals securely and locked the heavy door. Angus stood guard outside.

Before closing the door, the pastor managed to fill a bottle from one of the wine casks. He gave celebratory cups to all the men and women.

When all, save Angus, but including the good pastor, had returned to the warm mansion, the celebration continued. Scrooge drank more than he ever had. With his last drink, before he fell asleep in his chair, he had set the cup upon a footrest. He put his hands on his knees and bent his nose down to the cup, breathing in the aroma, and feeling enormous peace, if peace could ever be said to be of a particular size. His grin widened upon his face, and the wrinkles about his eyes crinkled, and he laughed as much as if he had inhaled laughing gas. He grabbed the goblet in both hands and dispatched the wine in one long gulp. He nodded, and the cup fell to the floor. Just before he slipped into a deep slumber, he could have sworn he heard the gentle, robust laugh of the Ghost of Christmas Present.

EPILOGUE

A MARRIAGE PENDING AND A NEW CASE

Hiram Grumbles straightened his coat and removed his hat before entering the Scrooge and Cratchit office. He noted the revised name on the sign by the door, which read inauspiciously, "Scrooge and Cratchit: Lenders and Crime Detectives." He steadied himself, for he was prepared to fall on his knees and thank the two benefactors who had saved him from the gallows. At last, he thrust open the door. There, he found Cratchit explaining the game of chess to Scrooge, the board and pieces having been spread across the papers and coins on Scrooge's desk. Coins lay about the desk in partial and tilted stacks and scattered among the captured black and white chess pieces. Lockie looked on studiously.

Cratchit was explaining, "So, there I was in the Wheeler home, and this tiny nine-year-old boy, Corny Wheeler, had my king pinned thusly—" He looked up and saw Grumbles and jumped, spilling the pieces off the board. He hugged Grumbles. "Such a good day to see you well and hearty, my fine fellow, I should say!" He shook his hand.

Scrooge was not far behind, having sped around his desk. He, too, hugged the man and gave him an enthusiastic handshake. "So good to see you, old man."

At this, the tears streamed in a torrent from Grumbles's eyes. "How can I thank you both for what you've done for me? I came here for a loan and found two men who went far beyond the extra mile that our good Lord encouraged, you went many miles. And I've learned much, indeed, enough from a Sheriff Wheeler who came to the prison and gained my release. He had five villains in tow, the Owsleys, a Wiltfang, a Moriarty, and a Dimwittle, and they were the ones who perpetrated the murder of dear Mr. Tamperwind, then they did in the miner, Smyth. Those criminals are in prison now, in my stead." The big man fanned himself with his hat, grabbed his kerchief and blew his nose with a great honk.

Lockie came forwards with a chair and invited Grumbles to sit, which he did, still fanning himself with his bowler.

"Hiram," Scrooge said, "may I introduce to you our new junior partner in the firm, Mr. Sherlock Holmes, who is betrothed to one of Erasmus Tamperwind's nieces and who also is an heir to the mine and its fortune, Miss Lucy Tamperwind."

Grumbles rose and shook Lockie's hand.

"Lockie, or Sherlock, at first," Scrooge said, "got the better of a highwayman on our way to the mine, and then was quite influential in solving the crimes and in saving Lucy's life and her cousin, Abigail's, life, as well as indirectly saving the lives of two men when he found a secret door in the old Hopworth mine. One of those men was our very own Bob Cratchit. In this one week that he has been a partner, he has brought in three new clients who took out sizeable, secured loans. He is a boon."

"I am dumbfounded, and I am indeed grateful to you for working to save me, Sherlock."

"Thank you, sir. 'Twas doing no more than my Christian duty. And you can call me 'Lockie.'"

Scrooge continued, "And our esteemed junior partner was going to wait a whole year to marry Miss Tamperwind, but now that he has this more prestigious position, he plans to marry her next weekend at St. Paul's."

"Yes," Lockie said, "and let me formally invite you to our nuptials. Had it not been for you and your plight, I would never have met the woman of my dreams, the woman of my future."

"Of course, I shall attend," Grumbles replied.

Cratchit brought out the brandy from his desk and poured four snifters. They toasted Lockie and his bride-to-be.

"Since I've come to know her," Lockie was beaming with pride, "I've found she is incredibly bright, is well-read in Latin and Greek, dabbles in chemistry, is a student of philosophy and of the theatre, and is an ardent supporter of helpin' the poor and less fortunate. Here I am, an unfortunate scoundrel, with no mum or pa, and who used to pick pockets for a livin' and hide in brothels, and now she's forgiven any of my wrongdoings of the past, and I'm marryin' a fine lady. I've come up in the world, and I am blessed."

"I'm amazed." Grumbles clapped his hands. "You have done well, young man."

"I must confess," Lockie said, "there is another reason for our movin' the marriage sooner. At first, I thought she meant it as a tease of namin' our first boy Mycroft, but she already has a child. You see, she was raped when she was but fourteen by a pirate who was livin' ashore and had ingratiated himself with her ailing mother. She told me he said he had killed Samuel's and Abigail's father, Mr. Sprogg. And the authorities captured a different man and hung him.

"When she told him she was pregnant, he tried to force her to get rid of her as-yet-unborn child because he wanted her mother to write him into her will. He even grabbed her by the hair and dragged her to an apothecary to give her a poison to kill the babe. By God's grace, she managed to escape. That very night, he was at a bar and got impressed by a press gang onto some sailing vessel and hasn't been seen since."

Grumbles blanched. "I supposed the world has always had villains and will always have them."

"So, Lucy was able to keep the baby, and she loves him dearly. He's a fine strapping lad of three years." Lockie looked up as to praise God. "Mr. Tamperwind and his wife, having no children of their own, provided care for Samuel and Abigail after the death of their parents when they were younger, boarding them in a fine Christian friend's home until Samuel could establish himself in the tea importing business. Now, he'll be running a mining operation, assisted by his sister and by my future bride.

"As for me, I turned eighteen years on New Year's Eve, and Lucy has recently turned eighteen. Were she to wait another year, people would start calling her an old maid. So, it's fortuitous for me and her to marry now. I shall adopt her son, Mycroft, and give him the Holmes surname."

"And do you plan on having other children?" Grumbles chuckled.

"Yes, indeed. We've settled on six, and the first boy will be called 'Sherlock,' named after me. If my father, whoever that was, had no namesake, at least my son will."

Grumbles finished his drink, and Bob poured him another.

"Along the lines you just told me," Grumbles said, "I am using my own skills and connections to attempt to lobby Parliament to exact laws to protect the young people who labour as much as adults in the mines and workhouses. I have pull, you know, in high places. I am confident we will save many young lives. I'm sure of it."

Scrooge looked out into the foggy streets and thought, *So, this is why he needed to be saved. He will help bring a halt to the depraved abuse of our nation's children.*

"Bravo!" Scrooge shouted. "I would say no child under fourteen should ever be forced to work in a factory or mine. Only on a farm should children be allowed to do such chores as is appropriate to keep the farm in working order."

"I agree with that, Scrooge," Grumbles said. He took out a small pad and pencil and wrote down Scrooge's remarks. "In addition, I am in contact with Miss Angela Burdett-Coutts, the heir to the bank fortune. She has in her mind to open a home for prostitutes, so that they may escape their horrible travail and start their lives anew."

Grumbles winced, seeing the surprised expressions on the three men's faces.

"Wait," Lockie said at last, "the plan may have its merit. I know many of these women, and all of them would rather do somethin' else. It's the only means of livin' they can get, or they and their children would starve. They need a fresh start workin' as a milliner, a weaver, or a maid. Or even doing piece work, makin' matches or boxes."

"But be they not fallen women?" Cratchit admonished.

"Yes," Lockie said, "degraded and fallen, but not lost. In a new home, away from their previous trade or the need for it, they could have the means for a return to happiness within their grasp. Think of Beebe Grave. Was she not instrumental in stopping the criminal varmints and alerting the town to save it from a fire?"

"I see," Cratchit said. "I'm all for giving people second chances. Hear, hear!" He raised his glass, and all the men toasted.

"Or third and fourth and fifth chances," Scrooge said. The men toasted again.

Grumbles stood. "Let us toast this new year, which is full of bright promise."

"To the new year!" All the men said, clinked their glasses, and downed the brandy.

At that moment, the door of the business burst open and in rushed a female of about twenty-five years, her hair all bedraggled, one sleeve of her elegant dress torn at the shoulder, and red clay mud on her shoes.

Panting, she cried out, "Which one of you is Mr. Scrooge? And which one is Mister Cratchit? And are you truly detectives?"

"Yes," Cratchit stepped forwards and indicated for the woman to sit. "I'm Robert Cratchit. There is my esteemed colleague, Mr. Ebenezer Scrooge. There, our junior partner, Mr. Sherlock Holmes, and, seated there, a dear acquaintance, Mr. Hiram Grumbles."

"Call me 'Lockie,'" Lockie said.

"Enough with the formalities!" the young woman exclaimed. "My name is Evangeline Peabody. My husband is missing and may be seriously hurt or dead."

Scrooge sat at his desk and immediately began writing notes. While Lockie gave the woman a glass of water, he wrote: *torn sleeve, woman obviously has been running, twenty-five years, dark brown hair, sickly pallor, mud on her shoes looks to be from near the river Thames.*

Evangeline downed the water. "My husband is Peter Peabody. He was just now playing at a game of bowls. It was a Twelfth Night party in the street with many people attending. I was there in the crowd, watching. One of the balls ran over his foot in the game. He was limping and needing aid. I went to fetch help. When I returned, he was nowhere around. Not a single person could tell me where he was. Then I saw large drops of blood in the snow. The police say there's nothing they can do. And, and ... I need someone to help me find my husband, and possibly save him."

"Ma'am," Scrooge said. He looked at Cratchit and Lockie, who nodded approval. "We will take your case. Give us the details, then we will discuss payment for our services."

"Yes, thank you."

"Hiram," Scrooge said to Grumbles, "I know you must be on your way, but you can count on me to support your efforts financially. Good day, sir." He waved off his friend. Scrooge was driven in his desire to solve the crime.

Grumbles finished his drink, gathered his hat, and bade all a good day. Stepping out into the fresh January air, he smiled broadly. A great future lay before him.

When the door closed behind Grumbles, Cratchit quickly sat beside the woman and began asking her questions regarding the mysterious disappearance of her husband.

Scrooge was labouring to keep up in taking notes. He first wrote: *The game is*, followed by a dash, for he had forgotten what game she had said her husband was playing. He then wrote: *a foot.*

Lockie, looking over his shoulder, read the words. He said, "The game is afoot."

Acknowledgments

Special thanks to Becki Kinch and Sandra Timm for their editing and excellent guidance that very much helped me in the writing of this book. I also thank all my friends in WWG and my amazing publisher, Mindy Kuhn. She always listens and offers sterling advice.

Dear reader,

I so appreciate you reading this Christmas mystery, and I wish you all the joys and love of the season and all year long. If you enjoyed this book, I respectfully ask you to write a review of my humble tale of two erstwhile, yet fumbling, detectives and their pickpocket friend. Please submit your reviews on Amazon, barnesandnoble.com, and/or Goodreads. Writing a review takes about three minutes and I would greatly appreciate it. Thank you and may God bless you abundantly.

CPSIA information can be obtained
at www.ICGtesting.com
Printed in the USA
BVHW042303161122
652180BV00003B/20